MW00846804

TROUBLE AT BRAYSHAW HIGH

USA TODAY BESTSELLING AUTHOR

MEAGAN BRANDY

Edited by: Ellie McLove, My Brother's Editor

Proofread by: Rosa Sharon, iScream Proofreading Services

Cover Designer: Jay Aheer, Simply Defined Art

Dedication

*To the one brave enough to be
weak for those you love,
your crown is coming.*

BHS

"You don't belong."

No words whispered in anger have ever rung more true.

They're the Kings of Brayshaw with the world at their feet, destined for greatness and in need of control.

I'm the girl from the ghetto with nothing to offer and as defiant as they come.

They say it doesn't matter, that I'm one of them now, and nothing could ever change that.

Not even me, should I dare try.

But they're wrong.

They underestimate how far I'll go to protect them.

Trouble is coming...and they have no idea.

Dear Reader,

Trouble at Brayshaw High is the second book in my Brayshaw series. In order to follow and enjoy this story, you must have read book one, Boys of Brayshaw High, as this will pick up where the other left off. Thank you so much for reading!

Chapter 1

MADDOC

I GRIP THE ENDS OF MY HAIR AND PULL, TRYING TO LESSEN THE pounding at my temples. My body and mind are exhausted, and my head is taking the heat from it.

It doesn't help a damn thing, so I drop onto the bar stool and look to the clock.

It's past three a.m. and still, no sign of Raven.

Captain is pacing the fucking house while Royce keeps walking in and out the front door with his arms crossed over his chest.

I shake my head. Only hours gone, and the three of us are losing our damn minds. This girl, she's got us all sorts of fucked up.

She had slipped out front only minutes after coming downstairs, and I was seconds from following her ass, but didn't. I kept my feet planted and gave her the time I convinced myself she needed to build back the sass or fire she was ready to throw.

When fifteen minutes ticked by and she still hadn't walked back in, I knew without looking she took off, pulled a fucking Raven and made a solo decision.

And a solo decision meant a stupid fucking decision.

That's the thing about Raven Carver, she does whatever the hell she wants, makes shitty judgment calls in a snap that you never see coming, and hopes it'll all work out in the end, fuck the consequences.

I can't fucking stand it.

Her ass has to stop taking off without us when she knows there's nothing but trouble waiting in the dark. This is something Bass fucking Bishop should have thought about before he asked her to slip away from us and meet him at the warehouses last night where she ended up getting fucking jumped.

He may be our bookie for all events out at the warehouses and a damn good one at that, but that's my fucking girl. He should've known better.

I might talk to my brothers about blacklisting his punk ass for that move alone – everyone on hand is replaceable, Raven is not. He should have fucking thought of that.

The second we realized she ran, we tossed him out, called up our boys, and went searching.

The problem, Raven's spent the better part of her life sneaking around others. We knew we'd only find her if she wanted us to. Going to look was more us hoping her ass was walking around to clear her mind.

Hours ticked by and she was nowhere in sight, so we came home to wait her out while our boys kept looking, hitting random house parties around town in search of her.

"I still think Bass is hiding something," Royce spits, tilting his head to look along the porch. "Little bitch is out pretending to hunt for her, he prolly knows exactly where she's at."

Captain shakes his head. "If he does know something, no way will he give it up now." He looks to me. "He knows we'd ream his ass for not talking last night after she got her ass beat on his time."

My jaw locks at his words, and I grind my teeth.

He's right, we would. I might for the fuck of it at this point.

My phone dings against the countertop and all our heads snap toward it. I jerk, quickly grabbing and unlocking it, completely fucking annoyed when I read my boy Mac's message on the screen. I toss it back down.

"Mac got a hold of that Mello chick she went to The Tower with. She's in fucking Maui – hasn't talked to Raven since we dropped her shit off."

Cap looks to his phone right then, frowning down at the screen. "Leo said he just searched the school grounds and park again." He stuffs it back in his pocket. "No Raven."

Fuck. Fuck it.

I jump to my feet, glancing from Captain to Royce. "I'm going to look again."

Royce has his keys in his hand in seconds, but Captain's features tighten.

"What?" Royce drags out suspiciously.

"We've got a game to play tomorrow, or fuck, today now." Cap licks his lips, glancing back our way. "We have to be ready for it."

Royce's brows snap together. "Cap. No." He shakes his head. "Maddoc, tell him."

Shit. The game.

When I don't say anything, Royce slices his eyes to Captain. "We're not fucking going if she's not back!"

Cap is cautious with him. "Royce—"

"Don't fucking Royce me, man," he cuts him off. "The fuck you actin' like you're calm, when I know you're not?!"

Captain glances from him to me. "We watched on the surveillance cameras, we know nobody took her. She ran. And you know if it weren't for the game, I'd be in the damn driver's seat already, but we need to be there, and we need to play well."

"And if she shows up, packs her shit or something while we're gone?!" Royce shouts, a frenzied look in his eye. "I'm not fucking leavin'!"

Fuck.

I rub at my temples. Cap's right, we have to play well, but damn, this is Raven we're talking about.

When we brought her here, we never expected her to fit. We sure as fuck never imagined wanting to keep her or to be unaccepting of her leaving.

We were told to make sure she fell in line the way the others my dad accepted into the houses did, but she fought us at every turn from the first fucking day.

She was different, and I knew it instantly.

It was in the way she didn't peek up at us but stared full-on, her chin held as high as ours if not higher. She gave lip when we demanded silence. When we pushed, she pushed harder, stepped in closer and lit our asses on fire in a way nobody ever had. She tested us more than we have her and without even trying, maybe even completely unaware.

At the thought, the pulse in my neck throbs harder against my skin as my anger boils higher with each passing second.

The fucked up part is I know Cap is on the same level we are right now, but he has more to lose, so he's in a fucked up position.

I know my brother, he'll be kicking his own ass later over even suggesting we stop looking for the night.

Still, with his inner struggles now in our face, Captain nods, looking between us. He's ready to ride even though he wishes we'd listen. "If we play like shit, we lose."

"Yeah," Royce mocks, not allowing himself to feel the guilt that'll hit later for our being selfish right now. "We lose, we jeopardize the season and Graven Preps stats raise, and piece of shit Principal Perkins will cause problems, and Dad will get on our fucking cases from a five by nine cement cell, and it'll all fall harder on your shoulders because of Zoey, man, but— " His mouth clamps shut when a click sounds.

Our heads jerk when the front door slowly creeps open and Raven steps inside.

She's measured in her motions, taking her sweet ass time to close and lock the door, prolonging what she's expecting to come at her – the fucking firing squad.

I quickly meet my brothers' frowns with my own before shifting it back to her.

I clench my jaw, forcing myself to wait until she turns around and looks at me, but Royce jumps in before she even can.

"What the fuck, Raven?!" He rushes forward.

Captain grips his shoulder to try and calm him, but he jerks free waiting for her to meet his glare. When she refuses, a sour laugh leaves him and he kicks over the coffee table, sending shit flying before storming up the stairs.

"Raven," I call her eyes to mine, but she only blows out a deep breath and looks to the left.

"I needed to clear my head," she rasps. "And in case you forgot, I don't have to ask anyone's permission to do it."

"Are you for real right now?" I growl and push toward her. "After all the shit from the last few days, you wanna play this fucking game?"

"I'm not playing games."

"Then fucking talk!" I shout, moving even closer. "You can't just run off whenever—"

"I can, and I will!" she yells back, trying for her usual defiant self, but her voice cracks without permission and her eyes quickly dart to the floor in a very un-Raven-like move.

Every muscle in my body locks, a sudden sickness spinning in my gut.

What the hell...

I glance to my brother, hoping for a sign of what he's thinking, but his stare is just as wary as mine.

"Raven..." I try again, a little calmer this time and finally her stormy eyes hit mine.

My lungs constrict as I get a good look.

Her makeup has worn off, eyes are puffy and red, a silent scream bristling, a flicker of something I can't quite read sitting at the edge, ready to burst.

I bite into my cheek to keep my mouth shut, fighting for some damn restraint when it's the last thing I want to do.

I had every fucking intention of ripping into her and not letting up but staring at her now, standing in front of me all beat up and bruised, emotionally drained from whatever is running through her mind, and physically from being attacked at our underground ring, I can't fucking do it. My shoulders fall.

"I need ... a shower and sleep." Even though she says it, she doesn't move right away.

She doesn't move at all until I take a half step toward her. That kicks her into gear and she hustles for the stairs.

Both Cap's and my eyes follow until her feet are no longer seen on the steps.

He turns back to me, speaking low. "I knew she was off earlier, but I can't convince myself it has anything to do with the fight."

"Cap." My fucking body is weighted, ready to drop. "Tell me it's not because we weren't there to help her. Tell me she doesn't look at me and see a man who can't keep her safe."

Captain grips my shoulder, looking me dead in the eye. "She left on her own, man, she purposely stepped away from us. The question we need to be asking is, was it because she needed a minute to herself" —he lifts his brows— "or because she needed to take care of something she didn't want us to be a part of? And I don't know the answer, my man. But what happened to her last night? That shit wasn't your fault."

"What if it was?" I argue. "What if she was jumped because of what we've made her?"

Cap laughs lightly, but it's defeated. "We didn't make her anything, brother. Raven was born who she is. Yeah, we brought her into our world, but she came in strong and determined. It's why she blended instantly. All we can do is try to understand the fucked-up way she was raised to think. Maybe down the road, she'll understand she's not alone anymore."

I narrow my eyes on him. "Why do you sound like you know she pulled some shit tonight?"

He sighs, releasing me. "I don't know, but I feel like she's in her head right now. Last time she was like this was when we tried to force her hand the day her mom showed up and she purposely tried to get herself kicked out of the Bray house, all to prove a point. That she was in control of her own moves."

"Things are different now," I all but growl.

We're not fucking dispensable to her. I know it.

I fucking feel it.

His eyes widen as he lifts his brows. "Exactly. It was all about her then and she still made a move that would be bad for herself, get her ass sent back to the hell she lived in, out of spite, but she's one of us now. Even if she hasn't said it out loud, she knows it, and look what she did for us when she didn't give a shit who we were... Pushing the girl in the pool at that Graven party, roping up the chick who had the video of Coach and his girl, the shit at the warehouses when she tried to let us get out without being seen, the cabins..."

When my brows dig in, he nods.

"Now, imagine what she'd do for us now that she cares."

Fuck. He's right.

I run my hands down my face and I push past him. "I can't

think about this shit right now, Cap. We'll figure it all out tomorrow or fuck, tonight, after the game."

"Yeah," he sighs. "That's probably a better idea."

He follows behind me, disappearing into his room.

I stop by the bathroom, finding the water still running, so I head for mine to rinse off real quick.

I don't know if anything Cap said holds any merit, and I sure as fuck plan to find out, but right now I'm gonna lay with her, fuck her if she needs it, hold her if she lets me, and we'll worry about the shit that happened tonight tomorrow.

RAVEN

I CRAWL UNDER THE COVERS, PULLING THE FLUFFY COMFORTER up to my chin, clenching it as armor when the sound of his footsteps pad against the floor in the hall.

The handle turns, but only as far as a locked knob allows, and I hold my breath.

What seems like a never-ending beat of silence follows, and I bite into my cheek, denying the pathetic tears trying to fight their way to the surface.

It turns again but slower, quieter as he tries one more time ... just in case.

Angry feet pound against the flooring and a door slams in the distance.

The second it does, I release a deep breath, pull my knife from under the blanket and flip it open. I turn it to run my finger over the blade while reading the inscription.

Family runs deeper than blood.

It's funny when you think about it.

Family runs deeper than blood, yet it's the ones we chose we'll so willingly bleed for.

I poke my fingertip until a drop of deep red appears, then run it across my lips. I rub them together, sliding my tongue along my teeth, spreading the metallic flavor left behind across my mouth in self-hate.

I'm sorry, Big Man. For today ... and what's to come.

Chapter 2

RAVEN

I KNEW AFTER WITNESSING PRE-GAME WARM-UPS THAT TONIGHT would be a messy battle, but I didn't expect this. This is just ugly.

For what must be the twentieth time tonight, the ball is passed to Maddoc in hopes of him adding some points to the board.

Switching up positions, he spins around a guy on the opposing team but loses his footing and slips. And like the last time the ball touched his hands, it's stolen right back.

Maddoc growls, his chest bowing out, but he shakes it off and keeps down the court.

I pinch my lips to the side, cringing when the visiting team makes yet another shot, Brayshaw now down by seven.

This entire game they've been playing catch up, but they can't seem to pull ahead. They're extremely sloppy, like I've never seen before, and unfortunately, it's trickled across the entire team.

Captain hasn't made a single shot he's attempted tonight, his frustration etched across his face. He's pretty much taken himself out at this point, and Royce is playing angry, which translates into foul after foul.

Right as I'm thinking it, another whistle sounds.

All heads turn to look down the opposite side of the court in time to see Royce get in the referee's face.

"Oh, you're not gonna call that on his ass, but you wanna call on me all night? I see how it is, ref." He bends his shoulders back a little, shaking his head mockingly. "It's cool, I know who signs your paychecks, bitch."

"Brayshaw!" the coach yells, but Royce ignores him.

I cut a quick glance at Maddoc and Captain, but they stay back, letting him do his thing.

"Man, let's go. We've got a game to win," a guy from the other team boldly – or stupidly – shouts and Royce whips around, the wild ass look in his eyes caught from here.

Within seconds he's shoving the dude in the chest, hard enough where the guy falls back against his teammates and I sit up straight, ready for a fucking brawl, but this is Bray's house, Brayshaw's town – nobody dares move closer. Nobody except Royce.

"Get in my face again, motherfucker, and you'll be eatin' metal."

The ref throws his hands out, a cautious look in his eyes as he officially ejects Royce from the game.

He flips him off with both hands and stomps over to the bench. He grabs his hoodie and water bottle, throwing it at the other team's coach, then slams his way through the gym door leading to their locker room.

Bass catches my eye and narrows his, but I dismiss him.

He can blame me all he wants for this shit show, he's just as guilty and he knows it. All he had to do was go to them with the news about the video, but he came to me instead.

I mean, I appreciate it, but I won't take his judgmental bullshit when he can right his wrong any time he wants. My guess, though, is he's not bold enough to know that he already held back information from the three who trust him with their dealings and money flow.

Maybe they shouldn't.

I find Maddoc on the court, who happens to look over right as I do, but he quickly cuts his eyes back, sliding into position before the ball is in motion again.

The way they're playing is completely my fault, I know that. I stressed them out, kept them up for almost two days now – doubt any of them slept last night. I know I didn't.

Maybe they're having a bad game today, but at least they got to play in it, right? I mean, if the video of the four of us getting frisky while also breaking into the Graven cabin was released, they could have been dropped from the team or be in juvenile hall or something.

There was no need to risk those outcomes when I was able to prevent it.

I'm realistic enough to understand my place in the world, and maybe it wouldn't have happened today or tomorrow, but the end game is never the girl from the ghetto ending up in a mansion to stay. I know that, and I accept it.

I'll admit though, I didn't expect the distance to sting so quick.

Maddoc hasn't spoken a word to me all day, Royce or Captain either, and they still have no clue what's in motion.

I can't even begin to imagine what happens from here, but the damage is done, and I'd do it again if I had to.

I shake off my thoughts and focus back on the game.

Asshole Leo makes a basket and everyone cheers. With a new shot of energy now flowing through the room, all eyes trail the Brayshaw Wolves as they follow the other team down the court.

One of our guys leaps up, blocking the shot attempt, and the ball falls into our hands. The Brayshaw player heads toward their basket, faking a throw down court only to toss it back to Maddoc, who shoots and makes a solid three-pointer.

The crowd jumps to their feet in excitement.

Elbows are thrown around, rougher than should be allowed, but after Royce's blow up, the referees seem not to want to call fouls on either team.

With Maddoc's new lead, the Wolves are fighting back.

There are seventeen seconds on the clock – a lifetime in basketball.

Come on, Big Man.

I lift my chin to see over the teammates who hop to their feet in front of me, jerking my head to the side when Principal Perkins plants himself directly at my side.

"Hello, Raven."

Unease washes over me, but I force my eyes back to the court, and sure as shit, amongst the crazy, Maddoc and Captain both spotted the piece of shit move my way.

"What do you want, Perkins?"

"I got a very interesting transfer slip on my desk this morning, Ms. Carver."

I freeze, and I'm pretty sure my eyes widen, because Maddoc's frown deepens, but he takes off, the ball now in his possession and I shift to see him better.

In the same second, Perkins lays his hand on my arm, and I spin, yanking away from him.

"Don't fucking touch me," I spit through clenched teeth and a mocking laugh leaves him.

The crowd groans and when my eyes flash back to the court, Maddoc's hands are swiping down his face in frustration, the ball now with the opposing team as the final buzzer sounds.

"Thanks for all your help, Ms. Carver."

"Don't get it twisted. I'd never do a damn thing to purposely help you."

He steps down, turning back to face me as he does. "You have a good night. Can't wait for the next game." He smirks and walks away.

I wish I could tackle his ass to the ground.

I look to the scoreboard.

There goes Brayshaw High's Varsity Basketball team's perfect record. The last chance the boys had at a seamless high school season.

Everyone will assume they simply couldn't pull it off, they'll say they were bound to have an off game at some point during the season.

Nobody around knows about the events of this weekend.

I had more than a few curious glances in school today, caught several staring at the cut on my lip and bruise on the side of my face that started to show even more the longer the day went on. The concealer I have is cheap, so I couldn't keep it covered all day. When you mix my appearance with the way the four of us sat staring into space at lunch today, the crazy of tonight's game, and Perkins' fake friendly smiles just now, I guarantee the rumor ring's firing on all cylinders right now. Not to mention how the three are known to tune out the world when on the court in uniform and were seen paying more mind to me than the game tonight. Yeah, people are gonna talk.

Fuck them.

I don't even consider moving from my seat as the team exits and the crowd disperses.

As I expected, Bass attempts to talk to me, but I shake my head and look away. He knows damn well I'm not interested in his backward worries – too little too late.

The guys take longer than normal in the locker room this time, likely getting reamed by their coach, and when they do come out, they're the only ones to step through the double doors.

All three sets of eyes zone in on me, making sure I'm still where they left me.

They slow their steps enough for me to catch up and together we head for Captain's Denali.

Once we're all seated, they take a few deep breaths before turning the engine over.

My stomach turns as anxiousness begins to grow inside me.

Any time now they'll start in, demanding answers, and no matter how many times I've played out the conversation in my head, preparing myself for possible questions and coming up with preplanned answers, none of them are believable.

I'm not even sure I could flat out lie to their faces when it came down to it.

Thankfully, they seem just as damn done with the day as me.

Captain heads straight for the house, dinner is skipped, and everyone moves for their own rooms. They lock themselves inside, so I do the same.

I throw myself back on the mattress, sucking in a lung full of air.

Perkins said he got a transfer form on his desk today. That happened so much faster than I anticipated.

My time with them is almost up.

Chapter 3

RAVEN

AFTER AN HOUR OF SITTING ON THE COUCH, WAITING FOR AT least one of the boys to come down, it's clear not one of them plans on going to school today, all three are likely burnt out after the last few days with little to no chill time. And I sure as shit couldn't care less about going, so I head into the kitchen to try and find some kind of food I can make on my own.

I scan through all their fresh ingredients and weird worded foreign shit I've never even seen before, let alone tried, digging out an old pack of Eggos. I'm pretty sure they're covered in freezer burn, but I go for it anyway. It's not like I've never eaten old or expired food that people claim is still good.

Nothing in my house ever lasted long enough to get old, but everything that came from the church was a solid week or more past the 'best by' or expiration date. The only thing that didn't come expired was the milk, when we were lucky enough to get it.

I was always the one to have to go down on donation days.

Being a kid all alone in a line full of mostly adults, their bleeding hearts felt bad and they'd give me more than the others, something they thought would brighten my eyes a little. It did. The one extra box of semi-stale cereal or a jar of canned jelly to go with the cheap Peter Pan peanut butter would honestly make my day, and sometimes my month when a spoonful of each was what held me over at home until the school days where I'd eat free meals in the cafeteria.

I stopped going to the donation centers though when I saw one of the other moms from my trailer park, who was there with her youngest kid, get turned away for lack of goods.

I'd heard my mom try to turn her out once, but she wasn't one to run tricks to buy her drugs like my mom. No, she chose to sell her food stamps instead. So, without the church's food, her kids simply didn't eat. She was never hungry since her drug of choice was meth, so I doubt she even noticed all the times her kids would make their way to other neighbors' houses hoping for an invite to stay and eat that didn't always come.

They were only five and seven. I was nine.

I left my box on their steps that day.

I think that was the moment I realized other people had it worse than me.

If I could go back there and pull all those kids from their homes, I would.

People think CPS steps in and saves little kids, but that can only happen if someone cares enough to call. Unfortunately, most around us don't. Their situations are usually shitty in some way too, and they don't want anyone in their business, so mouths stay shut when maybe they shouldn't.

I only remember ever seeing one kid getting removed from his home, and that was only because his dad overdosed, and the dad's girlfriend didn't want him there. Sucked when he left. He would sit outside with me at night sometimes, waiting for the louder clients of my mom's to leave.

With my plate of slightly soggy waffles in hand, I tiptoe back to my room. I drop onto the bed and take my time eating, then grab my stash from the drawer and roll a joint. It's a pinner, all I have left is the shake from the bottom of the bag, but it'll get the job done.

I grab the old water bottle from the bedside table to ash in and drop in the chair next to the window. I unlatch it and push it open ... and a piercing ring hits my ears making me cringe.

I slam it shut, but it keeps going.

I growl, jumping when my door is thrown open and Maddoc appears.

He pushes a button on his phone and the earsplitting alarm – that they must have had installed or activated today – stops.

He stands there a minute with hair the perfect kind of fucked-up, puffy lips and sleepy eyes. Shirtless and in nothing but tight briefs, his morning wood still very much present, and suddenly I'm hot in all the right places.

But he gets me in the gut when fire doesn't fill his eyes, and instead they slowly drop to my doorknob before purposefully lifting back to mine and holding.

Anger and cageyness stare back but he blinks them away, a mask now slipped in their place. He walks away without a word.

I jerk forward, ready to go after him but I force my feet still, reminding myself the shift in the house is my fault and the way I'm reacting to it isn't who I am.

I'm not a frail girl affected by the actions of a broody boy.

So, I locked him out twice now, so what?

With a sigh, I toss the weak ass joint to the carpet and drop back on the mattress where I stay for the remainder of the day.

Yeah, I'm not even fooling myself.

This is gonna suck.

Chapter 4

MADDOC

I'm stuffing my phone back in my pocket right as Cap walks in. "That was Leo," I say.

"And?" Captain pushes.

"He said Coach ran into Perkins' office and slammed the door shut."

"The fuck?" Royce steps closer.

"I have no fucking idea."

"We can't even miss a fucking day anymore without shit going south." Cap shakes his head, annoyed by all the bullshit.

Raven comes down the stairs right then and all our stares lift.

She stops in her tracks, her eyes flying between the three of us as her slow steps carry her farther down. While her features remain perfectly expressionless, I know those eyes and dread bleeds through the stormy grey.

"We leave in five." I don't look at anyone as I say it, and

I'm in the car before they've even had a chance to grab their shit.

I glare at the traitorous orchards as I wait.

Until two nights ago, I liked the seclusion of the trees that surround us, blocking us from the outside world, but the dark blanket it provides helped her get out without tipping us off to what direction she went.

Where'd you go, baby, and why you pulling away?

I groan, running my hands down my face.

She's making me a weak bitch. Maybe the distance she's forcing is what I need to fucking detach a little.

Maybe I should tie her ass to the bed, legs spread, arms out, and show her some pretty pain to make her talk?

A grunt leaves me, and I hit the steering wheel, hiding my eyes behind my shades as the three exit the house.

They slide into their seats, and knowing something is happening with Perkins, we skip the donut shop and are pulling into the parking lot of the school in minutes.

"What's our plan here?" Royce questions angrily.

"No plan," I tell him. "We go in and figure out what the fuck is going on."

Royce nods and steps ahead, Raven following behind him.

Cap trails a little slower, so I stay at his pace, meeting his stare when he looks to me. "I've got a bad feeling about this."

I frown at the building thinking the same damn thing.

"Let's go."

Leo meets us at the door, Royce already standing there grilling him, Raven at his side.

"Coach is out now, but they're already in the gym getting ready for the assembly," he tells us.

"Fuck." I shake my head. "I forgot about that shit."

Leo nods. "I think you should wait until after."

"I think you should keep your thoughts to yourself," Royce bites back with what the three of us are thinking.

Leo tenses, but quickly shakes it off, moving out of the way with a tight shrug.

I meet Cap's stare.

"Let's go in, we'll pull his ass out." Royce yanks the door open and we step through.

Soon as we're inside, the bell rings and people rush to take a seat, but we head straight for Coach.

He quickly breaks from Perkins and rushes our way, his face etched in anger. "Sit. And stay sitting."

"Talk, and talk now," I demand.

He glares but does as he's told. "Your dad called. I'll explain, but I need you boys not to fight me on this, no matter how bad you want to." He looks between the three of us, his eyes pausing a brief moment on Raven before he walks off only to turn back one more time. "Sit."

Royce's jaw clenches, but he only groans and moves for our seats – the first-row of bleachers in the center of the rest.

Captain moves next.

Coach Brail is one of the only people we trust around here when we're forced to count on other people, but even I admit right now it's real fucking hard to keep my cool when tension is so fucking high between us all. To say we're on edge is an under-fucking-statement.

The office lady turns to usher Raven off, but I stop her before she can speak on it. "She sits with us."

The woman clamps her mouth shut and gives a tight-lipped nod.

As soon as I drop my ass down, Coach catches my eye, narrowing his own. He tips his chin.

"The fuck's he trying to say, Madman?" Royce hisses beside me.

I shake my head slowly. "I have no fucking clue, but he wants us to stay in line."

"Fuck him," Royce quips and I can't say I'm not on the

same wavelength of thinking. "It's our fucking line, he's lucky we let his ass on it."

The crowd dies down as Perkins pulls the microphone to his mouth.

"Good morning everyone," he addresses the room. "It's an exciting time, and even with our ... unexpected and disappointing loss this week, we're going into playoffs tonight as the number one seed over Graven Prep."

The students go fucking nuts, shouting out their excitement while Perkins looks pissed we still managed to pull ahead based on points earned and points allowed through the season.

Fuck him.

Perkins goes over some bullshit about the hype the next few weeks will bring, reminding everyone that schoolwork comes first and other shit he doesn't believe in but preaches to save face, and then the music starts, and he moves aside as the cheerleaders take center court.

Chloe, front and fucking center as always, makes damn sure not to cut her eyes our way while she shakes her ass or pops her tits in some sex-infused move she's thrown in the middle of their routine.

They do some crazy acrobatic shit and people go nuts whistling and clapping.

"Now that's some flexibility," Mac muses a few spaces down and Royce chuckles.

He ain't lying. The cheer squad, or dance team you could call them, has won at state the last three years, ever since Chloe started choreographing. She never lets anyone fucking forget it.

Soon as they're done, they throw their poms at the team's feet – not a single pair land near me – then crawl to some cheesy fucking wolf calls to retrieve them.

Captain kicks the pair near his feet away with the shake of his head.

He looks past me before meeting my eyes. He nods his chin, so I shift to look at Raven.

My brows hit at the center when I find her zoning out, eyes forward and focused on nothing.

"What—"

I go to call her out but stop short when Perkins flicks the mic on again.

His eyes instantly hit mine, and I glare.

"All right! Thank you, girls, that was lovely," Perkins starts, way too fucking giddy for me.

My brothers and I lean forward wearing matching frowns.

"Now. We have an announcement to make. It's not usual," he continues and my pulse kicks. "And it took some digging into the rulebooks, but I'm more than happy to say it's all been worked out."

"Maddoc..." Captain trails off.

Perkins' stare slices to mine, triumph growing in his eyes.

"Please," he pauses, the corner of his mouth tipping up. "Help me give a warm welcome to the newest member ... of Brayshaw High's Varsity basketball team."

There's a beat of silence in the room, but a deep ringing in my ears tells me to stand.

My brothers rise with me.

The door tucked away in the farthest corner from us is thrown open with a loud thud and in walks Collins Graven – wearing a fucking Wolves jersey.

My body starts to shake as anger fills every inch of me, but my feet have turned to lead. I'm rooted in my fucking spot.

Royce and Captain must be too, because they've yet to move.

He dares to walk in here?

The whispers start, growing louder and louder until the entire fucking student body is gasping and talking shit behind us.

Collins stands tall, slowly stalking forward, his eyes scanning every face he can find in the stands from left to right.

Then they stop, right on fucking Raven at my side.

She slowly pushes to her feet, and my eyes snap her way. She doesn't look at me but keeps her blank stare on his.

Mine move back to him. The corner of his lip rises as he studies her and I take a step forward, but all of a sudden, Coach is right there, pushing me back, blocking my body discreetly with his. He drives his shoulder between me and Raven and turns his head to my ear.

"Do not fucking move," he growls through his teeth. "He wants this. You move, he starts over you next game."

I have no idea what's said after that, all I can focus on is the blood pumping through me at an increasingly dangerous level.

Raven takes a step left, a step away from me, and I push my chest against Coach's.

"Raven." I glare.

She licks her lips, taking a half a step forward.

Her hands rub against her jeans and unease flares in my chest.

"Raven..."

My head snaps straight when her name flies from Graven's mouth.

I see it when she resolves herself to whatever the fuck was going through her mind.

Her chin lifts, shoulders square.

In one swift motion, she whips her sweater over her head, a black jersey with teal trimming – a Wolves jersey, a fucking Brayshaw High jersey – with the large number one on it covers her frame. A jersey identical to the one Graven is wearing.

And I see red, blood fucking red, and it's about to be his blood everyone else sees. I'll paint the fucking floor with it.

He reaches out and she steps closer to him.

He's dead.

My brothers dart forward first, but our teammates move in. Mac and Leo are hardly able to hold back Captain, but nobody can contain Royce.

And that's my fucking girl beside that little bitch.

Fuck starting. Fuck everything.

I shove Coach to the ground, half leaping over his body as I rush him, but I'm yanked back by a group of my teammates.

It takes a second but I'm able to throw them off one by one and dart forward, but I skid to a fucking halt when my eyes lift.

Royce stands braced to fight, trembling in a rage he's about to unleash on the preppy prick in khakis.

Only a five foot six, dark-haired piece of fucking trouble stands before him.

Against him.

Against us.

Fury flares and before I can think better of it, I'm yanking her by the wrist until she's right in front of me. Any normal girl would have shrieked, frightened eyes flying to the guy jerking her around. Not Raven.

She has control of her stare, purposely taking an extra, careless moment to meet mine.

Hard. Unwavering.

I heave her even closer.

There's gasping behind me, and I know how this must seem.

Raven's face and arms are bruised and beat and now they see me manhandling her, but I couldn't give two fucks what they're thinking right now.

"It's nothing personal, Big Man." There's fire dripping from her words as if she's baiting the fucking enemy. Determination screams behind her eyes, but what she's hoping for is unclear, even to me. "Just business."

"Let her go, Maddoc," comes from my coach who is now at my side.

Raven's lips smash together and as I start to loosen my grip, she begins tugging against my hold, drawing away from me.

I quickly let go, darting forward and using both hands, I grip the jersey she's wearing by the collar. I pull, shredding it from top to bottom, forcing the fucking thing from her skin. She's twisted around and falls against the floor with a thump, nothing but a sports bra on her upper half.

"Maddoc!" Royce yells, bounding forward. "The fuck, man?!"

My shoulders fall, my eyes frozen on her exposed skin, and I swear time stops fucking ticking.

Royce's shoes squeak against the flooring as he skids to a stop beside me. "Holy shit," he rasps.

"Raven..." Captain drawls out quietly, stuck where he stands, but I sense it when his eyes harden and slice to me.

Large bruises, one the perfect imprint of a boot, covers half her stomach, smaller ones trailing down her abdomen and up her chest.

"What the hell happened to her?" is whispered to someone behind me.

Baby—

My body jerks toward her subconsciously, but Captain and Royce are gripping me by my arms and dragging me backward in the same second. They toss me back, shoving me forward when we reach the door.

We're in the truck and smashing down the road in the next minute.

"The fuck just happened?" Royce shouts, panic and anger threaded in his tone.

"I don't know," Cap seethes, picking up more speed.

"Her body." I look to them. "Her fucking body!" It looks ten times fucking worse than it did the night it happened.

"You see what someone did to her?!" I yell, punching the dash.

"Yeah, man," Royce growls. "We saw."

"Everyone fucking saw, Maddoc," Captain barks and my muscles grow tight. "And now they probably think you beat her ass, you dumbass! Nobody knows she was jumped!"

"Fuck them and what they think! She was wearing his fucking number!" I turn to Cap. "She is mine, Captain! And we just fucking left her back there ... with that little bitch!"

"Is she though?" Royce sits forward, spitting venom with every word. "Maddoc, she knew he was coming. That was fucking planned. She just served us on our own damn court."

"There has to be more going on here," Captain adds dryly, completely unsure of his own words.

"The fuck are we missing then, Cap?"

"I'm telling you, she fucking played us!" Royce shouts back. "We trusted her, man!"

"Stop," Captain snaps. "Don't cut her off yet, Royce. We need to find out what the fuck is going on."

I look back at Royce and as soon as my eyes meet his, he shifts his glare out the window.

"We never should have trusted someone outside of us," he spits, the muscle in his jaw ticking against his skin.

Trust has always come harder for him, but he better be fucking wrong here.

Captain's phone starts ringing, and I grab it, frowning. "Blocked caller."

Cap pulls over and answers, putting the phone on speaker.

"Dad," he calls out.

"Are you with your brothers?" our dad asks.

"We're here," Royce adds, sitting forward in his seat.

"Where are you?" he asks.

"What the fuck is going on?" I demand.

Fuck his question.

He obviously fucking knows we aren't in class – he never interrupts us at school unless something went down and he got wind. "How is he at Brayshaw? Why is he at Brayshaw?"

He stuns us when he says, "I gave the okay on his transfer request."

"Without talking to us first?" I bite out. "You let us get completely fucking blindsided in there! How do you expect us to keep control and order if we're not fucking aware? You made us look like fools!"

"Maddoc," Cap hisses.

"No!" I shout, looking between them, then back at the dark screen. "Fuck this. Man, fuck you for this, Dad. Why the hell would you agree to letting him in?"

"Why the fuck would he want in?" Royce adds.

Our dad speaks again, "It was either him at Brayshaw ... or her at Graven."

Our eyes snap up meeting each other's.

"Yes," he answers our silence. "I'm aware of what's happening with the girl, but you figured as much, I'm sure."

"She's not just some girl." Cap frowns. "She's ..." He trails off, not knowing the right words to describe what she's become. What we thought she had become.

"She's important to you?" His voice calmer than normal, almost troubled.

My brows pull in.

"Has she grown close to one of you specifically?" he questions warily.

"All of us," I snap at him before they can answer.

"Or so we thought." Royce glares at me, mouthing what the fuck.

Our dad's quiet a few seconds.

"Listen to me," he starts cautiously, and instinctively we all lean closer to the cell phone. "Be smart, think before you act, but do not hold back if you need to handle business. You three are Brayshaw, if people need to be reminded, show them what that means. Don't let them forget who's in charge, Graven around or not. They're digging, and they may have discovered some things they weren't supposed to yet. Keep him there, right under your nose where you can watch him."

"You expect us to let that little bitch run in our halls?" Royce questions. "Run on our fucking court?"

"Yes," our dad's answer is instant, but he pauses a moment before adding, "Make no mistake, Collins Graven has changed the game. I'm afraid it's not about you anymore."

"What do you mean?" Royce asks, his eyes hitting mine.

Captain's features grow dark and he slowly looks between the two of us. "Raven."

Why would he go after her other than to get to us?

"Boys," our dad stresses. "Do not lose her to them."

"She's not exactly easy to control," Captain barks.

"And she just played us, could have been this entire time. We can't trust her," Royce spits. "She's a liability at this point."

There's a deep sigh through the phone and then, "Do what you must, sons. Hold tight. Everything is in the works."

The line goes dead.

"The fuck does that mean?" Royce hits the seat and drops back against his own.

"I don't know." Captain puts the SUV in drive and we're back on the road in seconds. "Guess we'll find out."

I turn to look out the window.

If she thinks she can fuck us over, she's got another thing coming. They both do.

She wants to fuck with my head? It's worked.

She wants to prove a point? She's done it.

She thinks I'll back down? She's fucking wrong.

My jaw clenches, a heated poison burning in my veins at the thought of her with him.

Don't lose her to them, he said.

I'll lose her to no one.

Raven Carver is mine whether she wants to be now or not. Period.

She wants to pretend she doesn't see me the same, I'll force her fucking hand, in time. Problem is, I'm far from patient.

Go on, play your games, baby. I've got more moves than you can handle.

Chapter 5

RAVEN

"Don't look so glum, Rae."

"Fuck you, Collins."

"Begging again? So soon?" He stuffs his phone in his pocket. "It's only been two days since you fucked up their world on their own turf, sweetness."

"You're a fucking fool."

"But I'm your fool, right?" He laughs and drops down across from me. "Great job, by the way, not sure I told you that yet. I'll be honest, I wasn't so sure you'd follow through."

"I said I would."

"People say a lot of things, but you know that." He grins and I want to slap it off his face. "You see how quick they gave up on you? Bet you didn't expect that. You probably thought they'd tear you right back, right away, yet here you sit, wearing the same shit you did two days ago and still ... no Brayshaw to the rescue. Not even one out of three."

I clench my teeth as discreetly as possible.

I don't know what I expected, but I won't show this chump my regret or the pathetic ache his words cause. Not that he'd read it right, he's too blinded by his need to win a war he's nowhere near equipped for. I'm almost curious if he wants it or if it's simply because he craves notoriety.

Or maybe it's acceptance?

Makes me wonder what he saw and heard as a kid.

I break our stare off and glance around the room.

This is a big ass house both empty and cold, more of a showroom of sorts. No color or real sign of living other than the ring around the coaster on the coffee table. Stone colored statues and ugly ass art fills the place.

Maids likely come in each day and out each night, cleaning up after the parties he throws almost on the daily – his need to have people close – and leaving him food to reheat in the fridge.

Maddoc had said, other than Collins, it was only his mother and grandfather, the last Gravens standing outside their men around town, but there's no sign of them anywhere.

"Your dad really dead?"

His glass tumbler freezes at his lips – yeah, he's that guy, does the whole ritzy shit, bourbon on the rocks like a typical rich boy trying to play like his pops. Sipping on it like a bitch.

He can't shoot a shot like mine do.

Another twinge hits in my chest at the thought, but I shift my body to hide it.

Collins sets his glass beside him, leaning forward to rest his elbows on his knees, eyeing me.

He's far from a bad looking guy, I've admitted this before. He's found attractive to even the pickiest of females, I'm sure, with the typical preppy boy look – too perfect hair and text-book teeth. His face is clean and sharp, never a sign of yester-day's shave or shadow even. No small cuts or scars to be found – bet he uses wrinkle cream already, too. Of course, he's also fit like a basketball player, trim frame and decent height, sculpted to ego feeding perfection.

"I assume you know the story of how Rolland and his boys became Brayshaw, how their families were brought in before they were born?"

I'm well aware none of the boys are blood Brayshaw, and that Rolland, Maddoc's biological dad, was brought into the family when he was younger. I know damn well that after Rolland's best friends were killed, he adopted their sons to raise as his own, giving each his earned Brayshaw name.

Three boys, not one blood related, but brothers by choice.

I know who the fuck they are.

"Yeah, you must," he continues when I say nothing. "But what is it you think you know about my family?" He eyes me. "About my name?"

A laugh bubbles out of me instantly, and I roll my eyes. "Please, pretty boy. Tell me you're not dumb enough to think I'd answer that?" I lean forward to meet his glare. "I may be sitting on your couch, but don't fool yourself into believing it's where I want to be."

"You might wanna work on changing that, it's where you should be."

"Hard pass."

He laughs lightly, his chin lowering. "Did you know it was a Graven lawyer who got Rolland Brayshaw convicted?"

I give him nothing, but even still, he nods.

"Yeah, you did. But did you know that lawyer was my father?"

I force an impassive expression when every muscle inside me locks. "Nope."

Holy shit. Not just any Graven put their dad away, but Collins' dad himself?

"Case didn't even go to trial." He smirks at my frown – so much for a blank face. "Daddy Brayshaw denied, denied,

denied up until the very last second. Then, right before he was set for court, he changed his tune, pled guilty and took the deal."

"Maybe he grew a conscience."

"Or maybe he had a completely different reason to admit to a crime he swore he didn't commit." He arches a brow.

I force myself not to swallow but color me intrigued. "And what might that be?"

He simpers like he's privy to something I'm not, picks up his glass and tosses it back in one gulp. He stands. "Now you're the fool if you think I'll tell you, but maybe, in time, Rae. That depends on you. Get up and let's go."

"Where?" I snap.

"Shopping." He lets his eyes run over my form. "Can't have my woman looking like she stepped out of a low budget music video."

"Why not? I've gotta walk next to a guy who looks forever ready for a round of golf."

He laughs lightly, and I frown. "Class doesn't mix with trash, Rae."

"Yet you were ready to pay me for my time, Collins. Weird, right?"

"Get up and get in the fucking car, this is non-negotiable."

"I'm not dressing like some prep school princess."

"You'll dress how I say," he snaps with a glare. "Don't forget, you agreed to do this my way, now get up."

I take my time pushing to my feet and move to stand directly in front of him.

"You think you'll win this little battle, but you won't."

"Yeah, and what makes you so sure?"

A slow smirk finds my lips and his brows meet at the center. "Respect can't be bought or earned when blackmail is in the mix. Everyone at your feet is paid or pushed while everyone at theirs is proud to be where they are. Ever ask yourself what happens when those guys you had jump me feel the need to brag and do because you haven't earned their loyalty? Or when they get a higher offer somewhere else and drop you like the bitch you are? You—"

"Watch yourself, Rae." He pushes closer, the muscle in his jaw ticking. "I can keep this easy or I can make this hard, your call."

I meet his one step forward with two of my own. "You watch, Collins. I don't know what you thought you'd get from me or what put you in this mindset, but you're an even bigger clown than I knew if you think for a second easy is what I need."

I step back, watching the fury rise in his eyes with each step taken. "The ball may be in your court but consider me the referee in this game. You didn't gain yourself a soldier, you earned yourself a snake. Don't get bit, Graven."

His frown holds for a moment, but slowly a malicious grin takes its place.

He makes his way toward me, stopping to whisper near my ear. "Oh, this is bound to be good, Brayshaw. I can't wait for all the sweet little lies to come out. That pretty little head of yours is gonna spin, baby, but if you're a good girl, I might just hold your hair back when the vomit makes its way up."

He pushes past me, snatching his keys off the side table before storming out the door, leaving me with nothing to do but follow his punk ass out like a good girl.

Dick.

"YOU BETTER BE CURLING YOUR HAIR REAL DAMN PRETTY IF IT'S taking you this long to get ready!" Collins snaps from the other side of the door.

I roll my eyes and take one last hit off my joint before

putting it out against the comforter, making another burn hole straight through the cliché silk covering.

I can't believe I'm actually staying in this fucking house.

I'm half pissed at myself for not just taking off on my own, but I can't do that to the guys. They've earned every bit of my loyalty, something I've never given to anyone, even if they don't know it.

That's the difference between true allegiance and the need to stay at the top of the game where the strongest sit with ease – honest loyalty doesn't need to be seen or stated. It's just as powerful if not more so when given in silence.

I don't need them to be aware of why I'm really here. I need them oblivious and untouched by this asshole's current piece of blackmail.

"Two minutes. That's all you get," he says as if his words mean shit to me.

There's some shuffling and then stomping of feet down the obnoxious spiral staircase.

I watch the clock, waiting for a solid three minutes to pass then drag myself to stand, gliding my feet in the pair of slides I hid in the ridiculous shit Collins bought yesterday to help "raise my stature."

Fucking, please.

He's so clueless it's unreal.

I turn to the gold trimmed mirror, glaring at myself.

The stupid girl who can't stand the thought of letting go of the three she's pushing away.

Oh, the irony behind the change of events.

I grab my backpack from the floor and drag it out with me, squaring my shoulders when I hit the last step.

Collins spins around, doing a double take. "What the fuck?"

He takes in the dark purple cashmere sweater dress he picked out, now cut down the sides and loosely tied back together to show my black tank underneath. His eyes fall to the 'stockings' he bought, now with strategically placed holes at the left outer and right upper thigh, disappearing under the material.

It's also missing a few inches at the bottom now.

I didn't curl my hair like he was hoping, but I did pull it back in a tight ponytail – only because it kept getting stuck to the fucking material.

He dared to ask me to cut off the blue tips, and I kindly told him to fuck off.

"That was a four-hundred-dollar dress." He glares.

"That I told you not to buy. Besides, that's chump change to you, right?"

He gets in my face. "I need you to look the fucking part. You agreed to this."

"These people piss Armani and puke fucking Prada. They'll smell a fucking foul ten miles away."

I shake my head and move past him, but he grips my elbow and I jerk around, yanking free.

"I should let your punk ass make a fool of yourself!" I seethe.

His features tighten in question and I shake my head.

"Are you so unaware, you honestly think changing me to fit you will be convincing? That they'll praise you or be jealous? Because they won't. I may have agreed to all this to keep your rat bastard mouth shut, but don't think for a fucking second, you've got it all figured out. Those boys? They know me."

"Yeah, clearly they all do," he tries to get in a dig, referring to the video.

I hold my head high and shrug. "Yeah, you're right. All fucking three dropped to their knees ... for me. Thanks for reiterating my fucking point. They know me. They know how I think, what I need and when, and yeah, how I fucking like to be touched – completely irrelevant right now, but still true, dick. I'm not hiding that. I don't need to, Collins, because the only people I give a shit about didn't judge me for needing, and yeah, enjoying something they gave me. This is all about keeping people from finding out we were in your cabin while you partied only feet away, none the fucking wiser."

"Fuck you."

"Fuck you," I throw right back. "It's like I said, they know me, and if I show up there only days after being at their side, now at yours, wearing a fucking dress and flats with curls in my hair and smile on my face, looking like another carbon copy of the basic bitches you're used to, you'll be eating cement quicker than you can say concede."

"I'd never concede."

"And I'd never conform," I spit. "You want this believable, let me be me, because I'd never be anyone else for any-fucking-body. I may now be the untrustworthy bitch in their eyes, but they are far from dumb. Give them the credit they deserve. You're only making a sucker of yourself if you don't."

I don't bother waiting for a reply but turn and head for his little bitch car and slide inside.

He's in his seat in the next few seconds. "At least you attempted to hide the bags under your eyes."

Asshole.

Chapter 6

MADDOC

I BOUNCE ON MY FEET AND SHAKE MY BODY OUT, ONLY TO STEP in again for another combo.

The chain clashes against the beam, the punching bag bounding against my gloveless hands, the cracks at my knuckles ripping deeper, the blood trickling down my forearms and onto the rubber mat beneath my feet.

I keep going – one, two, uppercut. Left, right, kidney shot.

His cheek, his jaw, his fucking temple. Lights out, bitch.

My right knuckle splits completely open, and I clench my jaw, wrapping my arms around the punching bag to catch my breath.

I can't fucking believe this shit.

Three damn days without seeing her and it feels like three damn years. Why or how we agreed to stay sitting fucking ducks, I have no idea.

It's fucking torture.

"You 'bout done, boy?"

My chin drops to my chest and my arms fall to my sides. I swing my glare toward the door, knowing my brothers are standing right behind her.

Really, fuckers?

"Nuh-uh, child," Maybell reprimands and moves forward with a first aid kit. "Don't be lookin' at them like that. They did right, calling me. You look as bad as you did when you found out the green Power Ranger was leaving the show."

I crack a smile despite my shitty mood and my brothers chuckle behind her.

She smiles faintly, then waves her hand over her shoulder, signaling for Royce and Captain to shuffle into the room.

"Got some work done, I see." She looks pointedly at the tattoo on my left pec, following the trail that wraps over my shoulder blade. It's only half done – ten fucking hours in the chair. I had to pass the time somehow.

"I did. I just took the wrapping off last night."

She winks and we all move to sit.

Maybell kneels in front of me and starts working on my hand with peroxide.

"So." She peers up with an eyebrow raised. "She's gone."

"You heard he put Collins Graven at Brayshaw?" I ask even though I know the answer.

"I did."

"You hear she left with him day one?"

Her hands pause their movements and I cut a quick glance at my brothers. They caught it too.

She didn't know.

Our dad's known to tell her everything, almost always before us, so, why would he keep this from her?

"Your father is a smart man," she answers the question I didn't have to ask. "If he's being choosy about the information he shares, there is a reason. Believe that."

"We do," Captain tells her, but then shifts to frown out the window. "Problem is we didn't expect this, and it doesn't feel right. She's not ... it just doesn't feel right." He licks his lips and stands, moving to the other side of the room.

Royce leans forward, his elbows on his knees.

"Boy?" Maybell calls him, wanting his thoughts, but he only continues to glare at his folded hands.

He shakes his head, giving nothing.

Maybell sighs and spreads some skin glue over my knuckles, patting me on the thigh as she stands. She stares. "Your old man tell you to do as you felt needed?"

I nod.

She gives a grim smile. "Well, seems there's only one move at the moment."

Cap spins around to look at her and Royce's head raises. She looks from one to the next, settling on me. "Make her regret it."

"And if she doesn't?"

Maybell lets out a little laugh and turns for the door. "Come on, boy. No need to fish for reassurance, it won't take much to hit her where it hurts. No one knows that girl like you, maybe not even her. You boys are the only weapon that would work against her."

Maybell throws away the soiled gauze and grabs a towel from the rack in the corner, moving toward the blood on the mat, but she stops before bending down and scowls at the three of us.

"Wash away the self-pity and stand tall, like you were born to do. I've watched you take down a corrupt judge and get a congressman to give up his seat, a seventeen-year-old girl will not break you." Maybell's eyes travel between us again. "Watch her when she can't see you, force her hand when you need to. Make her think of you at every moment, every day – bet she already is. Stay in her face and get dirty if need be."

"Why?" Royce asks her, and she looks to me.

My eyes bounce between hers, and I answer, "Because that's what it'll take."

Royce pushes to his feet and Captain walks closer.

"To what?" Cap asks hesitantly.

My brows furrow and Maybell tips her chin.

I look to my brothers. "To break her."

"Is that what you want to do?" Captain asks me, an angry glare he doesn't try to hide behind his eyes. "You want to push her 'til she falls?"

"And catch her on the way down, yeah."

"And if she falls the wrong way?" Royce questions, unsure.

I clench my teeth together. Not an option. "Then we'll make sure it hurts when she hits the ground."

Captain pulls into the school and parks. "Look at these fucking people, standing around just waiting to see what happens next."

Royce shakes his head, frowning. "We need to set shit right here, and quick."

Captain glances my way and I jerk my chin, telling him to spit it out.

"You sure you're up for this?"

"Up for what? This is our fucking school."

"Yeah." He nods with a glare. "And that's your fucking girl who will be on the arm of a Graven. Collins fucking Graven," he spits and my jaw clenches. "Like I said, you up for this?"

"I'll snap his wrists, Cap."

"And we'll be right there to help you, my man, but we can't ignore the fact that she made the choice. Do what you need to, but don't forget where she slept this weekend."

My eyes harden, and he shrugs, but his eyes show disappointment.

"You need to hear this, brother, who the fuck knows what'll happen from here." He eyes me.

"We already talked all this shit out, we go in there, treat her like the rest of them and play it by ear."

"Yeah," he nods. "I know we did, but I also caught the way your teeth started grinding the second we pulled into this parking lot, and the bounce of your knee, and the fists your hands are making right now."

I throw my door open and climb out, turning back to lean in and grab my bag. "Point fucking taken."

He gives a weak ass grin and they both follow my move.

We step in front of the SUV, Mac and Leo moving toward us as we do.

I look from Leo to the old Thunderbird he's been driving. It's a piece of shit, but still...

On a part-time paperboy's salary?

"How long'd you have to save for that?" I jerk my chin toward the car but keep my eyes locked on Leo.

He shrugs, glancing back at it a moment. "'Bout six months, but I'm making payments."

I nod, shifting my eyes toward my brothers.

Royce looks from me to him, holding out his hand. "Badass, bro. Making it work."

Could be true.

Mac steps in for props, right as Leo starts talking.

"That was some crazy shit at the rally the other day, huh?"

"We knew Collins was working his way in." Royce shrugs and starts walking, so we all move with him, forcing Leo and Mac to stay behind or follow.

"But Raven, who would have thought," the bastard keeps going, shaking his head.

"Every-fucking-body would have thought." I swing a careful expression his way when I'd rather be pouring bleach down his throat for thinking he can speak freely on her. "She's the daughter of a whore, what else would you expect? You really think we'd keep her around long?"

Acid lines my tongue at my own words, so I turn away before he sees the shift in my gaze.

"Speaking of whores," Mac changes the subject, meeting my eyes a quick moment. "You guys hear Tisha Stevenson got caught sucking the judge's dick at the cheer competition the varsity girls went to this weekend?"

"No shit?" Royce entertains him to help save face as Mac intended.

Leo gives a stiff laugh. "Yeah, we heard the coach walked in on it."

Cap looks my way and I frown, following his stare when it shifts.

A group of girls stand in the middle of the hall chatting and I groan.

Fuck.

'Course they'd all be ready and waiting day one.

I don't bother covering my annoyance and keep toward my locker, but then laughter has me glancing down the hall in time to see Chloe step up to Mac and Leo and the others at the end of the hall.

Hmm...

I shift to Royce.

"Chloe?" He frowns, glancing down the hall and back, looking at me like I've lost my mind.

I shrug. "Why not let her run free on her, see if Raven cracks."

"Not that I think Chloe's brave enough to come hard at her, but this is Raven we're talking about." Captain glares. "She doesn't crack."

"Yeah, she cracks other motherfuckers." Royce shakes his head, but then his attention is pulled down the hall and he frowns. "But if you wanna test the theory..." He looks back to me, anger and anxiousness taking over his features. "Mask your face, brother. She just walked around the corner. With him."

I slowly shift my body to face the direction he's looking, and as if lava was injected in my veins, everything inside me burns.

My eyes trail over her and my fists clench. My mind has been so fucked I didn't even stop to think about how all her shit is still at our house – he must have set her up with clothes.

Keeping my cool is fucking useless and a deep crease takes over my forehead.

She tried to make it here, but these people know money when they see it.

Her head lifts and her eyes hit mine, but she doesn't falter, not even for a second.

The hairs at the base of my neck tingle and my shoulders grow taut.

My eyes snap to Collins and sure enough, the little bitch is staring right at me.

His smirk is slow, and so is his hand as he moves to wrap it around her waist.

Oh, so he wants to get his ass fucking kicked, does he?

Instantly, her eyes pop up to mine, but she doesn't flinch at his foreign touch and she doesn't kick him in his fucking nuts like my Raven would do.

No, she lets his fucking hand touch her.

I take a step forward, but Cap half blocks me with his shoulder, hissing, "Chill. Not yet."

They pause in the hall, and Collins moves to open what must be his fucking locker, conveniently right across from Perkins' office door.

I force my stare away when movement catches my eye, spotting Chloe headed right for me.

I look back to Raven who has her blank stare locked on the

back of Chloe's head, daring her to make a move, pathetically wishing she fucking would.

Chloe stops right in front of me, so I reluctantly look down.

She smirks. "Good game the other day, Maddoc."

"We lost."

She doesn't falter – she also doesn't give a shit about the game. "Maybe you feel like coming to the country club tonight? All the members have a benefit dinner across town, so it'll just be a group of us there." She steps closer and I let her, her tits brushing against my shirt.

I glance to Raven, finding her eyes now on mine.

I stare right at her as I move my arm, placing it exactly where Collins had his on her. I lick my lips knowing Raven is watching for it. "Maybe I will."

I pull back, purposefully giving a deep smirk and Chloe's eyes darken.

This girl craves power and gets off on getting what she wants. Her hand lifts and she runs it down my chest.

Again, my stare locks on Raven's.

Hers tighten around the edges, but then quickly jerk right, and mine follow to find Leo watching her.

What the fuck is going on with these two?

I shrug Chloe off, now that Raven's attention is elsewhere, I bound forward, but she feels me coming and shoots up straighter, a smokescreen dropping over her eyes.

Collins knocks his locker shut and grabs her hand, pulling her down the hall, but I catch up and yank her by her free wrist, dragging her back to me.

She jerks from Collins' grip, letting me pull her against me.

"Rae," he barks behind her, but she doesn't fight my hold in any way. She takes a deep breath and looks me right in the eye.

She blinks slowly and my pulse kicks.

"I'm watching you," I force past clenched teeth, pushing even closer to her. "Every. Fucking. Move."

I swear her lip tips up slightly before her eyes sharpen, and she whispers just for me, "What makes you think that's not exactly what I want?"

My brows crash together, and she uses the moment to free herself of my hold.

She walks backward, turning when she reaches where Leo stands and steps right in his face.

He stands tall, lifting his chin and a slow smirk stretches across her lips. She laughs in his face then looks back to me.

"Rae," Collins snaps and she spins, falls in line beside him and together, they walk away.

And I'm stuck where I stand.

"Nothing to see here people, move your fucking feet," Royce shouts and everyone around scurries off, the bell had already rung for first period.

Captain steps in front of me with a frown. "Yeah, you got it under control, huh?"

I shrug past him. "Fuck off."

I storm out the double doors and head for the outdoor courts.

Fuck class right now, and fuck Raven.

I grab a ball from the wet cart and charge down the court. I jump up to slam it into the net, grip onto the sides of the rim, and pull my body up only to drop back to my feet.

I growl, moving to grab another ball.

What the hell was that about? And what the fuck did she mean by maybe she wants me to?

Am I playing right into her hand?

Does she want me to pay close attention for another reason?

Fuck!

I move forward, stopping for a three-pointer, making the shot with ease.

Goddamn, I sound like a little bitch. I don't let my mind get run by others, and I sure as fuck don't plan on starting now.

Problem is Raven fucking Carver's not just in my mind, she's the resistance in every muscle in my body, fighting against every move, denying my push farther, closing me off to progression. She might as well grip me by the fucking balls and squeeze.

I pull my phone out and text the burner my dad has in his cell, asking him to call me tonight if he can swing it.

My dad's tone conveyed he was wary of Raven getting close to us, but he asked us to keep her from Graven.

Perkins is involving himself in our business more and more, not that he isn't always snooping, but specifically now where Raven is involved.

Maybell is being left out of the loop.

There're too many fucking things that aren't sitting right.

I need answers, but I don't even know the right questions to ask anymore.

She could very well be the poor girl who took the money and ran and there's nothing to figure out.

I mean, fuck, all we offered her was a temporary place to lay her head, right?

I laugh at myself, that's fucked if she felt that way.

She was more than that.

More than we ever could have thought.

More than we ever could have wanted.

Everything us three cold-hearted assholes needed.

I stuff my phone away and grab my backpack off the ground, heading for class.

Raven Carver is mine.

Chapter 7

RAVEN

ONE DAY.

Day fucking one and I'm ready to beat these bitches' faces in.

I've never possessed so much self-control in my fucking life.

Actually, now that I'm thinking about it, I didn't even know I had self-control.

Every class was a damn nightmare, but I didn't once look up from my papers – thank hell for dumb ass district testing week.

It's lunch now and the floozies are flying high and coming hard.

And I'm pretty sure I'll explode if I don't do something about it.

Right when I think it, like the flashing sign I needed, shiny black and teal in the form of an oversized bow catches my eye as Chloe sashays in the cafeteria like my mother when on the hunt.

I glare, tracking every swing of her step. Her steps carrying her straight to the boys' table.

I jerk from my chair before Collins can stop me and swiftly move toward her.

I purposely step forward as she does, causing her to bump right into me, not missing the way the noise dies down the second I do.

She's jolted back, and I'm nudged to the side slightly, but I recover easier than her.

Her cheer bag falls from her shoulders and she growls, looking from it to me, but her eyes widen just the slightest when she sees I'm the one she 'bumped' into.

"Watch out," she snaps, but I smirk when her fingertips instinctively move to the tips of her itty bitty ponytail.

"How you likin' the short look?" I goad her.

Her hand swiftly falls to her side and she stands tall. "Love it," she lies through a nasty grin. "Thanks for the cut."

"Anytime," I say back, but I feel my eyes hardening the longer we stand here.

I take a step closer, and a zing shoots up my back, wrapping around my shoulders and making my head buzz.

Yes, I missed this feeling.

Her pupils grow, I can only imagine how my eyes have changed to evoke fear in the ice queen.

I've got a lot built up and haven't let it out in a cool minute.

My body is tingling to, begging me to snap so it can crash – the troubles of virtually no sleep in days.

"Back off, Raven," she whispers, her body leaning away while her feet stay planted.

I should. She only knocked into me, and because I made sure it happened while also making sure it looked like it was her fault, but we girls are as smart as we are dumb. They'll understand.

"It's Rae." I snatch her bag off the floor and toss it in the garbage can beside me. "And I can't do that."

She gasps and darts forward, but I slide in front of her.

I stuff my hand in the side of my dress, pulling what I need out of the waist of my bottoms, making sure to close my fist around it so she can't see. I hold my hand out over the garbage can.

"What are you doing..." She edges closer but freezes when a darkness passes over me. "My uniform is in there."

Without taking my eyes off hers, I slide my lighter up and blindly flick the flame on.

Her stare snaps between me and the flame as she nervously licks her lips, attempting – and failing – to give a careless shrug. "Whatever, I'll just pull out a replacement."

I nod lightly, hiding my annoyance for not considering that beforehand, but when she shifts from one foot to the next, I tilt my head.

"No harm, then, hm?" I bait her quietly, my hand dropping an inch closer.

"Yeah, but—" She reacts before she can stop herself, clamping her mouth shut before more can be said.

A chill runs through me, and I drop my hand until the flame touches the edge of the bag folded over the edges.

She fights it, I give her that, but her bravado cracks, her shallow breathing giving her panic away. "Wait! Our signs are in there! Our music, props, everything we need!"

When I give her nothing, her eyes grow glossy, both anger and frustration front and center.

She's angry because she knows she can't stop me. "We fly out tomorrow night. There is no way we can replace all that in time!"

A better person would feel bad, pull away and let her digging in the trash be enough to get the point across.

He's mine.

"We worked all four years toward this!" she shrieks, shifting forward but freezing in place when my glare intensifies.

The smell of burnt plastic fills my nostrils, and I inhale deeply. It only takes another second for a napkin to catch and in an instant, the entire thing is on fire.

There's shouting and screeches across the room, but I simply put the lighter back in my waistband, wait another minute until the crackling of the metal zipper can be heard as the flame fights its way through her bag, and then step aside.

She darts forward, but she can't do anything, it's as good as ash.

"Should have said, please," I mock her, and she growls through her angry tears behind me.

She knows it wouldn't have mattered.

Principal Perkins bounds around the corner as if he was already close by and watching, headed right for me, but to my surprise, he drops back when he sees Collins step up first, not even flinching when Collins is gripping my upper arm hard enough to leave a bruise. "You're gonna pay for that, Carver."

"Kiss my ass, Graven."

A hostile chuckle leaves him, and he hisses in my ear, "Oh you'll be kissing something, in seconds in fact. I know what the fuck you just did and why. Reassurance is needed now."

"I don't—"

I'm cut off when I'm shoved into the lockers and a hard right hook shoots across Collins' jaw.

He falls back, banging against the metal beside me.

Collins spits and rushes for Maddoc who holds his hands out, inviting him in.

Students hear the commotion and rush into the hall, but Captain and Royce create a brick wall, forcing them back and slam the cafeteria doors closed.

When I hear a deep groan, my eyes snap back to the two.

Collins nails Maddoc in the gut, but he laughs and bends

slightly, gripping Collins under the leg and behind the shoulder. He lifts him, slamming him sideways into the wall before letting him crash to the floor with a loud thud.

"Grab her like that again, motherfucker and I'll break your arms."

Collins' eyes fly to mine quickly, and it's written across his face.

Fix this.

Damn it.

I bite through the soft flesh of my cheek, hard and quick, until blood trickles down my throat. My cheeks will be raw by the time this is all over.

Maybe if my body bleeds, my heart won't.

"He can grab me however he wants," I say, and I'm surprised it's come out so strong when in my own head it feels like a filthy fucking whisper.

Maddoc swings around, his eyes wide and wild. He has to convince himself I've just said what I did.

Royce and Captain are now taking slow steps closer, deep frowns directed at me, and I didn't miss Perkins slide in on the other side of the hall.

I'd swear he wears a smirk.

Maddoc's shoulders tense, but he moves toward me.

Anger and uncertainty.

God, what am I doing? This wasn't supposed to hurt them like this.

I release a deep breath and take a half step toward him, but Collins jumps to his feet and steps forward.

Maddoc glares down at me, his hands twitching at his sides.

Students have shuffled in now.

"Rae..." Collins calls, the fakest tenderness I've ever heard ringing through loud and clear for all these fuckers to witness.

Can I do this in front of all their people? With the enemy?

Do I have a fucking choice?

I drop my eyes from his, unable to look him in the eyes this time, and step past, but of course, his hand shoots up and he stops me at his side, shoulder to shoulder, my front facing one way, his the other.

We both shift to look at each other.

His grasp shakes against me as his nostrils flare.

I see in his eyes what I feel.

This is torture.

"Madman," Royce says quietly.

It works, Maddoc snaps out of it, a shield suddenly hiding his eyes from me, and I'm released. He storms down the hall.

Collins steps forward and I grind my teeth discreetly as he grips my hand and feathers my fingers over his lips. He pulls me away with a gentleness he fights hard to keep.

Fake ass bitch.

As soon as we're around the corner, he shoves me into a dark classroom and gets in my face.

"Are you fucking kidding me right now?" he growls, slamming his hand against the wall beside my head like he expects me to jump.

I don't.

"Why do I keep having to remind you to keep your ass in line?" he seethes.

"Because I'm shit for a listener."

"Well you better fucking learn, or else the video will end up not only on the damn school website but on the evening fucking news."

"You don't have the balls."

"If you believed that, you wouldn't be here."

I shove him away.

"I know you do, baby," he says randomly, quickly moving in. He whispers, "Stay still, and do not look, Bray number three is about to be watching." His hand finds my waist and squeezes.

Bray number three?

He's a fool. There is no number three, there are only three number ones – each as strong as the next, none weaker than the other. If he's hoping to find a kink in their line, he'll be disappointed.

"I'm going to lean in, and you're going to let me. Do not push me," he warns quietly.

"You'll pay for all this eventually, Graven. In one way or another," I hiss.

He chuckles against me, his breath growing closer to my neck, his grip on my waist lifting higher.

I dig my nails into his bicep, enough to leave a mark and he tenses like a bitch.

"I promise, baby," he says purposely. "He barely touched me, don't worry." His lips slide across my jaw and I close my eyes so I don't have to see his face.

His mouth comes down on mine, and in the same instant, there's a loud bang in the hallway, followed by retreating footsteps.

I shove him away before his lips make full contact, my chest feeling like it's caved in on itself, and Collins laughs, moving to hit his knuckle beneath my chin.

"Good job, Rae." He smiles and walks out.

I drop my head back on the wall, slamming my palm against it, and allow myself a minute of misery.

I take a deep breath, and exit the classroom, freezing when I find Bass standing outside the door with his arms crossed, glare in place.

He spins his lip ring as he studies me.

"What the fuck do you want?" I snap, annoyed with everything and everyone.

He tosses me my backpack – he must have grabbed it from the cafeteria for me.

His eyes flick between mine a minute before he starts shaking his head and walks away.

Well, fuck him too.

I move toward my next class, a class Maddoc happens to be in, and push inside with my head held high, but my steps falter slightly when I find he's entertaining one of Chloe's minions.

I take another step, and her eyes snap up and meet mine.

A little shot of panic flashes in her baby blues and she quickly averts her gaze, pulls her phone out and waves it at Maddoc as she moves for her seat.

A sudden phone call, huh?

I smash my lips together to keep from laughing.

Right.

Maddoc leans back in his chair as I grow closer.

I slide into my seat and replay what's just happened in my mind.

I knew these girls were smart.

Yes, ladies, that's right. I may not be at his side, but you won't be either while I'm still forced to watch it.

The rest of the day sucks a little less, even if I am coming across as a shady ass bitch.

Chapter 8

MADDOC

Raven's really fucking sitting there, in a dark ass corner not five feet away, pretending we're not in perfect line of sight.

She keeps feigning busy drinking her beer, but it's been in her hands for the last hour – it's got to taste like warm piss by now.

Graven played this well, knowing we wouldn't run him out as long as she was in sight.

The only reason I haven't beat his ass tonight is because he stepped out back with a phone glued to his ear twenty minutes ago and she hasn't moved her ass once.

A couple people have tried to stop next to her to talk, fishing for something, but she dismisses each one who gets within two feet with the wave of a hand – even the chick from the home that somehow ended up here tonight.

The girl looked a little sour over it, but Raven didn't bat a lash.

A girl steps in front of me and the second she does, Raven's eyes finally swing my way.

I knew she was watching.

I don't recognize the chick, but her greedy stare tells me she knows exactly who I am.

The girl puts her elbows on the table, dropping her tits closer to my face like I'm some desperate motherfucker who can't control himself and has to look.

Raven's stare meets mine and she straightens in her seat.

You just gonna sit there, baby...not gonna come claim what's yours?

A crease forms between her eyes.

She knows exactly what I want from her, but of course she does the opposite and slowly sits back.

With a subtle shake of my head, I stretch my neck back to look at the girl in front of me.

Her eyes light up now that she finally has my attention and a smile breaks over her face.

She's not lacking in looks in any way, but she's desperate and trying too hard.

I lift my chin slightly, letting her know I've got something to say and she bites into her bottom lip like a typical girl fighting to entice when she's got no natural pull or appeal.

I keep Raven's eyes locked in as the girl shifts, bringing her ear to my mouth as requested.

"Tell me your name," I whisper, purposefully letting my heated breath waft over her skin.

Her chest inflates, and she leans in more. Every centimeter closer she gets, Raven's eyes narrow to match.

I push it more by bringing my right hand up, letting my fingertips run the length of her arm.

I touch my lips to her ear and Raven's hands grip the edge of her seat.

But suddenly her eyes snap left and mine follow to find

Morgan, one of the JV cheerleaders, standing a few feet away.

Morgan senses Raven's eyes on her and looks over, paling instantly before scrambling toward me and jerking the chick in my hands.

"Hey!" she shrieks, glaring at her friend, but when she catches Morgan's blanched expression, she tenses. "What's wrong?" she asks her.

Morgan gives a nervous half-grin, then leans over to whisper in her friend's ear. The girl I've got my hands on eyes pop wide, panic struck in every inch of her.

"Shit." She swallows, slowly pulling away from me and then the two quickly rush off, gather their friends from around the room, including the one Royce was fucking with, and all together rush out the door.

The fuck?

I glance at Captain right as Royce pushes forward glaring after them, then quickly turns back to us. "What just happened?"

"I'll tell you what happened."

We spin and glare at the chick behind me, but she doesn't recoil.

She stands a little taller.

The group home chick, Vienna.

I look to Raven, but her seat's now empty.

"That," Vienna starts. "Was a taste of your own medicine, buddy."

"Fuck you talkin' about?" Royce bounds closer.

She smirks. "You wanted a queen, you made one. One like nobody here has ever known. Just as strong as you, just as brave. But there's a clear difference between her and you guys."

"Keep fucking talking," I bark.

She laughs lightly, glancing between the three of us. "You're calculated, she's ... reckless."

Her words hit me hard, because I know exactly where she's going with this.

"They fear her now, just as you wanted. She has their respect, forced from the three of you from the beginning, but earned on her own. You thought the guys wouldn't touch her?" She laughs. "Welcome to the other side of the spectrum, Brayshaws. Your very own queen might just dethrone you." She looks across the room where Raven is exiting. "And with a Graven at her side, no less."

My body starts to tremble in rage, but I stretch my neck to the side to force it away.

"Get the fuck out of here, group home girl," Royce snaps. "And keep your little theory to your damn self."

She laughs lightly, shrugs, and walks away.

Royce frowns after her. "She's right, isn't she?"

I look to Cap who nods lightly.

Damn it.

"She might be."

"I can't believe she's fucking us like this," he spits.

Yeah, I'm over this shit.

I don't realize I'm moving until Captain wraps his arms around my shoulder and drags me into the closest room.

There are a few people inside, but Royce bounds through the door behind us and claps, signaling for them all to leave.

Once they're out the door, he slams it closed and Cap steps back.

"What the fuck, man?" I shout.

"You can't—"

"Can't what?" I throw my hands out. "End this bull shit, beat his fucking ass until he can't walk, force his ass back where he belongs and demand what's mine stays that way? 'Cause I sure as fuck feel like I can! I mean, what the fuck are we even doing? Fucking recon? Fuck this!"

"We don't know she's yours. For all we know, she planned

this shit."

"Do you really fucking think that, Cap?"

His lips form a flat line and he looks away. "I don't know what the fuck to think, but we can't push her. She knows things we can't afford other people to find out about."

Fuuuuck.

Zoey.

I DRAG MY HANDS DOWN MY FACE, SHAKING MY HEAD. "CAP … fuck, man I'm—"

He holds a palm up. "We'll deal with it if it comes."

"I think we need to get rid of her," Royce interjects, and we look to him. He hesitates a minute, then shrugs his shoulders. "She's with Collins. We can't look past that."

"There's no way this shit is so cut and dry. Look how she's acting? All the shit with Chloe and those girls out there? Vienna was right, they took off because they're afraid of her. If they think she cares if they come near us, how the fuck can we not?"

"Maybe you're seeing things you want to be there, Madman," Royce mumbles, looking wretched.

He doesn't believe what he's saying either, but he doesn't wanna feel the burn of losing her twice.

She reacted tonight, and in the hall at the school.

Or maybe I am trippin' like he says.

"Why hasn't Dad called again?" I ask them. "I texted and nothing. He said he was handling shit, and nothing. Why?"

Both frown, shaking their heads, at a loss.

"Fuck man," I mumble. "I'm over this shit. Let's leave."

They both agree and within minutes we're in the car, the party and Raven behind us.

Not a fucking word is spoken on the way home to the house that feels emptier than it should.

RAVEN

I SHAKE MY LIMBS OUT, ROLLING MY SHOULDERS AROUND AS I breathe in the cold December night air.

Fuck, I'm ready to explode.

I was ready to kill that girl. She's lucky her friend spotted me sitting there in the dark corner I was lurking in and ripped her ass away before I did it with a grip to her hair.

That's all I'd need right now. Collins was already on extra dickhead mode after everything at the school but fuck him. I gave his bitch ass thirty days max and then he's on his own in a pool of Brayshaw people.

Really though, what the fuck is Maddoc doing? It's irrational for me to be pissed, I left them – left him – high and dry with no word, but still. I can't handle seeing his hands on anyone else, maybe he knows it and that's why he did it, or maybe I was just another Bray Girl and in slides a new one.

All I know is I can't watch it, so they'll need to keep their fucking hands, feet and faces away until I allow more – which will be when I'm gone.

"What are you doing?"

I roll my eyes and spin around, holding my arms out. "Breathing, Collins. Just fucking breathing."

He laughs lightly and walks over. "Good job tonight, you kept your cool. I'm impressed."

"Gee, thanks. Goal fulfilled," I deadpan.

He grins and looks out at the dark night.

He nods, his brows pulling in. "We don't have to fight, Rae. This could go a lot differently."

I scoff. "So, you won't hold me in with blackmail?"

"No." He tilts his head, still looking off. "Still need to keep you where you are, but it doesn't have to be a miserable time for you, you know?" He looks my way.

I frown, and he shrugs.

"You and I would have been friends if it wasn't for them. Things between us would be good and our own choice," he says, his eyes bouncing between mine. "I'm not a bad guy, if you weren't in the middle of our problem, you would have seen that on your own."

"Maybe you're right." I consider his words and go for honest. "But I can't say for sure. All I know now is you're the asshole standing between where I am and where I wanna be."

He shakes his head. "You only want to be there because they got to you first."

My head pulls back. "Nobody got to me and we can't go back in time, now can we? I made my bed and I know the drill that follows. This is a pointless conversation. I'll be standing next to your car when you decide you're done sniffing around here."

"What if I told you I knew you were coming before you got here?" he calls out and I freeze.

I spin around slowly. "Then I'd say I expected that. I'm sure you watch their every move. I bet you have a PI watching their PI. Anything to get a leg up, Collins, but eventually you'll need to find your own moves and stop counting on the steps of others. An incapable man is a weak man, and I've seen nothing straight from your hands."

"Is that a challenge?"

"Challenge, observation, solid fucking fact." I shrug. "It's whatever you want it to be, Graven, but none of that matters, because at the end of the day, you're still you and they're still them. Stronger by count and courage."

I turn and walk away.

Fuck life.

Chapter 9

RAVEN

I walk into third period, the first class of the day I have with Maddoc and now Collins to find that my chair is missing.

I look up, meeting Maddoc's eyes and he tips his chin back, leaning lazily in his seat.

I glance to the teacher who purposely looks everywhere but at me – she knows who's in charge and it sure as shit isn't her.

I'm about to say fuck it and walk out when Collins gets a little braver than he should.

"Come here, baby," he says, and the entire fucking room goes silent. The teacher even freezes, arm stuck in the air ready to write on the board.

Collins sits back in his seat, patting his lap with a devilish look in his eye. "I've got a seat you happen to love."

I open my mouth to speak, not really sure what's about to come out when suddenly the choice isn't left to me and I'm drug from the room, literally, my feet sliding across the flooring as Maddoc yanks me by the arms from the class.

"Hello!" I shout at the teacher ... who turns away from the scene.

Mac rushes out after us, and for a half second, I think maybe he's considering stopping Maddoc, but he spins, pulls the door closed and holds it there, right as Collins reaches it.

Collins bangs on the small window from the other side, fighting to pull it open.

Maddoc continues to drag me along until he can shove me into a small concave in the hallway. He gets in my face.

"The fuck is going on?!" he booms. "And don't you fucking dare bullshit me, Raven. Talk. Now."

"Nothing to talk about, Big Man—"

"Don't. Call. Me. That—" he growls, stepping against me.

I think he expects me to fight him, or shove at him or to tell him the truth.

He definitely doesn't expect me to melt against his erratically beating heart the second it blends with mine.

He also doesn't expect it when I move to my tippy toes and yank his head down until my lips smash into his.

Maddoc snarls angrily at first, and then his growl morphs into a deep, territorial rumble, possessiveness pouring into me, off of him. My lungs finally open, greedily pulling in all his scent, the burn left behind from not having him finally soothing.

His tongue swallows mine as his hands take control, and he pushes against me.

Yes. Mine.

My eyes pop open.

Shit!

Not mine.

I bite his bottom lip until he yanks back and quickly slink under his arms, but he catches me by the back of my shirt, and I slam onto my ass.

He pulls me back up, spins and pins me to the wall with his

grip on my ribs, my feet dangling in the air, so I can't gain any leverage and try to slip past. His eyes are wild and crazy, the green almost gone as a blackness takes over.

He opens his mouth to speak, but Collins and Mac tumble down the hall, shoving and punching at each other and then there's another crowd behind him.

Maddoc squeezes me, only letting go once Royce appears out of nowhere and places a hand on his shoulder.

He drops me to my feet, and I stand there frozen.

Why did I do that?

"Keep your hands off my students, Brayshaw," Principal Perkins calls from the hall.

Maddoc moves right toward him, spitting in his face as he stalks by without a word.

The principal glares from him to me, and just like every other time when he's around, there's something extra hidden in his leery light eyes as he studies our movements.

I wink like a bitch, even though I don't feel cocky right now.

I feel like the wishy-washy bitch I'm acting like.

It takes a few minutes for the area to clear, and as soon as it does, Collins gets in my face. "What did he want?"

"Oh, you mean after you provoked him?"

Collins glares. "I said what did he want?"

"Answers." My eyes widen as my brows raise mockingly. "Asshole. He wants answers."

"And?" he grates.

I shove away from him. "And he didn't get any."

I spin around the corner, freezing when I spot Captain leaning against the wall.

He frowns at me, frowns at the ground, and then walks away.

My shoulders fall and I look to the ceiling.

Fuck.

"I THINK WE NEED A NIGHT OF FUN, NOT RECON AND DEFENSE," Collins tells me as he drops down in the patio chair across from me.

"I think you're an idiot."

"I think," he says, leaning forward. "You'd have a good time if you let yourself."

"Doubtful."

He sighs as if he actually hoped I'd be all for it. "Well, get up. We're going anyway."

I cut my eyes his way. "Where, exactly?"

"Just a pizzeria my buddy owns. Beer and bad music."

"Will the people you had jump me be there?"

"Maybe." He grins.

I can't help it and I scoff out a laugh.

I eye him, not at all understanding how his brain works. "Why do you do this?"

"What?" he asks, and I'd say he looks honestly confused.

"Pretend you want to be friends, like it's an option still on the table. Act like you're giving me a choice when we both know you'll make me go under some pretense that if I don't, you'll pull your extortion cards. You know you plan to make me, so say it upfront. You don't need to fake nice with me. I'd prefer you be real, even if real you is a privileged asshole."

His eyes tighten around the edges a moment as he stares at me. "Believe it or not, I'm asking because I'm hoping you'll agree instead of being forced, as you call it, but while we're on the subject? I see no ball and chain around your neck, sweetness."

I push to my feet, staring down at him. "Ball and chain or not, don't forget I'm here for three other guys, not one of them being you."

"Yet, you're sleeping in my house every night anyway,

something, dare I say, you should really learn to get used to if we're talking bigger picture." He grins and moves to stand beside me. "Not seeing how I'm the loser here. Get in the car, Rae, I'll even allow you to wear your ratted little hoodie."

He walks past and like the pathetic bitch I've become, I follow.

It only takes fifteen minutes to get to the pizza place, already loaded with sweater vest douchebags and their scarf wearing women.

I choose the booth in the farthest back corner, and after a few minutes of balancing the salt shaker, Collins comes over with the waitress.

When I don't order, he orders for us and suddenly a pitcher of beer is delivered. For a second, I wonder if he'd slip some Molly in it or not, but when he steps over to one of the dozen metal tubs full of ice and bottle beer, offering one to me, I decide it's safe and go for the fresh draft instead.

Surprisingly, Collins doesn't act like a dick to me in front of his buddies, probably because he knows I'd embarrass him should he attempt to. He actually makes an effort to get me to have a good time, offers me to join each new game of darts and makes sure I always have a fresh bottle of beer until I tell him I'm done for the night – I'm not stupid, I'd never get drunk and leave myself for him to handle. I thought maybe that was his plan, but he actually snapped at another blond dude when he set a beer on my table and asked the waitress to bring me a water.

I'm not sure what he's playing at by acting like a decent human, and I don't care enough to need to know why.

The others here tonight, though, they do.

They watch him discreetly as he returns to me for what must be the seventh or eighth time. I grin at how they're no longer able to hold in their evil eyes and instead toss them my way.

The queen bee of Graven Prep — who I plucked from the pack within the first few minutes of being here — is equivalent to Chloe from Brayshaw and just as pretty. She's also just as predictable in her territorial ways.

She glares and slides up next to Collins as if she expects me to give a damn, so I wink back with a grin.

He's all yours, princess.

As if she can read my patronizing thoughts, she flips me off, scooting even closer, but Collins glances at me and puts distance between them as if I care.

But I have no time to even roll my eyes at him because the girl's sudden move to the right leaves a gap, allowing me to see straight across the room where I couldn't see before.

Tucked away in the opposite corner is a familiar blonde with long legs and clothes that don't quite fit the crowd she's trying to mold into.

A tautness finds my shoulders as I squint to see better.

The girl shifts in her seat, turning so the guy beside her can stick his tongue farther down her throat, and my teeth clench.

My feet work on their own, leading me straight across the room.

She can't see me coming, not with her eyes closed the way they are, but everyone else in this place does.

I lift the glass of red wine — at a fucking pizza pub — at her side and pour it over her head.

She gasps, popping to her feet and spinning toward me.

In the same second, I shove her, sending her tumbling back into one of the ice tubs full of bottled beers. I lift my knee, jamming it into her abdomen as hard as I can, punching her clear across the jaw.

She whimpers and tries to shove me off, but when her frantic eyes pop up to meet mine, she freezes.

Yes, bitch. You recognize me.

Blood begins to dribble over her now quivering lips and hurried steps sound behind me.

In one quick, smooth motion, I spin my upper body, pull out and flick open my knife.

Every single person steps back.

My eyes snap to Collins who raises his hands slowly, cutting a curious eye from me to the blonde.

A crease forms over his forehead as he slides his hands in his pockets and moves farther away, and with their leader's okay, the others relax around him, moving even farther than he did.

I narrow my eyes at him, but he simply shrugs and nods his chin, telling me to get on with it.

This only makes my frown intensify and my adrenaline pump harder.

Wary and aware of all movement around me, I turn to the girl while slowly closing my knife, but keeping it in my palm.

"Not so nice seeing me again, is it?" I bend, getting into her face, twisting my knee more and more, watching tears fill her pathetic eyes as she sinks deeper into the container. "This is the life you craved? Hm?"

When she opens her mouth to speak, I cut her off.

"You gave him up" — my body starts shaking — "her up, for this shit? Free fucking drinks and Friday nights out?"

Her eyes pop wide, and she pales, tears spilling down her flushed cheeks.

I lift my other foot off the ground, putting all my weight on her and she weeps.

Her back should be good and cut-up from the ridges of the bottle caps and sharp ice by now, but even still, it's not enough.

She needs to hurt more, this is nothing compared to the bleeding mess she left inside Captain's chest.

I move my knife to my left hand, my right darting out to grip her jaw, my palm covering her mouth. I can feel the curve of her teeth as I squeeze her cheeks against them, so I pinch harder driving them deeper, deep enough to bleed, and her eyes slam shut, more muffled cries leaving her.

He missed his baby girl's first breath. Her first step and first word.

I swallow the rage before I do something I can't walk away from, like snap her fucking neck. I get in her face and she cowers, looking every bit as ashamed as she should.

"You're a dumb bitch and the world needs fewer people like you."

I kick off her and spin around to face the room, but much to my surprise, their eyes fall to the floor. Only Collins stares head-on.

I move past him, but he falls in line beside me and we walk out without a word.

He's quiet the drive back, but it's short-lived and the second we hit his driveway, he locks eyes with mine, shifting his body to face me.

"You know."

My brows hit in the center.

He knows?

"Know what?" I play dumb.

Suspicion grows in his stare and he shakes his head. "Wow." He drops back in his seat.

"What?"

He looks away. "Loyal to them – without needing them to know it – and you're still just an outsider with nothing but a slightly clearer view."

"Cut the bull, Collins, and lay it out."

He looks back to me. "You showed up at my house, going all fucking in, to protect these guys you hardly even fucking know, who clearly aren't giving you anymore detail than necessary."

"I don't need to know all their secrets to know I don't want them to fail."

"When they didn't offer information, did you ask what they stole from me?"

My ribs constrict, but I glare. "It was none of my business."

"But what happens in this town is?" He studies me in a way that has me curious about the delivery of his question. Almost like he's insinuating it is but wants me to think it's not. Cryptic as fuck. "You are so dead set on Brayshaw running this place when you don't even know the full story behind our families. We're only a few pebbles in a much bigger pond, and neither one of our names are as clean as we claim."

What the fuck does that mean?

I force a careless shrug. "If you have something to say, say it."

"Ask me what they took, and I'll tell you," he dares, but he's not being playful or arrogant. His eyes are clear as day, his features fixed in a serious manner.

My jaw sets tight.

Of course, I want to know what it was, but I don't want it to come from his mouth. He could make up something completely fucking random and I'd have no way of knowing if it were true or not.

"It doesn't matter what they took. I'll be out of here soon, so it makes no damn difference to me." I climb from the vehicle and slam the door, hurrying forward and stepping through the one held open for him like royalty by his doting little maid.

I keep my eyes on her as I step in next to her, but hers fall to the floor. I head for the room he's stuck me in and lock myself inside.

I plug in my headphones and lie flat on the floor with my flashlight beside me, staring up at the ceiling. I flip my knife open and closed, over and over again.

As expected, sleep never comes.

Chapter 10

MADDOC

Cap walks in, confusion drawing his features tight.

Both Royce and I push to our feet.

"What happened?"

He hesitates a minute, running his hand over the back of his head. "Fuck it." He shrugs. "I have Mallory on a 24/7 watch," he admits about Zoey's mom. "Have since the day I found out Zoey existed, before I even knew for sure she was mine, no plans on calling him off anytime soon either."

"Duh, man." Royce laughs.

I look to Cap who glares, but Royce leaps over the coffee table to stand right in front of Captain.

"Come on, Cap, she's the enemy. We all want her watched, and we knew you did."

"How?" his eyes snap between ours.

"You told us when you were piss drunk, said you couldn't hide anything from us." Royce smirks. "Even your conscience is a good boy."

Captain chuckles, shoving him away.

"For real, though, brother." Royce goes in for a bro hug and handshake. "We've known this whole time. Would have expected nothing less."

Captain looks to me like he's ashamed and I shake my head.

"Man, this is different, and you know it. There're some things that don't need to be said, Cap, and there's nothing wrong with that. And the fact that you just came in here and told us, means now you have a reason to talk about it. We knew you would come straight to us if there was something needing said. Quit feeling fucking guilty about it."

He nods, his eyes dropping to the floor, and when they pop up, they're focused. Determined and a little amused.

His lips pinch to the side. "Mallory got roughed up."

My forehead furrows.

Cap's eyes flick to mine. "Seems she ran into a fist last night."

Royce and my eyes jump to each other's, quickly moving back to Captain.

The organ in my chest starts hammering. "Cap."

"Raven rushed her, got in her face, smacked her around a bit. She went fucking easy from what I heard, but—"

"But why the fuck would she do that?" Royce rushes out.

"Exactly." Cap nods.

I spin around, biting on the skin between my thumb and pointer finger.

What's your game, baby?

With him, but hurting for us.

Giving us nothing but fighting for us.

For us.

I jerk my head, my chin low. They're fucking right. "Why would she do that?"

My brothers and I look between each other, a small nod passing between us.

That's the fucking question.

"Let's go to practice, boys." Royce grins, already pulling out his phone to make plans for tonight when we had agreed not to celebrate. "We need a venue." "Yo, Buck!" He laughs into his phone as he heads outside. "It's Royce."

Cap's eyes follow him out before he turns back to me. "Think he's good?"

"You ever seen him care for anyone, Cap?" I ask him but keep my eyes on Royce who's laughing on the phone in the driveway.

"Nobody but her. He liked having someone to talk to outside us. He felt comfortable being himself with her."

I nod. "Pretty fucking sure she was the center of his world."

"And then she was ripped away," he finishes, then looks back to me. "But we'll get her back."

Damn straight we will.

"Come on, fuckers!" Royce shouts from the front. "Quicker we're done the quicker night will come!"

We laugh and meet him in the car, but the mood shifts on the short drive to the park court knowing we'll share it with a Graven today.

Like we figured he would be, Collins is already jogging the court in warm-up gear.

"We should run his ass over," Royce grumbles. "Bet his knees have never hit gravel before. Pansy ass motherfucker."

Cap turns off the engine and shifts toward me.

"What?" I snap.

"We don't know what's really going on between them two," Cap worries. "He's gonna fuck with your head, man."

"Let him. Make him think he's winning." I turn my glare

out the window. "I told you guys before, I'll lose her to no one, now let's go."

Cap sighs. "We need to make sure someone mentions the party in front of him."

"Already handled, brothaman." Royce claps a hand on his shoulder. "Mac and Leo are on it."

Walking toward the field, Collins pauses at the far end, eyeing us with his hands on his hips as he tries to catch his breath – Graven Prep clearly doesn't work on cardio.

"'Sup, bitch?" Royce grins at him, dropping his bag on the bench.

Collins rolls his shoulders and starts jogging again.

We take our time getting our shit out and switching into our street shoes.

Right when I stand back up, the rest of the team and Coach arrive.

Coach Brail eyes us. "Brayshaw, early as always." His stare cuts to Collins, who makes his way toward us.

"Always, Coach." I roll the ball in my hand, eyes on Graven.

"All right, we're gonna get rained out, so a quick lap and then we'll go straight into a scrimmage."

The team waits for my lead, then follows us around the court, stopping in the center as Coach asked.

He separates us into more even teams, each a mix of starters and second string. When he adds Graven to a team, everyone takes a step back, every fucking eye landing on me.

Coach glares. "I said play," he snaps.

Still, they wait.

I walk toward Graven, slow and fucking steady, and he squares his shoulders, a slight tip to his lips, but I'm a fuckin' Wolf, I can smell his fear. Under that pasty ass skin and pretty-boy hair, he's trembling like a bitch.

He thinks he's showing strength, that his standing here puts us on edge and makes us and those around us see him as brave.

His fake ass, cocky attitude says a lot more than that to us, though.

He's making a mistake and he's too fucking dumb to realize it.

No Graven would set foot here like this, not unless they knew they had a safety halo hanging around their head, one we'd later use to noose their asses if and when needed.

Collins is well aware our dad asked us to play fucking nice.

The real fucking question is how and what else does this dick know that we don't?

I chuck the ball into his stomach, and he jerks, catching it like I knew he would.

"Go on, Graven." I tilt my head back lazily, walking backward to my position. "Start us off."

The corner of his eyes tightens as he starts dribbling and drops back to his place.

The rest of his temporary team still waits at the side, so I nod my chin, giving my team the go-ahead to play with him here.

"Let's go, assholes," Cap smacks our boy Mac on the shoulder, who was placed on the opposite side of us.

We talked to Coach last night and told him not to use our playbook or talk any sort of strategizing with him here. We'll run basic ass shit and nothing more.

So that's exactly what we do, run basic.

An hour and a half in, and he's only touched the ball twice, and one of those was for a free throw after he was fouled.

His glare flies to Coach. "You're willing to chance a loss just to appease these assholes by not exercising the entire team? I need practice before next game—"

Royce cuts him off with an obnoxious, nasty ass laugh and everyone stands to attention.

He grips the front of his basketball shorts and stalks toward Collins.

Collins' eyes tighten at the edges as he tracks Royce's every step.

"Next game?" Royce laughs again, but there's no sign of humor on his face. "Bitch, you really think you or your thousand dollar fucking Fendis will ever touch down on our court alongside us?"

Collins' head draws back the slightest bit.

"You'll never play as a Wolf," Royce tells him. "I don't give a shit what anyone says. Not Coach, not my dear old dad, not my brothers. Not when it comes to this. You, you punk ass bitch, played your last game of ball the second you decided to come into our house." Royce takes a step backward. "You're fucking lucky we have to play nice, Graven, or we'd have snipped you at the ankles the second your feet hit Brayshaw steps."

Collins stares at Royce, the muscle in his jaw ticking, but then his shoulders square and his eyes slide to meet mine.

My brows drop low as I gauge him.

I know where this fucker's about to go.

Push me, bitch. I fucking dare you...

"Work me out, Brayshaw." The corner of his lip lifts and I take a half a step forward. "Work me out today, and I'll give her the night off."

I'm in his face, nose to fucking nose, forehead to forehead in the next second.

"Boys—" Coach yells, but when nothing else comes from him, I know Cap or Royce cut him off with a single look.

"Don't be a cagey motherfucker, Graven. You wanna stand here, brave enough to run your mouth when you know I could lay you out in a solid fucking second, then be brave, bitch." I drop my voice to a whisper so only he can hear, driving him backward with my forehead on his. "You and I both know I have to leave you standing, for now."

He glares, but the sweat forming at his hairline tells me he's ready to piss his Moncler cotton fucking track pants. "Dunk on me, Brayshaw..." He licks his lips and edges back the smallest bit, but I lean with him, not allowing him the space he's searching for.

My hand starts twitching at my sides. I know he's about to throw what's mine in my face like she belongs to him.

"Dunk on me, and I'll let her sleep in a separate bed tonight, instead of mine—"

My fist flies, connecting with his jaw and he drops to the gravel.

I go to drop down on top of him, but Captain and Royce pull me back, shoving me toward the opposite side of the court.

"Fuck," Coach spits, tossing his clipboard. "All right, this half, stay on this side." He looks to me with a glare. "You boys stay on that fucking side. Fifty suicides. Go!"

I jerk from Captain's hold and he and Royce throw their arms over my shoulders laughing quietly to themselves.

I can't help it and a small grin takes over.

Fuck that fool.

"Yo, Maddoc!" I turn back, tipping my chin at Mac. "Car's confirmed. Party's at the Tower at eight, yeah?" he shouts.

Collins' eyes hit Mac in my peripheral and I fight a smirk.

"Yup, invite anyone you want, doors are open tonight." I turn back around, and Royce elbows me.

All fucking set.

RAVEN

· · ·

I shuffle through paper after paper, coming up with nothing. For a library full of files, the Gravens seem to keep nothing but worthless shit here. Pool boy and gardening receipts galore – useless.

With a sigh, I close the door back and head down the gaudy ass spiral staircase. The second I hit the marble landing, there's a knock at the door.

I stand there a moment, just staring at it, and then they knock again.

Fucking Collins, who is at practice causing problems, I'm sure, won't allow me and his maid to be here alone, so he sends her on her way every time he leaves. Probably texts her on his way home every time, heaven fucking forbid he has to hang his own coat.

The doorbell rings next.

Fuck.

A low growl leaves me, and I yank the door open with a frown, prepared to tell his buddies to kick rocks, but my brows meet my hairline when none other than Maria Vega, my so-called social worker, is at the door.

"Raven."

"Ms. V."

Interesting fucking timing.

She frowns. "Are you going to invite me in?"

"No." I lean against the frame and cross my arms. "Not my house."

"And you care why?"

I blink at her. I don't care – don't want to let her in either.

She sighs. "Fine. Listen, I'm here because I was unaware of your new arrangements."

I run my tongue across my teeth. "What led you this way, Ms. V?"

She blanches a second. "It's my job to know where you are."

"Yet you weren't aware of my new arrangements." I lift a brow. "Yeah?"

Her eyes tighten. "I ... look, we have to remove you and place you back in the Bray house, with Ms. Maybell."

We?

"That's not gonna work for me."

She hesitates before responding. "I'm afraid it's not your choice."

I eye her, already having had suspicions about her character, none of which I've confirmed, but still. I stand taller, grabbing onto the door with one hand and the frame with the other.

"How 'bout this? You call your people and have them come in and remove me?"

She observes me a moment, her voice a little less sugary this round. "Do you really want them to take you in and make you go through a hearing and replacement home, all because you wouldn't cooperate with me? I'm making this easy and offering to take you back to your original location."

I scoff, a small smirk coming out as I shake my head at her. "You're as full of shit as you are sure, Ms. Vega," I quip, and she fidgets under my unrelenting stare, a crease forming on her forehead. "You do what you need to, and I'll be here until I'm not." I go to step back but pause and instead step outside, right in her face. She doesn't cower away, but her pupils dilate just the slightest. "Since it's just me and you standing here, let me tell you this now. If you had or have anything to do with that little girl not being in her daddy's arms every night, you'll regret it with every bone in your body."

Her eyes widen, and I step back inside and slam the door in her face, moving to the side so she can't see me through the long window panel. I lean back for a breath.

Something is off with that chick, I know it, and she was damned surprised that I knew about Zoey. All I know is she better hope she's legit with noble intentions or she'll have more than three Brayshaws raining down on her.

With a sigh, I pour some of Collins' big money bourbon and knock it back, dropping onto the couch.

I close my eyes, taking a calming breath when I'm on the brink of flipping my shit.

I'm in deep and falling deeper, like a fool.

I need to let these people go.

All of them.

Problem is, I'm not so sure I know how. Every day away has me questioning what the hell I'm doing here, with Collins and in this place.

A smart girl would have left by now.

The door bursts open and a sweaty, angry Collins barges through.

Surprisingly, his shoulders relax when he sees me.

"How was practice?" I raise a brow, reaching back for the tumbler and pouring myself another half glass.

He grins. "Fine, dear."

I scoff and drop back again.

His eyes run over me, and he smiles wider.

"What?" I grow suspicious.

"Your outfit is perfect, you know, for your kind of crowd," he says, not taking his eyes off my black jeans ripped at the thighs and plain white, baby doll T-shirt. His stare moves over my hair, and the French braid pigtails I threw it in when I got out of the shower. "Hair too."

"For what?"

"Didn't you hear?" His smirk has me sitting forward. "Tonight's Maddoc's eighteenth birthday party, and you're my pretty little date, sweetness." He heads for the stairs, leaving me fighting for air my lungs suddenly deny.

I didn't even know him long enough to know when his birthday was.

"We leave in thirty! I guess you can wear those ugly ass boots, too!"

Holding in whatever it is trying to claw its way out, I lay back and close my eyes.

This should be interesting.

And by interesting, I mean a fucking nightmare.

I take another shot.

Treacherous bitch.

That's me.

MADDOC

She came with him, just like we fucking figured.

Glued to him and a little unstable on her feet, they slip inside quietly – like Buck, the guard dog here at The Tower, the club we rented out for the party tonight, didn't text me the second her used Timberlands hit the cement.

My blood heats, my muscles flexing just from looking at her.

She's pure fucking natural fire.

No effort from her reads as pure purpose to everyone around her. Tight ass pants and a slice of skin showing above her waist, hair long and twisted back in two, ready to wrap around my fists, the blue tips shining against the light of the room. Effortless sex appeal.

Now if I went off the look in her eye, I'd say she looks like shit. Just as exhausted as I had hoped, and miserable like I wished. She looks as fucked up as she deserves to be for the moves she's made.

Still, looking at her, all I see is mine.

Yet, she's not here with me tonight.

She's with him, the dick that wants to take my family's power. The guy who wants to push Brayshaw out and regain control of this town with his family's name, so he can run it dirty and in a way that makes him rich and powerful, not respected and feared like worthy leaders, like Brayshaw.

Like we fucking are.

He doesn't want to help the weak grow stronger so long as they stay in line, doesn't want to watch the local business in this town thrive and create a better, tighter community of local life. No, he wants to reign over all and shit on the little guy along the way. That's not a society people want to be a part of – that's how an era ends.

We're not the only power families around, there are several of us spread across the state, protecting the lives we live and the towns we created. It's how we live under our own laws, we have others who look out for us just the same.

But our town, we're the last split in two, the only one left with a power struggle among founders. According to our dad, it's up to me and my brothers to put an end to it before the other families step in and help decide for us. Only one name can lead, and it will be Brayshaw.

The Gravens were pushed out for a reason.

They're dirty and know no loyalty. They fuck over their own in a heartbeat if there's a means to benefit from it. Our town, our family and populace was built on three things: honesty, loyalty, and respect.

Collins would trade all three for more green in his pocket – as if the sole heir needs any more than what his grandfather will be leaving him with when he croaks.

Greed brings lies and deceit and if this place turns to anarchy, we'd all fall down. The surrounding cities and their head makers won't hesitate to step in if we can't control our own people.

Question is, did money already speak louder to my girl than I could?

I glance at Tisha, one of the chicks in Chloe's little pack of peasants, perched on top of the bar so she can chat up the bartender.

"I'm done waiting, let's test this shit now."

I look back to Raven, who tries real fucking hard to hide her body behind the bar stool.

"You sure about this?" Captain speaks low so only I can hear. "That chick should be here anytime."

"I need to know."

"I'm with Maddoc." Royce gives a jerky nod, his body swaying a bit as the alcohol kicks in.

Cap eyes him before sliding his stare to me, his concern easily read. "And you're ready for this?" he pushes. "What happens if this doesn't roll the way you want?"

"Then she'll be begging for her trailer when we're done with her."

Cap sighs, his shoulders falling slightly as he nods and Royce rubs his hands together, shooting for confident and ready, but I know he's nervous as fuck. He's been downing shots since we got here.

I down the rest of my drink and push to my feet. I haven't drunk this much in months, and I'm not trashed, but I can't say I don't like that my body is finally chill after days of nothing but pure fucking tension.

Tisha sees me coming and her back shoots straight.

I give her no warning other than my eyes on her as I grow closer, then I'm gripping her behind the knee, and yanking her to the edge. I step between her legs and she gasps, her eyes widening.

"You've had your eyes on me the last hour, Tisha." I lean closer. "You got something for me?" I whisper, sliding my hands up her thighs and she tenses.

A nervous laugh leaves her, and she recoils, her eyes flying right briefly.

"I..." She starts pulling away with a shrug. "Look, I've been dying for this, and maybe I was looking at you, but that's all. Before, I'd have been all over this, but things have changed. I have a shoot next week, and I can't risk getting my ass beat. Sorry." She hops off the bar and walks away.

"You're an idiot."

I spin around to find Vienna behind me. Cap and Royce walk over to us.

"I told you to be here at ten," I hiss.

"And I had to wait for Maybell to pass out, then hitch a ride here because I don't got it like that. But..." Vienna licks her lips and smiles up at me. "I'm here now."

"Why'd you even go for this?" Royce questions, studying her with his cloudy glower.

"Like I told you guys before, I happen not to like her newest move. She shouldn't have gone against you." Her hand reaches out to touch my bicep and I glare. "I don't believe she's as scandalous as her little trade-off paints her." She steps closer to me, her palms now planted on my chest. "So, like I said I would, I'm gonna take one for the team here, Brayshaws, hoping that it helps you get what you want."

My brothers reluctantly take a few steps away, both mumbling something under their breaths as they do.

Vienna hesitates a moment, then cautiously pulls herself up on her tiptoes and slides her lips across mine.

It takes me a second, but I force my hands around her and pull her body against mine.

She grins and covers my lips with hers, driving her tongue inside my mouth. I kiss her back, forcing my tongue to meet her careful swipes.

It's all fucking wrong.

My baby would never be careful or cautious with her mouth.

She's demanding, punishing and eager.

And she hasn't stepped in to fucking stop this.

Goddamn it, Raven!

I pull away from Vienna's lips, but hold her there a minute, jerking my hands away from her when she smiles up at me.

She reaches up to touch her lips, hesitates a moment longer, and then disappears down the hallway toward the bathroom.

Captain and Royce move toward me again.

Anger and annoyance mixed with flat out fucking disappointment slices through me, the same pained expressions clouding my brothers' eyes.

Captain sighs, dropping his chin to his chest while Royce's jaw sets and looks away.

That was it, Raven didn't make her move. She let it happen, stuck to the little bitch's side all the while. I don't know what the fuck I thought would happen just now, but what I didn't expect was the sharp ass pain hitting my chest. A sting so deep my facial muscles tighten, forcing my eyes to squint.

She might as well have rammed that knife of hers into my gut and twisted. Something tells me that would've done less damage than standing here knowing it's not where she wants to be.

Raven for real just stood back, watched this chick stick her tongue down my throat and did nothing.

My Raven would never stand for that.

Guess she thinks she's no longer mine.

Royce kicks a stool and it knocks to the floor, but the music is so loud and the lights low, it doesn't create a scene.

He storms off.

Cap picks it up, signaling the bartender for another round.

Fuck this shit.

RAVEN

BRAVE LITTLE BITCH.

And she tried to front like she had a thing for Royce. I knew she was too easily roped in by the glitz of their world, she showed it in her envious words at the very first party the group home girls dragged me to at Collins' house.

She's just like the rest, waiting for a turn with any Bray they can climb on.

I should break her fucking nose.

I slip out the door and start back down the dark hall, but I'm yanked to the side and shoved against the wall – a move he's getting far too fucking comfortable with.

Collins gets in my face. "What the fuck are you doing?" he growls.

I jerk from his hold in the same second and shove at him, stepping into his face. "I told you, Collins, you put your hands on me again, without my permission, which you'll never fucking have, I won't hesitate to stick a four-inch piece of metal through your lung and laugh as you drown in your own blood."

His head draws back a second before he glares. "You think I didn't notice what you just did? That I didn't watch the entire fucking thing, same as you, and then trail your ass when you disappeared in the same direction?"

"Like I fucking care."

He growls. "You can't run around acting like the jealous little girlfriend! You belong to me as far as these people are concerned."

"Back the fuck up, Graven."

Both our heads snap right to find Royce swaying slightly on his feet, eyes dull and bloodshot.

Fuck. Did he hear that?

"Fuck you, Brayshaw. Just getting some time in with my girl, here. Dark corners are my favorite—"

Royce swings before Collins sees it coming, landing a hard one across the jaw.

I step back, giving him more room, and Collins shoots me a glare, rubbing at his jaw.

Collins lifts a hand, pointing at Royce as he starts walking away – he knows better than to pick a fight with them here. "Let's go, Rae," he commands but doesn't stand there waiting.

Royce does, however, and as soon as Collins is around the corner, he steps closer to me.

"Back off, ponyboy," I force past my lips, taking a step away. "None of your business."

"It is my fucking business. We brought you in, trash," he slurs angrily, but it's the ache laced in his tone that has a twinge hitting against my ribcage.

"We gave you a place, twice, and you wanna fuck us over? You wanna fuck my brother, then let the guy trying to fuck our family stick his dick in you?" He creeps closer. "You're loosening it up real good, now aren't you? Trying to get on your mama's level?"

"Enough," Bass barks, now joining the party.

I grow rigid. The last thing I need right now is for him to spill what he knows.

I slide my eyes his way right as Royce spins to face him.

"Fuck you, Bishop. Bet your ass was in on this shit too, huh?" He gets in his face. "Poor little punks like you two stick together, don't you? I should kick your wannabe ass."

"You're drunk." Bass blinks at him. "Just go."

"You go, bitch." Royce grips his belt stepping closer, his eyes narrowed to slits. "Don't forget where you are."

As if this isn't bad enough, the door to the restroom flies open and Vienna appears.

She jerks to a halt at the sight of us all, her eyes wide, lip still bleeding.

I freeze where we stand, we all do, minus Bass.

No, no, no. Fuck!

I told her to wait five minutes ... five fucking minutes ago.

Finally, Vienna jump starts and rushes away.

That kicks Royce back into motion and his head snaps my way, but I can't bring myself to look at him.

He's motionless a minute, but then a light laugh leaves him, and he stumbles off. "Well, fuck me, baby girl..."

Bass slowly follows him down the hall, glancing back at me once on his way.

I fall against the wall and close my eyes. "Shit."

MADDOC

CAP AND ME DOWN TWO SHOTS AND JUST AS WE DROP THE GLASS and get ready to go find Royce, my shoulder is bumped, bloody tissues tossed in my face.

Vienna squeezes by us, blood trickling down her lip and slightly smeared over her T-shirt. "You're welcome," she bites out in a hissed whisper. "And you owe me one."

Captain whips around, looking down the dark hallway that leads to the girl's bathroom, where Vienna disappeared to and just came back from.

Royce rushes from the same hallway, headed right for us with a fierce expression, but my eyes cut behind him.

Raven steps into the light, her face blank, but her eyes are wild.

Her eyes snap up, crashing into mine with a fire so bright my shoulders stretch wide.

If she could reach, she'd catch me across the jaw.

My baby is jealous, and she wants to fight about it.

Suddenly her eyes leave mine, and her feet carry her away, back to the bitch who is gonna burn.

Collins hisses something at her, gripping her wrist and I push forward, but Cap stops me with a tight grip to my shoulder.

He dips closer to her with a hard expression, but she jerks away with a solid fuck you mouthed in his face.

A zing shoots down my spine.

The fuck is going on here?

In the next second, we're exiting the club.

"We're missing something," Royce slurs right as we hit the pavement out front, not entirely convinced but desperate to believe it. "We need to find out what."

The driver we hired for the night, one of our guards from the warehouses, rolls up and we silently slide in.

I agree, something is fucking wrong. There's a reason for this and we need to find out what it is, but it's not just with her actions, but Graven's and our dad's, too.

But back there? That was what tonight was about, bringing her loyalty to light by playing off her weakness, just like Maybell said.

Tested.

Reacted the only way she knows how.

Impulsive. Uncontrolled. Reckless.

Mine.

Chapter 11

MADDOC

LIKE CLOCKWORK, THE SKINNY FUCKER SLIDES OUT THE GATE of the warehouses right at midnight to make his check-in call. He adjusts his leather fucking jacket, those dumbass headphones around his neck, like always, and pulls out his phone.

"We should jump his punk ass." Royce sits forward.

I grip the steering wheel tighter. "Grab him."

"Why?" Royce laughs. "Not like he won't come in on his own if we tell him to."

"He doesn't get to be asked tonight. He's fucking lucky I don't run him over right now."

Royce starts for his handle, but Captain unbuckles his seatbelt.

"Let me get him," he insists and steps out.

Me and Royce look to each other.

"This shit's messed him up, Madman. If we're reading this wrong, if Raven really is playing dirty, or fuck, bartering even, she could tell everyone about Zoey." Royce looks out the window. "Kinda fucked up we can't ever have anything for ourselves. He shouldn't have to share baby girl with nobody until he wants to."

"You think she'd do that?"

I frown when Bass spins around, trying to punch Captain as he reaches out and grips his jacket, but Captain spins him and slams him against the fence.

Bass finally sees it's him and chills some, but he still acts like a prick and forces Captain to push on him to get him over here.

"Not in a million fucking years, brother, but I didn't think she'd ever be where she's at either," Royce says then pushes open the door.

Cap shoves Bass inside and slams the door before he has time to move and Bishop's head smacks against the window.

Royce grins and sits back, eyeing him. "'Sup, bitch?"

He gives us a careless look. "What do you need?"

"I need you to sit there, say not a fucking word and watch your mistake unfold," I start, shifting to look back at him. "You can beg to keep the life we've given you after."

"The fuck you talkin' about?" he draws out.

"He said sit, Bishop. Not speak. You're the dog, we're the masters," Royce adds with a malicious smirk.

I get us back on the road.

"If we're leaving, I need to let—"

I cut him off. "Already let everyone know you won't be back tonight."

Bass moves his glare out the window.

We called our PI the minute we woke up sober enough to reprocess and regroup after last night's shit.

He had what we needed in an hour, but Cap had a date with Zoey today, so we waited. It was the better choice anyway. This way we catch them good and fucked up, right before the end of the night when bravery and the sense of invincibility has come and gone.

"You didn't wanna look like the rat, yet you went to Raven for a reason. Loyalty. That's what we asked from you when we hired you. You fell short, Bishop." I meet his eyes in the mirror. "We take a hit, you take a hit. That's how this works."

I pull over up the street to let Captain and Royce out and they slide into Captain's SUV – always better to have a second escape if needed – and head for the edge of town.

He doesn't say anything but his jaw clenches, a deep crease taking over his forehead.

Like Raven, he comes from nothing and holds only self-pride.

He keeps to himself, stays out of drama, can read people the best we've seen – it's why we let him run our cash flow.

He gets respect because he handles business the way it should be handled, quick and quiet. Clean when he can, merciless when the situation calls for it.

Bishop's no bitch. He's a smart and solid motherfucker, we wouldn't have him on our team if he wasn't, but he sure as fuck is acting like one where Raven is concerned.

Thing is, the way this world is run, you keep your people tight and your lips tighter.

Your word and anonymity is everything. People won't follow you if they think you'll throw them under the bus when the heats on your neck.

He should have thought about that before he decided to hold back on us.

He's hiding something, and that's cool. At this point, we don't need his ass to figure out what it is, but better believe he'll be seen – the rat that led the way.

He can work himself out of that on his own.

We pull up behind a row of parked broken-down Hondas.

I spin in my seat to face him again. "You know who lives here, Bishop?"

"Nope," he bites out.

I smirk. "Good. Now get the fuck out."

The three of us step from our vehicles and rush for the door, an alert Bishop a few steps behind us.

We bust through the door and several around the room jump from their seats with slurred shouts.

Me and Cap pause in the center of the room while Royce moves for the sound system, yanking the cords from the wall and slamming it into the TV.

Captain tosses his bat in the air, catching it at the end and pointing it out at the few who attempt to step closer.

They pause once they realize who we are, then Bass steps through the door and his eyes widen as his gaze travels the room, spotting people who run in the outside circle.

"Fuck," leaves him on a quiet note.

Yeah...fuck me, I fuck you, bitch.

"Benny Rodgers." I lift my arms out, spinning slowly. "Where the fuck is he?"

When nobody speaks, Royce grabs the closest guy to him, forcing him to his feet.

He jerks the drunk's head down as he lifts his knee, slamming him in the nose and watching him crash against the floor.

The girls scream, and a few more guys stand.

I look around the room again. "Who is going to tell me where Benny Rodgers is?"

"Upstairs, second door on the right," a scrawny, younger guy mumbles under his breath.

I step in front of him and he looks up. "Show me."

The guy swallows but does as I ask, and I follow him up the stairs.

I kick in the door he points to and charge right in.

The girl riding on the dick that must belong to Benny hops off with a yelp, but she doesn't bother to cover herself.

"Get out!" she shouts.

"What the fuck?" He sits up quickly, reaching for something at his bedside.

I dart forward, grip his ankle and yank him off the bed, letting his head bang against the edge.

I drag his ass down the stairs.

He fights me every step of the way, but I quicken my pace until I'm tossing his naked body onto the lawn of what we're told is his own damn house.

His partygoers rush out behind us, the girl he was fucking cussing up a storm and still buck ass naked.

"Get your ass in there and put something on!" Royce shouts at her.

But she ignores him, reaching into a pot by the door. She picks up a rock and chucks it at me.

I duck and it hits the car in the driveway.

Royce sighs and grabs her by the arms.

Benny stirs by my feet but freezes when I look to him.

The chick instantly goes off the fucking wall and starts screaming, so Cap rushes to the SUV, pulls out some duct tape, and tosses it to Royce.

He goes to rip off a piece, but she throws her hand up, clamping her mouth shut.

Cap points to some girl. "Go get her something to cover up with."

The girl nods, running back inside the house and out just as fast with a blanket from the back of the couch.

Royce wraps it around her, and I look back to Benny.

"Benny Rogers, nomad in town who is supposed to lay fucking low or get the fuck out of our town, right? That was the deal you made when you moved here?"

"I do lay low!" he shouts, his embarrassment making him brave.

I laugh lightly, swiftly moving to push my shoe against his Adam's apple.

He squirms under me, his eyes wide.

"I asked you a question," I growl.

"He can't answer you! He can't even breathe!" the girl shouts, fighting against Royce.

"Quiet," he shouts, and she clamps her mouth shut.

One of Benny's buddies attempts a step forward, but Captain lifts his brass knuckle covered fist, spinning the bat in his other hand and the guy freezes.

I let up a little and he gasps for air. "I'm gonna ask you again, are you Benny Rogers?"

"Yes."

"The same Benny who called Bass Bishop, the mother-fucker standing in the background right now, about my girl?"

His brows snap together, and he opens his mouth to argue, but his eyes shoot wide in realization. Beads of sweat instantly form on his forehead and he frantically shakes his head. "I didn't know, I thought it ... oh shit."

"Yeah, Benny boy. Oh shit." I bend down. "Tell me exactly what you told Bishop and I'll leave your balls intact. Lie or hesitate, even for a second, and my brother is ready to smash your nuts with a Louisville Slugger."

"Maddoc—" Bishop starts but cuts off.

I can only imagine Captain leveled him with a look that said not a fucking seed planting word.

"I didn't know it was about her." Tears fill the bastard's eyes and he swallows. "I only told him I heard a video was being shopped around for those interested in a blackmail piece."

"What fucking video?"

"Maddoc—"

Bishop tries again, but a slam is heard next. "You had your chance to speak. Open your mouth again and I'll fill it with brass."

I quirk a brow at Benny.

"You really want me to say it out loud?" He looks from me to the bat in Cap's hands frantically.

I stand up and nod to Royce.

He shoves the girl in the house, ripping the blanket from her as he shuts the door.

He tosses it in the grass, and I nod my head toward it.

Benny quickly grabs it and covers himself, cutting a glance at the people around us.

"Leave," Captain tells them, and they scatter in seconds.

Royce hops off the porch and the three of us crouch in front of Benny.

"Talk."

"I called Bishop." He sits up, glancing at the fool himself before looking back to us. "I told him I heard about a video being shopped around of his new girl." When I growl, he throws his hands up. "I didn't know she was your girl, man! I only knew she was one of his newest fighters."

"Just keep talking," Captain snaps, throwing a frown at me.

"I told him there was a video of the girl who had been fighting out there, and you three ... fucking. All I knew was it was being pushed as Brayshaw blackmail material, but it didn't sit right with me because how would a video of you three getting with the baddest bit— " He cuts himself off, clearing his throat. "The baddest chick we've seen out there be black-mail material? More like a good ass porno, you know?"

"Wait." I shake my head.

"Video of us fucking..." Royce's eyes hit mine and then widen.

I frown looking from him to Captain. "What?"

"The cabin."

My muscles lock.

The fucking cabin.

Graven.

Fervor spreads through my body and a tremor follows.

Benny recoils in fear.

"Look, man," he rushes out. "I called Bishop on purpose. I knew he was in charge of running shit at the warehouses for you guys. I thought he'd go to you." His eyes bounce between the three of us. "I was doing a solid, I swear!"

I push to my feet and move for the truck, my brothers on my heels.

I grip Bishop by the neck and slam him against the door so hard his head snaps back against the glass, hard enough for it to bounce right off.

He doesn't fight me, he knows he fucked up and takes it.

"You better fucking pray or grasp for some kind of straw, Bishop."

I toss his ass to the ground, moving to the front of the vehicle to talk to my brothers quietly.

"Bishop is fucking dead," Royce growls.

"Raven earned his trust like she earned ours. We can't fuck him up for that," Captain reasons. "We wanted that for her, but we can fuck him up for not telling us this the second she took off."

"Fuck!" Royce folds his hands behind his head, looking to the sky. "She did it again. She fucking protected us."

"But at what cost?" Captain says quietly. "This is Collins we're talking about."

"I'm going to get her."

"Now?" Royce asks eagerly.

"Right fucking now."

Cap and Royce move for his SUV

I climb in mine, and Bass slides in the passenger seat.

My heartbeat hammers against my ribs – the fucking cabin.

Shit.

Captain leads down the road, but I hit the gas, swerving on to the wrong side of the street to pass.

Bass grips the handle above his head, his glare snapping my way briefly.

Captain shakes his head as I fly by him – I know that's why he wanted to lead.

But this is my girl we're going after.

"Where we going?" Bass asks.

"Shut the fuck up, Bishop." I glance both ways, zooming through the red light before the cars have a chance to cross, looking in my rearview mirror when Captain honks his horn. He throws his hands up, letting them come down to smack against his wheel.

My phone rings in the next second, but I don't fish it from my pocket. I already know he's gonna ask me to pull over and wait.

He's fucking trippin', I couldn't calm myself if I tried, and I'm not even gonna attempt to.

Raven is the most stubborn fucking girl I've ever known.

She's venom in the water. Not the snake itself, but the fatal liquid that floats across the top. No matter where you step, if even twenty feet away, she's finding her way inside.

She's in me.

She's in my brothers.

And she's in the prick next to me. Why else would he feel the need to warn her, a girl he hardly fucking knows, when he's been working for us the last year?

Our dad had his file sent over the second one of his men got word of what was going on in his home. Turned out his dad beat his ass, put him in the hospital for the last time, all for defending his little sister. Our dad always got wind of these situations before whatever county these kids come from did.

Pick of the fucked-up litter.

We caught up with him before they could.

He liked what we offered, but he didn't want his sister involved in anything illegal now that she had a chance to be free of her parents.

They had an aunt that wanted her, but she couldn't afford any after-school and summer programs for her and she worked for a living, so we took care of it. She was sent out of state for a better life and he moved into the Bray house. Worked for us since.

"What's Collins got to do with this?" Bass asks, his voice a little tight when we're finally racing across the bridge.

"You fucked up, Bishop. You'll be lucky if we don't ruin you for it."

I blast the radio so I don't have to hear his voice anymore.

Song's pretty fucking fitting and I grow more antsy.

We're getting close, so fucking close and my pulse starts to drum in my ears. My blood is pumping, flowing straight into my muscles and making me shake if my grip on the wheel tells me anything.

I can't even feel my fucking body right now, I'm so amped. I feel nauseous but empty and ready to go.

I cut the corner sharp and the tires skid. I drive right up into the fucking grass, clipping his parked piece of shit Lexus. Throwing the door open with the engine still running, I barrel my way inside the fucking house in one fucking run.

Raven's shriek hits my ears and I rush around the entryway, into the living room where she stands shocked as shit, and wide a-fucking-wake.

Her stare hits mine and instantly becomes overwhelmed with emotions, her body visibly sagging in the same second.

She knows I'm here for her.

I spin and quickly jump over the table before Collins even has a chance to run his fucking mouth.

The screech of tires sound behind me, but I don't look away.

I grab him by the throat, lift and dip his ass back down on the glass top table beside him.

He groans and there's blood coming from somewhere, but I don't care.

I draw my fist back and smash him across his fucking face.

His arms shoot up, one pushing on my jaw, the other, coming across for a weak shot to my cheekbone.

My head doesn't even move – I feel fucking nothing.

Collins tries to lift his legs, an attempt to wrap me up, but I sprawl across his body, so he can't get a grip, and drop my elbow into his nose.

There's blood everywhere now, his eyes hardly open, both almost swollen shut.

"Maddoc!" Raven shouts.

"Come on let's get you—"

I grunt, pushing up quickly and slicing my eyes to Bishop. "Get the fuck away from her!"

I spin back around when Collins starts to roll, but I tuck my hand under his throat and flip him back on his back.

"You think you can put hands on her? And more than once?" I punch him in the ribs. "Corner her in a fucking bathroom?" Left side of his jaw. "Fucking blackmail?!" Right side and he spits, his chest bouncing beneath me.

"Fuck you," he wheezes, and I head-butt him, sending his eyes rolling back

And I lay into him. Over and over and over again.

Until he can't fight back.

Until he stops trying.

Even after his body grows limp.

I don't remember stopping, but suddenly I blink and I'm being dragged across the grass, Raven pushing on my chest,

Captain gripping my right arm, Royce at my left, and then I'm in the passenger seat of my own vehicle.

Bishop is driving, Raven is on my lap and my brother's tail-lights are visible in front of us.

The low whine of an ambulance rings in the distance.

A soft, warm hand slides up my chest, and I look to the contact.

My shirt is ripped, my skin exposed, the imprint of her tiny fingers blended into the blood splattered across my chest.

I look up into her eyes.

Glossy grey.

She nods, her fingers spanning out against me and my eyes close in an adrenaline crash.

My girl.

Chapter 12

RAVEN

WITH SHAKY HANDS, I MOVE MY FRESHLY SHOWERED HAIR FROM my face and take the mug from Captain when he holds it out for me, his eyes focused on anything and everything ... but me.

I know what I did to him and I can't take it back.

I had one of his most precious of secrets at my disposal, and for a minute there, I'm sure he thought I'd use it against him. I misused the trust I forced him to give me, that he had only recently relinquished on his own.

I did this to all of them.

For a few short days that felt like a lifetime in my own head, I placed fear and anger in the first people who ever seemed to care enough to look past my forever flaws and unbreakable stupidity.

I'm a perpetual fuck up. I know this.

I warned them of this.

My mother did a number on me and it seems I'm not the only one who will have to deal with the aftermath.

I go to cradle the drink in my lap, but Captain finally looks at me, but only for a second to deliver his glare. "Drink it, Raven, you're shaking. I put some chamomile in there to calm your nerves."

I nod and bring it to my lips, blowing lightly before taking a small sip.

Maddoc still hasn't come down yet and we're all waiting around not saying but thinking the same damn thing – this is all my fucking fault.

He climbed out of the car and went straight for his room to rinse off, so I slipped into the hall shower quickly.

Royce tosses his phone onto the coffee table and it continues to vibrate against the wood.

Cap sighs. "One of us is going to need to answer."

"We need to wait," Royce responds.

Footsteps have our heads jerking toward the stairs. Maddoc's voice floats to our ears. "Hello."

He's answered his phone.

He's visible now, still descending the steps and my ass cheeks clench in expectation when I meet his frenzied gaze.

My stomach turns, but I don't dare look away – couldn't if I wanted to.

"Yeah," he rasps into his phone. "I will."

He hangs up slowly, not stopping until he's directly in front of me, glaring down the length of his nose.

Naked anger and unreserved foreboding has my throat growing tight.

"He wants Maybell here," he speaks, looking at me but his words are for his brothers. "Can you guys go get her?"

"Yeah, man," Captain mutters and he and Royce head for the door.

"Take your time," he adds, and they hesitate a second before walking out, closing and locking the door behind them.

The second they do, he grips me under the armpit and

tosses me in the air, catching my hips in his rough hands. He turns, taking the steps two at a time until we reach his room. He bumps into the dresser, shoves everything off with one full sweep of his elbow and drops me on top.

He pushes closer, pulling me flush against him and my body heats – a strange mix of fear and excitement flaring inside me. I'm not afraid of him, but I admit, I have no idea what he's thinking, what he believes or what truths he knows.

His knuckle finds my jaw and he holds my head in place.

"What. Happened."

"Nothing—"

"Try a-fucking-gain, Raven." His chest rumbles with his growl. "And start with the part where you first left, the night you were jumped."

I lick my lips. "Bass told me to meet him out at the warehouses, he was too cryptic for me to ignore him, so I went. He told me about a video of us breaking into the cabin, but he didn't know that part of it, just thought it was of the four of us hooking up. I was jumped leaving." I pause, not sure I want to tell him the next part considering I'm pretty sure Collins is in the hospital right now for the little he did know.

"Keep. Talking."

"One of the guys whispered something before they ran off."

"Which was?" he prompts, crossly.

"That I don't belong, it was the same thing Collins said to me in the bathroom that day at the restaurant."

"Wait." Maddoc's frown deepens, anger vibrating through his voice. "Are you saying ... Collins is the one who had you fucking jumped?"

"Yes."

A deep growl leaves him, and his palms find my thighs, squeezing fiercely. "You hid this from us. You went there without us. Without me."

"I had to," I admit.

"Tell me why."

"Isn't it obvious?"

"Say it," he demands.

"To protect you."

His chest rumbles and he starts shaking for real— a crack in his unbreakable armor.

A sudden and strong warmth spreads in my chest causing deep creases to form between my eyes.

His lip curls. "And what were you planning to do to protect us, to protect me?"

I tell him the honest truth. "Anything."

A shuddered breath leaves him before he rips away from me.

He rubs his hands across his hair and down the back of his skull, gripping his own neck. "Did you fuck him?"

"No."

"But you would have, if what, he took it?" His eyes bore into mine. "You'd have given him what I'd just fucking made clear belonged to me?"

I'm not proud of the decision, it should probably tell me to run and run fast knowing I'd give myself over for him – that can't be a good thing – but ... "If I had to, yes."

With a deep roar, he spins and punches the wall, planting his hands against it. He bends his body, his chin dropping to his chest.

I wait a minute, hop down and walk to him. Slipping under his arm, I slide down the wall, knees bent, until I'm low enough to look up and meet his stare without him having to lift his head.

"You're angry." My eyes shoot between his and his nostrils flare.

"I am beyond. Fucking. Furious," he confirms slowly, and I nod.

I glide up and his head lifts to follow.

"Show me," I whisper.

He tenses a moment, his features tightening as he quickly flicks his eyes between mine.

His head draws back slowly. "Raven—"

"I said," I cut him off. "Show me. Now."

His brows drop even lower, but with a deep rumbly roar, he lifts me, quickly tossing me on the bed in complete abandon.

He yanks his shirt over his head and my lips part.

He got ink.

Wrapping around his pec and left shoulder, the tribal-like design is thick and bold. Angry swirls and sharp edges with woven tethers of four ropes.

One for each of his brothers, one for him.

Who does the fourth embody?

My chest grows tight at the thought.

It's so sexy.

So Maddoc.

His basketball shorts and boxers drop in the next second, so I start to lift my shirt, but he catches my wrist and tosses my hand aside roughly.

He makes quick work of stripping me bare. Before I can settle myself, he's got my hips in his hands and I'm flipped over, landing on my stomach. His hand slips between my legs, cupping me and he pulls, lifting me by the pussy to my knees.

Two fingers slide down my center until they're pushing into me and I clench around him.

He growls, pumps them twice, then removes his hand, his fingertips now biting into my ass.

He aligns himself with my entrance.

He growls, pushing inside me in one deep thrust, only to pull out completely, all so he can do it again and again.

Rougher, faster, and I clench around him, an airy moan

slipping past my lips. My head drops back and he grips my hair.

He becomes frantic, deep growls leaving him, his breathing erratic and loud.

When my body starts to quake, he pulls out, smacking my ass cheek, then squeezing. "You don't get to come yet."

He slides his dick coated with my juices up and down my ass crack and I twitch. Maddoc slams back in and my knees try to close, but he nudges them apart more. Pushing my shoulders down until my chest hits the mattress, he scoots closer, drives deeper, my ass completely in the air for him to rub on.

"You denied me," he rasps, flexing inside me.

"Yes," I breathe.

"You kept things from me."

"I did." I squeeze my eyes shut, trying not to let go but, fuck me, I'm so close.

He grinds his hips against me, my ass cheeks spread as wide as they can go so he can get in me as far as the position allows.

He places his wet thumb over my hole and pushes, making me whimper.

He feels it, me about to come, my pussy clinging to his dick, begging.

Maddoc pulls out and I'm on my back, him sliding inside me in the next second. He grips my right knee, pushing it up to my side, and hot breath hits my ear.

I shudder beneath him.

"You protected me," he whispers, biting at the flesh there before kissing it gently.

I nod against the pillow, my back arching slightly, hips rolling to meet his.

He grinds against me. "I didn't need you to, but you did it anyway."

My heart beats faster, my hands shooting up to grip him by the ribs.

His pace slows, still just as deep, still just as hungry, but ... different. His next words have my heart stopping.

"You left me," he whispers.

My eyes squeeze closed a minute, and when I push on his chest, he lets me roll him over so I can climb up. I slide down on top of him, unable to keep from grinding against him and his hands slip up my stomach, cupping my breasts. I brush his hair back.

"I didn't want to."

He eyes me before a tightness covers his features. "I know. And that tells me everything."

I'm spun back to the mattress.

He breathes against my mouth. "Let me drive, baby."

I clench around him, unable to speak, so I nod.

He starts moving, slow and steady. He fucks me deep and filling, and when I moan against his mouth, his lips finally fall on mine in a punishing kiss I fucking love.

My body is shaking uncontrollably now, my thighs clenching against him and he releases my lips.

"You can come now, baby." He slides his mouth across mine, pushing in deeper than ever and I gasp. "Come with me."

His body jerks with mine and together, partners in crime, we finish.

I could never get enough of this.

We only get a few minutes to catch our breath before tires crunching gravel has our stares meeting.

Slowly we stand, clean ourselves up, and redress.

He pulls me against him, running his lips over mine, before gripping my cheeks and kissing me slow. Different. "It's time."

We get downstairs only seconds before the front door opens.

Captain and Royce walk in, Maybell slowly entering behind them.

She looks solemn as she tries to smile, but there is a deeper issue plaguing her. "You ready, boy?"

He nods, skims his lips over my hair and walks to her.

He kisses her temple and she wraps her arm around his. Together they walk out front.

Royce, Captain, and I follow a few feet behind, making it out onto the porch right as a police car creeps through the trees.

My eyes widen and I take a step toward them, but Royce wraps an arm around my shoulder. "No," he whispers. "He can handle this, RaeRae," he says meekly, kissing my hair and my features tighten.

The officer steps out, his face drawn up in uncertainty as he steps toward Maddoc. It's not a cop I've seen around here, but he seems well aware of who he's here to arrest, fear clearly etched across his face.

But Maddoc gives a curt nod and the man relaxes, signals for him to turn around then places cuffs across his wrists.

His eyes meet mine over the hood and hold, then shift to his brothers' before he's placed in the back seat.

Maybell climbs in front.

"What do we do?" I whisper as the taillights disappear.

"We wait."

"For?"

"Dad."

Chapter 13

RAVEN

It's been three days since we've seen or heard from Maddoc. Three days since we've seen or heard from anyone, actually, since we stayed locked inside waiting for contact that never came. Today, though, we had to be at school because of the game. The team would already be short Maddoc, and the guys refused to leave them hanging.

All fucking day these nosey assholes asked questions they had no right to the answers to – where the boys had been and where Maddoc was, but they never responded.

Royce had called Mac the day Maddoc was arrested and told him to drop word that the boys were out on business. Nobody ever questions their whereabouts, but with all the flip flop happening around here, these Brayshaw students couldn't hide their drooling tongues and wagging tales if they tried.

The boys handled their admirers better than I did the gossipy girls. I could only handle a few of the curious glances before I got pissed off and threatened to give anyone else who started matching black eyes, they could look at in the mirror all day if they wanted.

I get the curiosity. I mean, fuck, Maddoc tore off my top at the assembly, then grabbed me up. I'm sure to outside eyes it looked like a fucked-up situation, even more so with everything that followed and now here we are, back minus the leader. But fuck them, I don't give a shit about their petty rumors and neither do the guys. I just don't like to be stared at.

A whistle sounds again, bringing me back to the now, and the crowd starts shouting.

The boys rally well, Mac and Leo helping lead the team as starters today alongside Royce and Captain – there's still been no sign of Collins.

Captain's footwork is off, but his shots are on point, so he passes off and the team rushes the ball down the court. Royce passes it back to Cap who shoots for a quick point earned.

The opposing team gets the ball and charges forward, but Leo manages to block a pass, the ball ricocheting off his hand and straight for Mac's, who throws for a half-court shot, but it hits the rim and bounces off. Luckily, Royce is near and hops up for the rebound, shooting midair and making it.

The score is back and forth all game, they miss and allow more points than normal, but in the end, they're able to pull off the win.

The team quickly retreats to the locker room, but Royce and Captain don't follow.

I rush to meet them on the court and together the three of us waste no time, acknowledge no one, and head for Captain's SUV.

Royce throws himself back against the seat and takes a deep breath. "Maddoc would be pissed at how we played."

"No, he wouldn't," Captain tells him. "He'll be proud we played period."

The boys talk a little about the game on the drive home,

and when we park and climb out, Maybell steps from the house.

Tension lines her brows, but she tries to mask it and my stomach muscles tighten.

We all rush closer, desperate for her news.

"Your dad called," she tells them. "Maddoc finally gets to see a judge tomorrow. He says he should be granted bail, no problems."

The boys' shoulders visibly drop, and both look to the sky a moment, but not me. The tension in my stomach spreads through my ribs and wraps around my shoulder blades until there's a slight ache there.

Maybell, she isn't relieved. She should be, hearing one of her chosen sons is coming home. She won't hold their eyes long and she hasn't looked my way yet.

"He wants to make sure you're there," she adds and they both nod instantly.

"Why didn't he call us, too?" Royce asks her and she gives a small smile, but it doesn't meet her eyes.

She reaches up and touches both their cheeks. "He knew you'd be there, playin' the best you could with all that's goin' on here."

"So tomorrow?" Royce confirms again.

"Tomorrow. Doors open at eight." She pats them lightly and moves toward me.

She takes a deep breath, her eyes finally meeting mine. She nods glumly. "I told you, child. I told you, you belong here. I need you to start believing it, you understand?" Her eyes grow glossy, but she doesn't let her tears fully form. "It's hurting my boys when you don't."

I nod, but I'm unable to wipe the frown that's been in place since she started talking.

She starts down the road and turns back to the boys, but they're already moving inside, so I follow.

"I'm fucking beat, bro." Royce pulls off his hoodie and tosses it on the couch.

"Me too, man." Cap moves into the kitchen, pulling open the fridge. "Sandwiches and chips cool for dinner tonight?"

"Sounds fucking good to me." Royce plops down and flips on the TV.

Cap lifts his eyes to mine and when he does, his brows hit in the center of his forehead.

"Raven?"

"Yeah." I nod, fighting down the growing feeling. "I'm good with that."

"Raven."

I lick my lips. I'm not fine.

Maybell didn't share all she knows.

"Raven."

"She's hiding something," I blurt out.

They eye me, then each other.

"Guys."

Royce walks over to me and grips my elbows. "She has a lot of secrets, only spills when she needs to."

"She shouldn't hide things from you, it's not right."

Royce grins, but it doesn't meet his eyes, then moves to the fridge for a drink.

"I'm serious. I don't know if you guys have known many people who've been arrested, but my mom was, all the fucking time. You're in court within a day, sometimes released right after booking with a court date to return. This isn't normal. He hasn't called and he hasn't seen a judge. Something is off."

"If there is something to know, Maddoc will fill us in tomorrow." Captain looks up and as soon as he sees the annoying unease I can't hide, his light eyes soften. "I know things don't work as easy as they should in our world, but we have to believe the moves made without us serve a purpose. And Raven, I guaran-fucking-tee, if Maddoc could call, he would have, and if there was a problem we needed to worry about, he would force a way. He's sitting, so we're sitting."

"But doesn't his not calling make you wanna fuck shit up just to be put in there with him and find out why?" I ask and both boys laugh.

Royce walks over and kisses my temple. "We love you, our little scrapper, but one more day, RaeRae."

I look to Cap for confirmation, and he winks, saying, "If it doesn't happen how we want tomorrow, we'll fuck shit up, all right?"

I nod, all fucking for that answer and again they both laugh.

Cap makes quick work of finishing up our food, and we're done just as quick, each of us disappearing into our rooms.

I close my door, change clothes and slide in my bed. I tuck my knife into my sleep shorts, plug in my headphones, and turn on my flashlight.

I stare at the door.

Here's to another sleepless night.

Chapter 14

RAVEN

THE RIDE TO THE COURTHOUSE FEELS LIKE A MILLION YEARS, but in reality, it only took a solid fifteen minutes to get to the turn-off. Once we're within eyeshot, though, it feels way too fucking soon and nerves kick to life making me queasy.

"Raven, make sure your knife's not on you, we have to go through a metal detector," Cap reminds me.

"Got it." I slip my switchblade between the seats and glance out the window at the large brick style building.

Captain finds a spot pretty close to the front and the boys get out, but guilt – an emotion I'm not used to – has me delaying.

My hand is on the handle but unmoving, and Royce is the one that has to open my door.

When he gets a look at my face, he sighs and moves closer. He grips my ankle and wrist and pulls me to the door, wrapping me in a hug.

"I know what you're thinking," he tells me. "And knock that shit off. This ain't your fault."

My eyes pool with tears despite my best effort.

These boys are turning me into a damn mess.

I don't cry.

"That's not true and you know it. You're both mad at me and we haven't even talked it out yet." I pull back to look him in the eye. "Maddoc only went over there to fuck shit up because of what I did."

Royce moves back a little so Cap can squeeze in beside us.

"No." Captain shakes his head and reaches for my hand. I let him pull me out and to my feet. He bends down a little to look me in the eye. "Maddoc fucked him up because he did what he did. This week, next week, doesn't matter. You should already know, if you'd have done what you should have and come straight to us instead of acting brave alone like you're used to, he would have reacted the same. Maddoc is fucking fierce, Raven. He loves us. Would die for us, but we're his brothers. He's never loved before. This? This is what that looks like."

A breath lodges in my throat and I shake my head.

Cap shakes his right back. "We're not having this conversation, but I know my brother. Whether you know it, whether he fucking knows it, it's in there. Maybe not fully grown but Raven you're inside him in a way nobody ever has been. He will always act in defense first, especially when you're at the center of the threat."

I nod, glancing at Royce.

"Fists first, fixes later," he says.

"Kinda sounds like me," a laugh bubbles out of me and they grin gravely.

"And we were pissed at you, maybe still are, to be honest, but we understand now. We see what you did and why, and we love you more for it even though you made the wrong move."

Royce's eyes slide between mine, the honesty of his words hitting me hard and meaning more than I could express if I tried. "Now come on. We still have an hour but let's get in there, the seats fill up fast."

Together, three strong, we head inside for our fourth man.

MADDOC

Three fucking days.

They stuck me in a damn cell by myself for three fucking days. Not once did I get let out. No calls. No other inmate interactions, not that I wanted it, but still. Three days of nothing but a fucking guard who would stick a tray through the metal bars. He didn't even speak.

I have no idea what's going on at home.

I don't know if Collins and his lackeys came after my family or if Raven took off again for some stupid fucking reason she cooked up. I don't know shit.

I have never in my life felt more helpless.

And if I didn't get a message from our lawyer telling me I'd finally see a fucking judge today for bail, I'd have lost my shit and threw my name around, forced them to feel the weight of it until they told me what I needed to know. But I trusted my dad and waited it out, just fucking barely.

Right now, my patience is being tested again as I'm crammed in a room with seven others waiting to see the damn judge. Shitty part is this isn't even the only room, so who knows how long this could take.

If I lean forward a little and look to the left, I can see inside the room across from me where more inmates wait just the same.

The officer who led us in here stands in the center of the

hall, blocking us from the others. He hits both door frames with his little nightstick to gain attention.

"Listen up!" he shouts, pulling up his belt to cover the potbelly hanging over. "Last names A through H, line up in front of that door. Face forward, no turning or communicating with the inmate in front of or behind you." He points his toy my way, looking right at me. "You first."

My pulse kicks higher at being singled out with these people around. My name hasn't been said out loud in here. They have no fucking clue who I am and what would happen to them if they decided to act like brave little bitches and start a pointless fight for the sake of dick measuring. While I'd love to put someone in their place right now, I've got a lot of tension to burn, I need out of this fucking shit today.

Or maybe I'm fucking trippin' from being in here three days with no contact and he simply called on the first eyes he locked with.

I take my time standing and slowly shuffle toward the door, the clinking of other inmate's shackles echoing behind me.

They put these fucking cuffs on that bound at the wrist, a thin chain hanging down and connecting at the ankles, making it awkward to walk and cutting my strides in half. It's infuriating.

I stand facing a door and my senses kick in.

He just fucking tucked me into a corner and expects me to stand here blind. I don't fucking think so.

I start to turn when a hiss hits my ear.

"Do. Not. Turn around."

My muscles lock, my shoulders stiffening.

"Stay perfectly fucking still or we're made."

"The fuck?" I hiss back, but he silences me.

"There's no one behind me, someone's causing commotion, but I only have a minute before the rest are in line and you're brought into the courtroom. Give a tight nod if you were left alone?"

I do as he asks.

"Good. I asked for it, sorry for the no communication but I didn't want your brothers stepping in and trying to speed up the process. I made them keep you waiting until my lawyer could get me here."

I frown at the old wood in front of me.

"It took a lot of work, a lot of money and promises, but I'll be reviewed for a parole release today."

"Dad— "

"I'm sorry to spring this. This isn't normally how these things work, but it's the only way. Things are moving quicker than planned, and I need to be home now more than ever."

"What the fuck does that mean?" I snap quietly.

"Shh. You'll understand soon."

"All right, the rest of you, in line!" the officer shouts behind us and my dad curses.

"They're out there for you, son," he whispers.

Annoyance flares. It's not right to catch them off guard like this.

Cap is gonna freak if this goes how our dad clearly has planned. He'll be forced to tell him he has a daughter he hid from him for the last two, almost three years. Cap will worry this will affect the little visitation he does have with Zoey.

But the irritation can only get so far before it's replaced with anxiousness.

If they're here, she will be, too. And if she's not, something is wrong.

This also means my dad will see her. With all the shit going wrong lately, there's no fucking way he hasn't linked it directly to our newcomer. If he tries to push her out, I'll push back for the first time in my life.

If she's even here.

The door is pulled open and I bounce my shoulders quickly before we're ushered through a narrow walkway and then straight into the open courtroom. My eyes immediately find them.

Four rows back, three seats over.

And my baby is here.

Her eyes fly across my face and form and she breathes a visible sigh of relief her head dropping to Captain's shoulder a second when she finds I'm in one piece. Untouched.

No one can hurt me, baby.

I meet Cap's eyes and he nods. Royce tips his chin.

And then I tense, wondering if they'll spot him behind me, but when I turn around and face forward, being the first to walk out and first to reach my seat, I see he isn't there, but another inmate instead.

I tip my head back to look down the line as discreetly as possible.

He's not there.

My brows meet at the center and I face forward.

In the next second, the judge is announced, and she jumps straight to it.

She picks up the first file and flips it open.

Her eyes pop up instantly, a quick shift of her features as her face pulls tight.

Guess I'm up first.

I can't hold still, and spin in my chair and meet Captain's, then Royce's stare and their brows snap in.

Raven shifts in her chair, turning to whisper something at Royce.

"Forward, now." The guard walks over to give his demands and I clench my teeth, forcing myself to listen to this prick.

Bet he's tight with my dad but has to act all fucking bad out here, like he's the boss. Like what he says goes.

He's got on a pair of twenty-five-hundred-dollar Valentino

boots, and a fucking Shinola watch ... with a sixty-dollar mandated uniform.

He's on someone's payroll.

And this isn't me judging. This is Brayshaw.

"First case this morning: Maddoc Brayshaw. Charged with assault and breaking and entering."

I stand, making way the few feet forward to stand behind the desk as instructed.

Her hands shake slightly as she reads over whatever is in front of her, her shoulders visibly relaxing in the next second.

"Your case has been dismissed and no charges filed. Please, sir, wait for your paperwork and move back to your seat." She dismisses me and before I can even turn around, she's picking up the next file.

I glance at my family as I make my way to the clerk stamping some shit on my paperwork and they smile at me, but my brows pull in when I see a guard slipping into the row behind them, dropping to whisper in their ear.

Cap's brows furrow and Royce's stare slices back to mine in question.

I give a tense nod.

This has to be about Dad.

I'm pushed through the side door right as they stand and shimmy past the others seated beside them.

The door clicks and I turn, coming face to face with my dad.

I don't often get to stand near him, the few times he allowed us to visit, he's usually already sitting at the table once we're cleared to come in, and contact isn't allowed so there's no hugging and shit. Not that he's a hugger.

Hell, he could be, I'm not really sure, it's been so long.

Standing with him now, it's strange.

We're almost the same height, but he's got me beat by an inch. His build is the same as mine, though. Solid muscle without the fullness like Captain's or the trim cuts Royce has. We're more tapered around the edges.

Same green eyes, same dark hair only his is lined with silver edgings.

The door we entered through slammed again and I snap back to reality.

"Son," he nods, looking me over just the same as I did him.

He nods to the guard in the room who quickly comes over and uncuffs me.

"I had your paperwork processed early, that was more for formality and to get your brothers here. It's happening right now, they're bringing them to the hearing room down the hall as we speak."

The bag with my clothes in it is handed to me.

We're about to be forced to listen to our dad, innocent or guilty, talk about why he, a convicted rapist, should be set free.

Raven has to hear this.

Suddenly I wish I could warn them, not that they'd go if I did.

"It's fucked up, you're making us watch this," I speak my mind.

His eyes slope around the edges. "I know what I'm doing, son. You're going to have to trust me."

"That's not easy for me right now," I tell him honestly.

"I know, son. I know." He nods. "Change, exit that door and enter the first room on the left."

The guard opens the door to a back hallway, and he walks that way.

"Maddoc," he calls, and I look back to him. "Don't do anything stupid."

And he walks out.

I make quick work of changing and splash some water from the fountain on my face, then rush to where he directed me.

When I enter, I find my brothers and Raven already inside, a wary look on all three of their faces.

The door I came through is on the opposite side and I try to move toward them, but a guard tells me to sit and a line of people walk through the door.

My shoulders grow heavy, but I sit.

"Let's move into this quickly as this wasn't on the schedule," a new judge states as he sits.

The side door opens and out walks our father, but he faces away from us.

I look to Royce and Captain and they slowly sit forward, bracing their hands on their knees.

I can't say for sure if they recognize him or if they're curious as to what the hell is about to happen and why they were sent this way.

"Today, we're here on a motion for parole, Stockton, San Juaquin County versus," – the man swallows – "Rolland Brayshaw."

"The fuck..." can be heard from Royce and again I jerk around to look at them, Royce is trying to stand, but Captain reaches across a stunned Raven and pulls him back down.

Both move to grip the seats in front of them.

And Raven. Her face is lined with tension as she stares toward my dad.

I spin back around.

He faces dead forward, his eyes locked on the judge.

I can't see him fully, but the man can, and his fear shows it. He pauses a moment to lick his lips and discreetly slides his eyes to the guard. "Mr. Brayshaw, you were arrested and charged on one account of rape and grand theft auto and attempting to traffic cocaine, where you were found guilty, and sentenced to fifteen years. Served eleven. Mr. Brayshaw, step forward please."

He does.

"Mr. Brayshaw, I have here, three letters of support from your local community. It seems you've made some positive changes, organized some outreach programs from your position."

He pulls his lips between his teeth, and my stomach muscles tighten.

Why's he fucking anxious?

The same second I think it's gone.

His feet seem to widen despite the shackles holding them close, his shoulders expand, his posture straight. "I have." His chin lifts.

"I've opened what used to be my groundmen's homes to the youth, housing troubled teenagers or those who need to escape their living situations. All victims of some form of abuse. We have a boy's and a girl's home now, both up and running successfully for the last five years. We've also created a program that allows these teenagers to go to our schools and receive a higher level of education than offered where they come from. Our success rate for graduates through our program is very high and increases every year. I've learned a lot through the development. I've grown as a man and I'm proud of the work we're doing.

"And it hasn't just been me. My family has also begun the remedial process. In fact." He nods his head slightly, like he's convincing himself to continue on, and suddenly I'm not sure I want him to. "My sons are here today, one under unfortunate circumstance, the other two in support of us both."

The people on the panel raise their eyes to the room.

"And the young woman seated between them," the judge starts and an ache hits deep in my ribs.

I sit forward.

"She's a resident at our all-girl's home. We rescued her from her home just a few short months ago, where she suffered from abuse, both mentally and physically. She's also a victim of sexual assault."

I jerk around in my seat to look at Raven.

This can't be fucking true. I read her file a solid ten fucking times. There is nothing in that thing that mentions sexual abuse.

"She has come with them today to show her silent support as she's found comfort with my family and helped show them things I am unable to being locked in here. She's brought a woman's touch back into their lives, softened their hearts."

The woman on the end slides her eyes back to Raven and curiosity has her scooting closer in her seat. "Is this true, do you live in this girl's home?"

Shit.

RAVEN

What. The. Fuck.

My muscles work on their own and suddenly I'm standing.

The boys stand. Maddoc stands.

"Miss?" the woman tries again, but I ignore her, my eyes locked on the back of Rolland Brayshaw's head.

He said Stockton. My home town.

"And she too." My insides tighten when he speaks again, the familiarity in his tone now ringing in my ears and sending a sting down my spine. "Has learned from them. She understands now," he pauses, clearing his throat. "The importance of finding people you trust."

My airway is cut off, and fire burns up my tongue.

No fucking way...

He turns around to face me, the motherfucker boldly meeting my eyes and everything clicks. "She understands ... how family runs deeper than blood."

"Are you fucking serious?" I think I say out loud, but I can't be sure.

"Cap ... what is this?" Royce whispers.

Maddoc shifts like he's ready to jump the little picket, but the officer at his side slides in his path, gripping his waistband where his gun hangs.

"Do you or do you not live in one of Mr. Brayshaw's group homes?" The judge gets louder.

I narrow my eyes on the man who has yet to look away since the moment he spun around, not even to meet the eyes of his sons. He hasn't even fucking blinked.

The man whose home I'm living in.

The man whose son I'm fucking, just like he used to fuck my mother at night.

The man who gave me my fucking knife.

I force my eyes to the judge. My voice is low, but it's strong. "Yes."

I shake off Captain when he tries to touch my arm, likely about to whisper something I don't want to hear. I shrug away. "I live in the Bray house." Just not the all-girl's house.

"Ms. Carver, do you wish to speak on behalf or against Mr. Brayshaw? Perhaps on your experience at the home, if you feel safe there. It could help us make a decision."

The weight of Big Man's stare is on me, but I can't bring myself to look his way.

If I see demand in his eyes, I might do the opposite.

If I saw regret, I might walk away and never look back.

If I saw pain ... I might just fucking cry.

None of those are good and right now, this moment has to come from me.

I could lie, say that he's a great man with a good heart when I don't know this to be true.

I could lie, say I've never met the man. Tell her this is the first I've laid eyes on him.

I look back to him.

He has slight grey above his ears now, the rest a deep, dark brown. Almost black. His skin a little more weathered than I remember. Eyes a little more jaded.

I could tell the truth.

I keep my eyes on him. "I couldn't care less about your decision. Lock him back up or let him roam free, makes no difference to me."

Royce tries to touch the back of his hand to mine, in support or demand, I don't care to know right now, so I yank away from him.

The judge clears his throat, but Rolland doesn't turn back. He takes his time attempting to read me and when that fails, he finally looks to his sons at my sides, then the one to the left of him.

Suddenly it's hard to breathe, and my chest starts rising and falling rapidly.

I have to get out of here.

I quickly and without warning, leap over the back of my chair. I know if I darted from my seat, Captain would block me. I shuffle down the row and one of them reaches out to grip for my elbow, but I jerk away, rushing for the door.

Maddoc's call of my name and a slight commotion is heard behind me.

I don't turn around.

MADDOC

"RAVEN!" I SHOUT, SHOULDERING THE GUARD AS HE STEPS UP and grabs a hold of me. Royce stays on her heels and my heart starts hammering in my chest.

Fuck.

"Chill, kid," the guard hisses under his breath. "You'll be out of here soon. Keep this up and you'll go right back to that cell.

"I'm not your fucking kid." I jerk away from him, grinding my damn teeth as I swing my glare to my dad.

I don't even hear what's being said my blood is pumping so fierce in my ears.

I'm not given the chance to look my father in the eyes again to gauge his thoughts before he's done and being shuffled out the door.

The panel is next to walk out and then the guard finally backs away.

I hop the aisles and meet Cap in the center, a deep frown covering his face.

"You good, man?" I know he's asking about my last few days, but no time for me right now.

"What the fuck just happened?"

His eyes narrow. "I have no idea."

"I need you to sign your release papers, Mr. Brayshaw." The guard changes his tune and motions for me to follow him.

I look back to Captain.

"I'll be out front."

I frown and look away, following the officer.

He'll be outside he said, meaning like me, he's not so sure she will be.

Finally, a half hour later, my paperwork is ready and I'm free to leave.

A black Denali is waiting right at the curb when I exit.

Cap climbs out.

"Where is she?"

"Took off down the road. Royce called Mac, chasing her ass all the way. Finally forced her to get into Mac's car after they got a solid two miles down the road."

I growl and move past him, sliding into the driver seat of his vehicle.

We're both quiet on the ride home and not too long later we're pulling into the property, rolling past the Bray houses to our home.

Our dad's home.

Fuck. If he gets out, will he fight us on letting her stay?

Royce comes out the front the second we park.

He comes down the steps, gripping my hand and pulling it in, he pats my back before stepping away and looking me over.

"Get in any brawls in there?" he tries to joke in true Royce fashion, but the strain is easily caught.

"Nah, man. They kept me in a single cell all three days. No fucking contact with anyone, I'd have called, but they didn't offer, so I figured it was all part of the plan."

They nod, understanding.

"We had Mac smooth shit over at the school as much as possible," Royce tells me. "They just think we were out on business."

"Last time we disappeared from school for more than a couple days was when we went to find Zoey." I look from Royce to Cap. "You good, man? Stressin' out?"

"I'm not ready to think about that tonight," Cap says firmly, letting us know not to bring it up again until he does.

I nod and all our eyes fall to the dirt.

"Dad is the reason I was held in there for three days, he had me held so he could get there when we were."

"Did you know he'd be there before you saw him?" Royce asks.

"No, I was waiting in line to be led into the courtroom and all of a fucking sudden he was behind me telling me you guys were there. Even then I thought he was coming out, but then we were all thrown in that fucking hearing room."

"Raven flipped her shit. Locked herself in her room as

soon as we got here." Royce sighs, looking to the house and my eyes follow. "Won't come out. Can't believe he put her on blast with that ... you know, the abuse and shit," he says low, and my forehead creases.

I shake my head. "She has too much pride to allow anyone to see her as too weak to handle her own past. It's something else."

Royce scoffs. "Well, what I wanna know is how the hell we're gonna get her ass out of the room to find out ... without pissing her off more by busting down the fuckin—"

The door is thrown open, and the screen flies to the side, slamming against the paneling and a pissed off, puffed up Raven steps out.

Hair down, face fresh and clear. Sweats and T-shirt.

Ready to breathe fire down our necks.

My baby.

Her forehead pinches slightly like she hears my inner whispers, but she stays strong. "Did you know?" she asks point blank, but there are deep creases at the edge of her eyes that have me thinking the question isn't as standard as it sounds.

"Know what exactly?"

"Don't fuck with me right now," she snaps.

"I need you to break it down for me."

Her jaw clenches and she glances away. "I need a ride home."

"What the fuck?" Royce barks. "This is your fucking home!"

"My real home, Royce."

I move closer to her, and her eyes slice to mine.

"I'm not playing. Take me or I'll find a way. I'll jump out the second-floor window if I have to."

"Tell me why," I demand, unease settling low in my stomach.

She shakes her head. "That's not gonna happen, not right now, so it's your call."

"We had no damn clue he was doing all that today," Royce shouts, moving toward her in a slight panic. "And if you're mad he mentioned your past, well fuck, RaeRae, be mad at him, not us."

Her forehead tightens, and she bounces her left leg. "Are we going to see my mom or not?"

My eyes narrow and she finally meets my stare and holds it.

Defiance flashes in her eyes.

"Fine. We'll take you, but don't pull anything stupid when we're there," I warn her, an edge to my tone I didn't expect to use on her today.

Fuck man, I've been gone, not knowing if I was coming back to a Raven-less house again, and she's acting like a stubborn fucking brat. Hiding what's on her mind.

"Now?" she stresses.

I glance to Captain and Royce who both give curt nods, their features drawn up in an irritated confusion.

I look back to her and she nods, then disappears into the house.

Soon as we're sure she's out of earshot, I turn to my brothers.

"If we have to tie her ass up and drag her back here with us, we do it."

They nod in agreement and it's settled.

She will come back with us. Period.

Chapter 15

MADDOC

I WASN'T EVEN HOME FOR AN HOUR LAST NIGHT BEFORE WE were on the road.

Being winter break for Brayshaw High, there's no class for a few weeks, but we still have games to be played, so the quicker we get back, the fucking better.

"This is the exit," Raven tells Captain and we pull off the highway.

We put the address we had on file into the GPS, but Raven said it wouldn't get us to her side of town without taking us all the way around since there were no official roads to her mom's place. Apparently, the trailers are just thrown down on a random lot at the edge of the city, so we let her navigate. At least, Cap pretended to. I'm sure he figured out and memorized the way before even sliding into the driver's seat.

We take a left on a broken-down gravel road, turning into a dirt lot gated off by large sheets of mismatched tin, something you'd see on a cheap shed roof or surrounding a junkyard.

It's night fall, but barefoot kids still play out in the cold, nobody bothering to tell them to get out of the way of our SUV as we roll toward them.

Captain slows at the sight, almost to a full stop, but I pat the back of his seat and he meets my eyes in the mirror.

His features tighten as does his grip on the wheel and I know he's thinking about Zoey and where she could have ended up if we hadn't learned of her existence just in time.

Come on, brother.

It takes a few seconds, then he lets out a deep breath and continues forward.

A little farther down, we spot a group of men sitting around a beat-up, parted out car. They jump to their feet as we edge closer, cigarettes hanging from most of their mouths. Their eyes fall to the blackout rims before lifting back to the tinted windows.

"I told you we should have gotten a cheap rental or borrowed someone else's car." Raven keeps her eyes on the group as we pass.

"Which one?" Cap asks her.

She looks ahead. "Last one on the right, up against the fence."

My eyes follow her direction and brows dip low.

I never stopped to consider what the place Raven grew up in looked like, but even if I did, I'd have missed the mark. There's no little porch with an overlaying awning like the trailers we've seen. No space in front of it with a table and chair set for when you need to step outside.

It's nothing but a fucking rectangular box with tin foil in the windows and a layer of dirt so thick not even rain could wash it away. It's basically an RV without the fucking engine.

The 'fence' she mentioned is not a fucking fence, but an old wire wrap tied loosely to a few rotted wood posts.

On the other side are train tracks with a few broken down

carts laying at the edges of them. There's laughter and lights coming from one of them – I'm guessing it's used as a squat house for homeless or maybe where teenagers get fucked up. I can picture Raven going out there to smoke at night or just to get away. Maybe this is where her love for riding trains came from, her own fucked up playground she shared with dozens of others.

"Lights are on," Royce notices first.

Raven sits forward, her face tightening as she drops back against the seat. She sighs. "It's candles."

Captain rolls closer, stopping right in front of it.

"She's not alone," Raven tells us, staring at the door.

"How do you know?"

"Because when she's free for the taking, she leaves a pink boa tied to the door to let everyone know they can come play if they'd like."

My stare slices to hers, but she's not looking at me.

"And people just walk the fuck in, ready for her?"

Her tongue runs along her teeth as she glares at the piece of shit in front of us.

"And you're the first thing they'd see?"

Finally, her eyes come to mine. "Thank hell for my knife, huh?" she snaps.

My frown deepens at her accusing tone.

"This is why you don't fucking sleep, why you stare at the door all the time." My eyes meet Royce's for a quick second and his tighten. "Because people pop in at any hour and you never know when or what they'll do."

Her stare hardens and she forces her eyes forward.

Shit makes sense now.

The headphones she's always wearing at night, that's how she'd block out the noises. Her flashlight allowed her to see who would walk in, and her knife made her feel safe. Or fuck, safer than having nothing.

She couldn't have always been this fucking tough, so at some point, she was nothing but a helpless little girl.

This is why she's as hard as she is. She had no fucking choice but to be, there was no one else there to protect her.

She was on her fucking own...until us.

"What do we do?" Captain asks, pulling me from my thoughts.

"We wait," she tells him. "She won't spot us out here, not that she'd pause if she did, and she charges by the hour. It won't be too long."

I grind my teeth and force my eyes closed.

I can't fucking let myself think about Raven in this place with a piece of shit like her.

"What are we doing here, RaeRae?" Royce turns around to look at her, a mix of worry and anger covering his face. "For real, the fuck's this all about?"

She holds his eyes a moment before glancing away, but he keeps at her.

"We didn't ask any questions, brought you like you wanted, avoided talking about the last few fucking weeks on the drive and now here we are, waiting outside your mom's and we have no fucking clue what we're getting into." He watches her. "I'm not sure I'm up for any more fucking bombshells."

No surprise when she gives him nothing and he glares my way.

None of us are okay with what's happening right now, and we're sure as fuck not used to doing things without knowing every detail included, but this is Raven and we're trying to figure out why her brain works the way it does.

So, we're bending a little.

A real fucking little.

Raven called it right, less than an hour goes by and a big burly fucker with a long, braided ponytail steps out.

He pauses at the sight of our SUV, but then quickly starts tucking his shirt in as he walks away.

Raven pauses a moment, then slips her hands between the seats.

I frown when she pulls out her knife.

She flips it open, turning it to inspect the sharpened blade, and I meet Cap's eyes quickly, looking back when she snaps it closed. She squeezes it, her eyes stuck to the old metal before she slides it up her left sleeve, discreetly holding it there.

"Why do you feel the need to take that?"

"I take it everywhere," she says flatly.

"Fine. Then why ready and waiting like it is instead of in your pocket or waistband like normal?"

Her eyes hit mine. "You think I'm unpredictable? She's ten times me."

"No. You are ten times anything she will ever fucking be."

Her face contorts, a softness lining her eyes, but she washes it away just as quick as it slips. "She's uncontrolled in a different way than I am."

"You're not convincing me to let you go in there alone."

"You need to understand you're not in control here." She pushes open her door and steps out and I go to follow, but Royce's hand shoots out, gripping me by the back of the collar.

With a growl, I yank free, spinning toward him with a glare.

"Give her a minute. Maybe this is about what Dad said, abuse or some shit and her mind is all fucked up."

"Do you really think I give a fuck about that?" I shoot back.

"Maddoc," he growls, spinning fully in his seat, anger flaring in his eyes. "She just fucking came back, man, and only because we went and got her. Your girl, your fucking call, brother, but damn. I don't wanna lose her by pushing her. We all know how she gets when we do."

"I'm with Royce," Captain agrees.

I smack the back of the headrest and drop against the seat.

"Ten minutes," I relent, slamming my eyes shut. "And not a second fucking longer."

This is fucked.

RAVEN

Taking a deep breath, I pull open the broken screen door and step inside, letting it slam with a loud whack.

God, I don't miss the smell of stale cigarettes and filthy musk.

A muffled laugh has my eyes jerking right to the sofa that only months ago acted as my bedroom.

I frown when I spot her lying there, legs still laying open, nothing but a stretched out tank top on.

Dirty bitch.

I know what the candles being lit means, but flick the switch to be shitty and draw attention to it.

"Clientele is low, I see."

"Clientele is just fine, daughter, but there are more important things to pay for than electricity." Her words are sluggish, and I step closer to look her over more. She lies there limp, eyes glossy and hardly open. "Besides, the candles set the mood, hm?"

I scoff.

"I saw someone yesterday," I say slowly. "Only he had a different name than the one I knew him by."

She tenses, slowly pushing up on her elbows. Her eyes shift between mine a moment and she laughs lightly, but there's a blankness to it that puts me on edge.

"Oh my god. He was right." A slow grin takes over her face. "You really are just a girl under all that rot."

My brows pull in and she laughs more.

I keep my calm bravado going, but really my insides are turning.

"I've gotta hand it to the man, it was the perfect ploy on his end." She sticks a cigarette in her mouth and lights it, sucking in a long drag. "He thought it would look great for his case to have you around, forming a little bond with his boys. With three to pick from, guess his odds were pretty good. He knew what he was doing when he made his offer."

"What exactly are you saying?"

"Don't play dumb, daughter."

I move closer to her. "You used me to help a man who used to pay to fuck you, while I sat down the hall by the fucking way, who needed help getting out of prison?"

She laughs, but her eyes harden, and she blows smoke straight in my face.

Oh my god. "He paid you."

She scoffs. "He pays me. Think I'd give up my welfare so easy? He's been paying me for years, Raven. Little here and there. Paid off this trailer for me, too, 'course he refused to sign it over to me. Smart on his part, I probably would have sold it and ditched you along the way if he did. But I knew the longer he sat, the more I could squeeze from him. Monthly checks like clockwork for the past thirteen years. Finally got the deal I wanted from him. If the state wasn't gonna pay me no more, then he sure was."

Thirteen years? The judge had said he served eleven.

This doesn't make any sense.

She laughs, the sound weak and dead. "I see you're still missing pieces, daughter, but don't bother asking." She grins and shakes her head. "I'm on strict orders from the man himself. If I wanna keep getting my money, I keep my mouth closed when you come knocking." She tilts her head. "The bonus is seeing you desperate. Pathetic, like I knew you were."

"And what would have happened if I simply left?"

"I knew you wouldn't once you had a taste of life outside these walls. He knew it too. He's a very smart man. A life for a life."

"What the fuck does that mean, Ravina?" I push closer.

She shakes her head and tries to laugh, but it only comes out halfway and a lost look fills her eyes. "They'll never let you go. Not now that they have you."

When my forehead pinches, she sits up farther, the bruises lining her arms more visible now with the light from the candle flickering beside her.

She assesses me, and a deep frown mars her face. "You wanna stay. Raven ... don't be fucking stupid."

"Don't worry about me."

"Don't tell me you think those boys haven't known since day one?" My mother smirks, far too proud, hoping to witness the potential fall of her own daughter. "Why do you think they moved you in with them? Security. To make sure, when good ole daddy went before the judge he had a happy story to tell of how the very daughter of the woman who had accused him of rape has forgiven and forgotten, and she's even fallen for his own sons. A tale of how it brought you together, forcing one big twisted family."

Oh my god, I knew it. I fucking knew it!

I've been thinking since the second I stepped out of that damn courthouse. Stockton California, a rape and cocaine. Knowing the man as my mom's client, and hearing those details, I fucking knew. It all screamed my mother.

"He gave up his life, in exchange for the ownership of yours. A life ... for a life. He got you to fall and he wasn't even here to make it happen. Roped you from a hundred miles away, watched from other's eyes, and now he'll come home. He controls those boys, has their trust and loyalty from a prison cell. They do what he asks, follows his orders, trusts his judgment without his presence – just his voice and their desperate need to please him. You think it would take more than a simple seed planted for them to stand beside him looking down at you? You're nothing but a means to an end."

My throat tries to close at her words, but I won't show her the panic she's caused. "Don't pretend you'd care either way."

"Don't fuck with my money."

"I hope you rot in hell."

"Oh honey, you'll be right there with me. Don't be mistaken. The poison that runs through me, runs through you. You're your mother's daughter, through and through."

"I'll never be like you."

A smile lines her eyes. "I heard you almost did…"

My head draws back. "What do you mean you—"

"It might not have happened this time, but look what you were prepared to do, and for what? A couple hard bodies who make you feel wanted?"

"You talked to Collins Graven?" I growl.

She shrugs. "He may have made a small visit before that night."

"What the hell did he want?"

"To know how to get to you, I told him to play at your pride." She winks. "He called to let me know it worked and wired me some quick cash. He's a good lookin' boy, pays well, too."

I swallow, anxiousness climbing up my throat, threatening to close off my airway.

She's not lying. I did almost throw away all I want to be … for three boys I was never supposed to know, but was purposely placed in front of, dangled like bait he knew the wolves couldn't resist. But for him to know this, he also had to know me.

She eyes me. "Did you really think you ended up there by accident? That boys – men, from what I saw – like them, rich and powerful and destined to rule over people like us, would actually fall for someone like you? Trash with a mediocre face and figure. They could never want a girl like you. They tricked you, they're just as much bastards as the man that paid for you. Rich punks who care about no one and nothing but money and power while they wait for their time to reign—"

I dart forward, gripping her weak neck in my hands and she lets her head fall back, grinning through her gasp.

She smells like grease and stale smoke.

I squeeze her tight, the screaming pulse in her neck almost calming against my palm as I force her trachea to narrow at my hand, cutting the blood flow to her brain in half.

"You know nothing about them. Stay far the fuck away, don't even speak of them, do you understand me?" I growl in her face. "You touch one, even for a second, I will destroy the only thing you care about, mother." I let my knife slip from my left hand and flip the blade over.

She jerks in my grip, her eyes widening as they grow even more bloodshot.

I bring the cool metal up to her cheek and slide it across, never once taking my eyes off hers.

"I will leave you looking like the Joker went easy on you, and then I'll drop you on your busiest corner for all your men to see. What was it you always said to me, your seven, eight, nine-year-old daughter?" I give her the tiniest of pricks, aside her chin – just enough to draw blood, and her nostrils flare, but she doesn't flinch. "A girl is useless without a pretty face for all the boys to love..."

I shove her back, forcing her head to hit against the wall and move for the door.

A deep shriek leaves her, and a beer can slams against the

trailer door, inches from my head, the tail end and ashes from inside splashing on me and everything else in reach.

I jerk around, not missing the footsteps hitting the broken pavement outside.

"It'll happen eventually," she shouts. "Especially when your final day comes and you're nothing but a trophy, traded to adorn someone else's shelf!"

"You're not making any sense!"

"Just wait, Raven!" my mom screams. "Using what God gave you to get what you want is all you know. It's all you've seen! You'll sell your soul just the same!"

"I'd never sell my child's." My voice comes out scratchier than I would have liked.

She drops her voice to a deathly whisper. "Good thing you can't have any then, huh?"

"You're a vile woman."

"Mmm." She grins, hatefully. "True. Now go away, daughter, and hang the boa up on your way out."

I will never be back in a place like this.

Right as I push out, the door is yanked back, and I jump.

Three Brayshaws stand before me in one strong, solid unit.

Deep frowns cover their faces, but dare I say fear lines their eyes.

"Move, Raven," Maddoc growls, but I pull the door closed behind me and step more in his face.

He growls and goes to shove me out of the way, but I shift before he can.

I know them, and I know how thin these walls are – far too well for my liking – they heard every word spoken, but the can hitting the door is what got their feet moving.

Maddoc's eyelids twitch. "I will pick you up and fucking move you if you don't get out of the way."

I squeeze past him and while his glare jerks inside the trailer, he groans and follows, like I knew he would.

I spin around, walking backward with my hands thrown up. "Go on, Big Man, do your thing. Walk up in there, threaten the whore for telling your little secret." I stop at the back corner of the SUV where we're blocked from others to see and far enough away now she won't hear.

His head draws back a second before a murderous glint slides over his eyes and he moves closer. "You seriously think for a fucking second I knew? That any of us knew?" He gapes at me.

"Are you seriously gonna stand here and pretend that you didn't?!" I shout right back. "Are you really claiming mister 'I have to know every-fucking-thing about every-fucking-one and some' didn't know the name of the person responsible for putting his dad in prison?!"

He gets in my face, speaking through clenched teeth. "A Graven put him away, that's what I know. If it weren't for that piece of shit coming in and playing lawyer, he never would have been convicted. And just so you know, no. We didn't fucking know. Those files mysteriously disappeared from public fucking record, Raven, at his own hand!" He flicks his eyes across my face. "This isn't some playground, this is real fucking business, real life shit, and every Graven will pay for that one's mistake. Crossing a Brayshaw the way he did was over the limit. Seems your ma was the easy target they pulled in to start the process."

"Why would your dad want the daughter of the woman who helped nail down his coffin?"

"I have no fucking idea."

My nostrils flare, frustration and uncertainty threatening to boil over inside me. "Why the hell should I believe you?"

"Because I'm telling you to," Maddoc growls, and pushes closer. "Because I want you to. Because I fucking want you with me."

"Yeah, RaeRae—"

"Shut up, Royce," I cut him off, eyes on Maddoc. "Want me here so Daddy doesn't get mad at you for losing a handle on his ticket home, or should I call myself his possession?" I spit. "Maybe I'm meant to be his little plaything—"

"Watch it," he warns, his eyes growing more fiery by the second. "And that's not what I meant, and you know it." He inches closer.

Royce pipes up again. "You saw how we acted when you weren't with us. Bunch of little boys throwing tantrums. We need you here."

"People do stupid shit for good reasons, Royce." My eyes slide between Maddoc's.

"Maddoc," Captain warns and Maddoc's nostrils flare. "Tell her, man."

"Fuck. Fine! Were we expecting you?" Maddoc raises a brow. "Yes. Were you picked from a crop of misfits? Yes. Were we specifically asked to watch you? Yes, like we are all of them, but that's the point of having these houses, not out of the kindness of his fucking heart like was said yesterday. Do we offer them better lives? Yes, but there's a purpose. We find assholes like us, but who come from real life nothing, that value respect and loyalty because they know that's the only way people like them can survive and bring them into our fold. The ones who get here and don't fit, are none the fucking wiser. We leave them where they are until they age out or fuck it up on their own and are gone. We've been doing this on our own the last two years, and we've built a fucking fantastic team. When we're done, we'll be the strongest this town has ever seen, and no fucking Graven will be able to get in the way."

"You're creating an empire."

"We're building our fucking kingdom."

A chill runs down my spine and his eyes heat.

His knuckles find my jaw, and he runs them across my cheekbone, a rare gentleness seeping into his next words spoken. "You want more honesty, baby? Fine. Truth is, I'm not above something like this. I'd play someone even harder – anyone, anywhere, in a fucking heartbeat – if it meant saving my family, which now includes you. By choice."

The corner of my eyes tighten, and I attempt to look away, but he shifts his head to follow my stare. He locks me in with his jade eyes.

"If you think for a fucking second, this far down the line, that you're here for any reason other than because I fucking want you." He lowers his voice to a whisper. "Then you haven't been paying attention, baby. Trust me when I say, you were never part of the plan," he whispers. "You were a solid fucking mistake."

My pulse is racing crazy, my head swimming with questions and doubt.

I said the first chance I got I'd be gone. Away from it all, away from everyone who ever knew of mine or my mother's existence, yet it turns out, she too is tied to them.

I need to be stronger, resist him more, deny the depth of his hold, and battle the ache for his desire.

I need to shut down my stupid girl heart and open my eyes to the devastation this road is sure to lead to.

I need—

"Raven..."

So soft, so gentle and cautious.

I look left into tender, light eyes, worry and concern etched across every inch of his face, but he doesn't make commands. There's no glare or force behind his mask.

So, Captain.

I glance at Royce.

Dark eyes. Cool covered fear and feigned ease, but tension lines his forehead.

I look back to Big Man.

Anger and uncertainty. Defiance and demand. Want, need, and consumption.

The ability to swallow me whole.

The big bad wolf with claws that stretch from one edge of his city to the next.

The opposite of what I need, yet the only thing I've ever craved. If I hit the ground, it'll be in a painful crash.

I don't belong in this world of power princes and rising kings.

Still looking at him, staring up into those mystic greens, no warning could keep me away.

I grip his collar, pulling his lips down to mine, and bite into his flesh.

His chest rumbles, his arms wrapping around my lower back to pull me closer.

To have him today and tomorrow, but maybe not the next, be it from his hand or mine?

Worth it.

Chapter 16

MADDOC

At Raven's demand — she's lucky we were eager to get this shit over with, too — we drove through the night last night with a plan to grab a room tonight, so long as we didn't have to tie her to the fucking seats, so that's what we're doing.

When we pull in the hotel parking lot, Captain stops right in front of the entrance where he and Royce step out, but I hold Raven back.

"Climb in the front," I tell her.

She eyes me, glancing in the direction my brothers went before looking back to me.

I step out and instead of doing the same, she climbs over the center console, sliding down into the seat.

I pull out of the parking lot, stopping at a little corner store for a few drinks, and then we're back on the road.

We get about a mile down the road before she starts asking questions.

"Where we going?"

"Almost there."

"That's not what I asked," she snaps.

A chuckle leaves me, but I ignore her and not five minutes later we're pulling off the side of the road.

I unbuckle myself, then her, and pull her body over so she's straddling me on the seat.

"Talk."

Her eyes bounce between mine and then she bends, pushing the lever that has the back of the seat sliding down. Driving herself closer, she brings her lips to mine. "I don't wanna talk, Big Man."

She lays her chest against mine and my hand slides down her back to squeeze her ass, and she sucks in a deep breath.

"I don't care if you want to, you will either way." I slide my tongue along her bottom lip and she nips at it, making me grin. "But I'll be nice and make you come first."

Her grey eyes darken before me.

"Is that what you need?" I whisper, running my fingers over her collarbone. "Me to make that pussy clench?"

Her tongue slides between her teeth and she nods.

"Good. Now, spin around for me, baby, and drop right back down in my lap."

She doesn't hesitate. Only when she's thirsty for me does she do as she's told.

I slide my hand under her shirt and up to her chest, pushing her down so her back is flat against me, her head laying across my shoulders, ear right at my mouth.

"Move your legs to the outside of mine."

She does.

My hand slides up until it meets the base of her neck and I leave it there, while my other comes up and dips inside the front of her jeans.

"Unbutton."

With shaky hands, she listens.

"Close your eyes and don't open them."

She nods against me, her chest now rising and falling rapidly.

I push into her underwear and her hips lift a little, pushing me further.

The second I'm cupping her, her pussy clenches against my hold, and her lips part.

I dip inside her to coat my two fingers, then slide my hand back up until I can lock her clit between the two. I rub her, circling my fingers on each side of the sensitive nub. Double the contact, and I triple the pleasure when I start to squeeze.

Her head falls back farther, and she moans into the air. "I need this," she whispers huskily.

"You need me," I tell her, and she hums, licking her lips.

She starts grinding into me, chasing her orgasm but I take my time, working her slower rather than faster, only to slow down again when her muscles start to lock.

"Baby..." I breathe into her ear and she shudders against me. "Lift your shirt up for me, bra too. I wanna see how hard those nipples are for me."

"Oh god," she whispers, her mouth clamping tight as she does what I've asked.

She can't help herself though, and right after she pushes her bra up, her hands dart down to her nipples and she pinches them good and hard, a sharp breath hisses past her lips.

"I need to come ... I need—"

I bite her neck and increase my speed on her clit, and she gasps. Her tits pushing up into the air.

Her hands on her nipples start to shake and she moves to grip them tighter.

I release her neck and quickly lift my fingers to her mouth.

"Lick."

Her tongue swipes out, a deep moan leaving her.

I take my wet fingers and run them around her pebbled nipples, then pinch her hard.

I grind against her, my dick rock fucking solid beneath her and she pushes into me.

"I wanna feel you."

"You do feel me, I'm so fucking hard." I lick behind her ear and she whimpers. "I'm aching, baby."

"I want you inside me..." She trails off as she starts to shake.

I push on her clit with my thumb and stick two fingers back inside her so I can feel her pussy convulse.

She squeezes my fingers, riding my hand completely unrestrained.

I bury my nose in her hair, groaning. "Your cum is mine, Raven."

"Oh fuck," she gasps, and another moan leaves her, her orgasm setting off a second wave.

All her muscles tense a moment before her body goes limp against me.

Her hand flops down, hitting the door with a smack, and a husky laugh leaves her.

She jerks from the heightened sensitivity when I pull my hand from her pants.

A whistle sounds in the distance and her eyes fly open.

She jerks upright, glancing out the window, and then her eyes slice back to mine.

Not taking mine off her, I fix her bra, my lip twitching when she shivers as the back of my hand brushes her now sensitive nipple and I smack her thigh. "Out, or we'll miss it."

Her features tighten, and she hesitates a minute, but then she shifts and hops out, fixing up her jeans, and tying her hair back quickly.

I grab the bag I brought from the backseat and throw it over my shoulder, locking up behind me.

She eyes me curiously, but I grab hold of her hand and move for the tracks.

The train has started to slow and the first few cars pass, so at an angle, we walk closer until it's moving at a speed we can catch.

She yanks her hand free and we start running right along-side it.

"Now," I shout, and she cuts a glare at me before bursting forward, latching on right as she hops from the ground and I make a jump for the back side of it.

We both pull ourselves in at the same time, slipping against the inside walls.

She laughs loudly, turning to look at me.

Dark strands of hair lay across her eyes, but she doesn't bother fixing it. This time, before she can come this way, I dart across to her, grip her hips and spin in a circle until her back hits the corner with a soft thud.

She chuckles. "Well, isn't this familiar." Her hands move to my chest, and she looks up at me, but the longer I stare, her laughter disappears, discomfort taking its place.

Her touch slowly retreats, and she subconsciously pushes against the metal at her back as much as the space allows.

"Raven," I call her name when her eyes fall from mine and they snap right back.

Her features tighten, and she rubs her lips together, but the vulnerability she hates seeps through for a split second before her shoulders square and she forces it back. She lifts her chin, so I give her the space she's demanding.

"If you're lying to me, if you knew, I will ruin everything you're trying to do," she threatens. "I will fuck you harder than you've ever fucked anyone, Maddoc, I swear on my life."

Call me a fucking masochist, because goddamn if her words don't make my blood burn hotter for her. So fucking fierce and determined, strong and unafraid to go head to head, even when her ammo could never match ours if push came to shove.

It's exactly fucking why I was drawn to her when I never wanted to be.

I don't doubt her words for a second, and if anyone else on the fucking planet stood here and said this to me, I'd have thrown them from the moving train already and never looked back.

I push my hard-on against her stomach, and she takes in a slow breath. "I have no intention of fucking you over, Raven Carver," I whisper, my thumb coming up to pull her bottom lip free of her top one. "But I do plan to fuck you ... over and over." I kiss the corner of her mouth and her warm exhale hits my cheek. "And over."

I move back to look at her.

Her eyes bounce between mine a moment, and then she gives a curt nod. "Maybe I'm dumb, and maybe I'll regret this, but I believe you."

She drops her eyes down between us, and I step back slightly, my muscles lock when they come back up to mine and she says, "I have to tell you something."

RAVEN

It only took a half hour to be able to jump from the train, and Maddoc had a car already waiting to take us back to the SUV.

Once we get back to the hotel we dropped the boys off at earlier, we find Royce, no damn surprise, booked a flashy suite he could get with a fire pit on the balcony, and ordered room service to be delivered in perfect time for our return.

They joke lightly about basketball, both cringing when they finally get the chance to tell Maddoc about the game he missed.

As soon as everyone is done eating, the trays are pushed to the side and Royce passes around liquor from the mini bar.

"The video's real," I blurt out, starting the conversation off and they look my way, waiting for more. "I saw it, it's not the greatest, but it's clear enough and there's ... sound." I smash my lips to the side, but I end up laughing lightly anyway when Cap and Royce grin at me. "Anyway... I guess it was some outdoor style, night time camera."

"Even a phone is capable of that nowadays," Maddoc says.

I shrug. "I wouldn't know, but either way, what do we do about it?"

"Nothing." Maddoc sits up straighter, a frown splitting his forehead. "The video's trash, useless."

"How?"

"Why do you think he was trying to shop it around?" Maddoc asks in a flat tone. "He wanted the news of it to get back to you. He played on the only soft spot he saw. You for us, and us for you."

"To get our attention?"

"To get your attention," Captain confirms.

"He bet against us when he put word out of that video, and you fell right into his hand, proving him right," Maddoc says.

"Again. How?"

"By showing him you had to rely on yourself to fix it, making it seem like you couldn't rely on us."

"It wasn't about that," I shake my head.

"We know." Maddoc sits back. "He gets it now, but there never should have been a second where he doubted us. If you'd have done what you should have and come to us with the issue first, he wouldn't have," he snaps.

"Look, this is all new for me, okay?" I snap right back.

"You seem to love to forget that I didn't have this" – I play connect four between us – "where I came from. It was me, and that's it. I'm not gonna all of a fucking sudden be 'go team' because that's what makes sense to you."

"It's not all of a sudden," he bites out.

A laugh bubbles out of me even though I try to fight it, and some tension leaves his shoulders. I'd swear there was a soft side of him hidden in there somewhere, covered in anger and buried with bitterness.

"What I'm trying to say is I don't know how to ..." Shit.

Captain leans forward, his little whiskey bottle hanging in his hands. "How to be a part of a team?" he asks and I'm glad we're on a dark balcony with nothing but the fire between us for light.

My neck heats, in doubt or awkwardness, I don't want to know, but it's annoying.

"You don't know how to be a part of a team?" he tries again.

"No. I don't."

"Raven ... you stood with us when you had no reason to, fought with us, defended us."

"But I didn't do any of it on purpose," I whisper, a heavy weight on my chest making it hard to bring in a full breath. "I just did what I felt like doing."

"Stop trying to convince yourself that's true. Quit telling yourself that deep-down you didn't feel connected to us right away, because you did. You passed on the chance at a new life when Perkins hit you with that offer, something even we know you want, to stay with us. Then you went there, willing to give it all up to protect us, meaning you'd walk away with nothing." Captain glances at his brothers before continuing.

"You fire off on reflex, which is a really good thing most of the time, it means you're quick to the wit and can turn a bad situation into a favorable one when needed. Knowing that about you makes us more comfortable when you're not in our sights. But Raven, do not ever think you need to protect us from anything."

I hear what he's saying, and it makes sense, but that's not the point. I may not have thought it through completely, but I knew what was at risk and it far outweighed where I landed in the end.

I lean forward, hoping the urgency I felt is delivered. "How could I walk away that night, knowing what could have maybe happened if I didn't try to stop it?"

His brows pinch and then smooth out in the same second. He slowly stands, making his way over to me and my stomach starts to flip.

He drops down in front of me, and in the corner of my eye, I catch Big Man looking away.

"Raven ..." He trails off, his voice barely above a whisper. "Are you telling me, you did what you did, made a fucking deal with Collins, for my daughter? For my baby girl who you've never even met and owe nothing to?" He swallows, the corners of his eyes squeezing, like the damn strings to the heart I'm only just discovering.

"I ..." I drop my eyes to my lap. This shit's too much for me. "She's not the only reason."

Royce's light chuckle catches my attention.

I look to him and he offers a small smile.

"This is why you fit, RaeRae." My damn shoulders shouldn't ease at the nickname. "You're honest when most would lie, you're strong when others are weak. You're loyal without having to try, even if it was a fucked-up way to show it." He winks.

I grin and look back to Captain as he stands. He looks down at me, nods his head and disappears into the suite.

Royce stands and pats my shoulders, following after his

brother, and I close my eyes a minute, taking in a few deep breaths.

"Come here," I demand of Maddoc.

When I hear no movement, I open my eyes and look at him.

He lifts his chin, so I lift a brow. With a small smirk, he pushes to his feet, and slowly steps to me. Once he's towering over my seated form, I stare up at him.

Green eyes, shining in the dark, and swimming with too many thoughts to count.

I grip the bottom of his hoodie and pull, so he bends, placing his hands on the back of the little sofa style patio seat I'm sitting on.

My chest stirs, a tightness I'm not familiar with taking over, and a heavy exhale leaves me.

His slow blink has me swallowing.

"Sit."

"I was sitting."

"I didn't ask what you were doing. I said sit." I slide my hands under his top and press along his damn tapered waist. "Sit."

He fights me for a second, frowning down at me, but then does as I asked right as the boys step back out with new, larger drinks.

I glance at Maddoc, but he only stares, waiting for me to fill his brothers in on what I told him on the train.

I reach in the waist of my jeans and pull my knife out. I look to Royce and hold it up. His brows pull in and he nods his chin, so I toss it to him.

His eyes are slow to pull from me and move to the metal in his hands.

"Turn it over, Royce."

He flips it over and when he does, he freezes a moment,

drawing it closer to his face. He sees it, etched into the side in a classic cursive script: Family runs deeper than blood.

What I now know are the Brayshaw's words to live and breathe by.

Royce slowly pushes right back to his feet.

"What..." He trails off.

Captain snatches it from Royce's open palm, and his head snaps up, eyes meeting mine.

"This is your knife, the knife you've been carrying around here for months?"

"Yes."

"What the fuck does this mean?" Royce asks, cutting quick glances between the three of us.

"Your dad, yesterday wasn't the first time I've seen him," I tell them. "He goaded me in there, as if I could forget his face. He knew if he threw out the words I've read at least a handful of times a day since the day I first heard them, that I'd remember, but I didn't need that. I remember his face and his voice."

"Raven..." Captain visibly pales, his head shaking slowly.

"He was one of my mom's clients when I was younger. Came by once a week, every week, for at least a year. The day he gave me my knife was the last day I ever saw him." I nod at Royce, hold my hands up, and he tosses it back.

"When was that?" Royce asks.

"Eleven years ago." I lick my lips, glancing between the three.

The timeline still makes no sense as far as how long she said he's been paying her. "She must have pulled some shit right after that last night he was over. I won't apologize for what she did, I refuse to do that for her, but ... I am sorry you guys lost his physical presence."

"It's not your fault," Royce tells me, and I shrug.

With a frown, Cap stretches back, pulling his brass knuckles from his pocket. He leans forward and hands them to me.

Made of real silver, they're heavy. Expensive. There's a tiny anchor, matching the one on his knuckles printed into the side and looping through each finger slot, a thin engraving: Family runs deeper than blood.

My stomach heats and I grip the item tighter.

Royce moves closer, dropping to his knees in front of me. He pulls his hoodie over his head and flips his arm over, showing me the underside of his full sleeve.

Hidden inside the intricate design the words are blended, not to be easily seen or read, hidden there, just for him.

"I have a crest at home I used to wear around my neck, but I almost lost it once. Now, no matter what, my family is with me," Royce tells me.

Maddoc sits forward and pulls his wallet out, sliding a key from the inner folds and handing it over.

I flip it and there it is again, imprinted perfectly along the edge.

I run my fingers across it, taking a deep breath. "What's it open?"

"Don't know yet, maybe nothing, just a token of sorts," he says, pausing for a moment. "We didn't have to accept each other once we understood we came from different parents, but we are a family in every sense of the word. We chose each other." I look up, meeting Maddoc's eyes.

"And now we choose you," he vows. "He chose you."

"He only saw me at night when I was nothing but the dope head, prostitute's kid he had to distract with ice cream and a fucking movie. He didn't even know me, Maddoc, or the shit I did in the daylight, even at seven years old."

"He's intuitive."

When I start to shake my head, Maddoc grips it between his hands, a frown taking over his face once more. "Raven, that was not his knife," he throws out tersely. "I have never seen that knife before. Being a Brayshaw has rules, and if an item is given to you by a Bray, it was created for you, and not to be given away. Those words are sacred. If he gave you something with them written on it, it's because he knew, eventually, you'd be exactly where you are right now. With us."

"He bought me from my mom for who knows what reason, because she sent him to prison. Maybe even before if that's why he was paying her for two years before he was even arrested."

Maddoc shakes his head. "I don't know. His going to jail never made sense, my going to jail made no fucking sense if you think about it from our perspective. We're Brayshaws, that doesn't happen to us, so I knew he had some sort of plan behind it. And the one he had shocked the shit out of us. We thought maybe because he was arrested in another town that it made a difference, and that's why he wasn't released right away – them not knowing who he was – but learned later it wouldn't.

"Raven, we're not the only family like ours, there's several of us spanning across the state line like a barrier, blocking people from coming into our worlds. We all serve a purpose, live a certain way to have the lives we do," Maddoc says, then glances to his brothers before looking back to me. "But we will fucking find out where you fit into this. Your area is outside of our maps. I don't even know how he found you or your mom. None of the families connected to us have business that way."

I rub at my eyes and let out a deep breath.

The last two days have been a huge fucking information overload. My head is starting to spin.

I meet each of their stares, each a complete contrast of the last – dark brown, light blue, and jade green – but each hold the same intensity and promise.

One I chose to believe, even if it makes me a sucker in the end.

Family runs deeper than blood, and I think I might have found mine.

We all stand, and Royce and Captain both move in for a hug before disappearing inside to crash.

Maddoc grips my hand and pulls me behind him, not bothering to close the balcony doors on our way to our designated room for the night. Our door, though, he closes and locks.

Grabbing a hold of my other hand, he pries my knife from my fist, pulling it closer to his face. A frown finds him as he stares, slowly running his fingers across the words that mean more to him than I probably even understand. He nods to himself, then sets it on the table beside us.

Maddoc's eyes shift to mine. He tugs his hoodie over his head, drops his jeans, and then moves to relieve me of mine, not once looking away from me.

He steps against me, wrapping his arm around my lower back and pulling me in.

I halfway hate how I like it when he does this, touches me, stares at me with dark eyes full of more than I might ever be ready for.

He tips my head back with a touch to my chin and runs his lips across mine, nipping lightly, before he pulls back. "Don't think too hard on all this, baby. Just let it play out, and while it does, know something," he whispers, walking me backward to the mattress. I allow myself to fall and he drops down, hovering over me. "I don't care what happens tonight, tomorrow, or next fucking year. I don't care what anyone wants from, or of me. I decide what I want from you."

He wedges his knee between mine, bringing himself even closer as he runs his lips across my jawline, stopping to whisper in my ear, "And I'm bettin' on everything."

Chapter 17

RAVEN

I TURN OFF THE SHOWER AND STEP OUT, QUICKLY DRESSING AND towel drying my hair.

Last night was the best night's sleep I'd had in weeks and it has everything to do with the one who slept beside me, while my knife sat on the table beside him.

My knife that was given to me by his father.

What a crazy few fucking days.

I quietly step into the living room area of the suite, and as expected, it was Captain's footsteps out on the balcony that woke me.

He stands there looking over the foggy city a moment before running his hands down his face. He grips the railing, dropping his chin to his chest, and the sight has a pain hitting mine.

I knew he'd be the first up, if he ever even closed his eyes.

My footsteps give me away and he glances over, a wretched smile on his lips.

I pull my sleeves over my hands and blow into my palms, moving to stand beside him. We both stare out at the early morning city below.

"How many times have you asked yourself if he really did it?" My question comes after a few quiet minutes. I don't have to say what it is, he knows what I'm referring to just like I know what's on his mind.

He has a baby girl to love and protect, even if that means protecting her from his own father.

"Too many to count." He looks my way. "And every time I do, I feel guilty for it."

"And then you feel angry, followed by ..."

He frowns, but admits quietly, "Unworthy. Of her."

I clear my throat, wanting to look away, completely overtaken by the torment in his eyes, but I don't dare. If this shit's hard for me, must be ten times harder for him.

"Captain," I call his name, even though he's already focused solely on me. "Your dad, the man who saved you, who loved your biological father as a brother, like you do yours..." I trail off and his hand shoots out to grip mine on the railing, the corner of his eyes tightening. "He did not rape my mother. He is not a rapist."

His grip on my fingers tightens, and he starts to shake a little, so I step closer.

"Rolland was good to me, too," I whisper. "The only one that ever was, to be honest. He was the first person I ever felt any kindness from, I remember that clearly. The knife? He gave it to me because he said he wanted me to be able to protect myself. I was just some kid he didn't know and had no tie to, and he wanted me to be safe." He tries to fight it off, but he can't, and his frown grows a little glossy.

"If he wanted that for me, some random kid in a beat-up trailer, imagine what he would do to protect his own grandbaby, packman?" I whisper. "I'd bet he'd die for her."

He pulls his lips between his teeth, nodding as he takes his eyes from mine. A deep, ragged breath leaves him, and his head falls back, a heavy chuckle escaping him. In the next second, he yanks me against him, hugging me tight.

I let him hold on until he's ready to let go, but even when he does he only pulls back a bit.

"Raven—"

"Don't," I cut him off. "Don't thank me. You deserve to know all that. He's your dad, Cap, and that's your daughter."

He sighs. "My mind, it's been fucking with me lately. I knew something was coming, I get that nagging in my gut right before it does, every damn time. I didn't know what I'd have to do. I love my brothers, and I love my father, but if he was guilty of what they said, I ..." He trails off taking a deep breath. "Zoey is everything to me, Raven. I'd—"

"Stop. You don't have to say it."

He nods. "I know they'd stand with me, whatever I needed, they'd do it beside me without question, it's who they are, who we are as a unit, but I'd hate to of had to be the reason they lost our dad a second time."

"Yeah, well," I try and make light of things. "My mom sent your dad to prison for eleven years, Cap, and look where I'm standing right now."

The corner of his lips tip up, some light coming back in his blue-green eyes. "Yeah, pretty sure it could have been you yourself who did, and you'd still be standing here."

I widen my eyes teasingly, happy we're back in territory I'm comfortable with. "Because I'm awesome."

He gives me a playful shove. "Yeah, Raven, you kinda are." His eyes fall another minute before coming back to mine, a newfound softness to them he's yet to show. "I heard about your little run-in with her, that's how we knew you were still ours."

I look away with a shrug, doing my best to keep my emotions in check.

"Raven."

"I said stop. It's not a big deal."

"Oh, it is a big deal, but fine. I'll stop." He laughs, searching out my eyes again. A heavy exhale leaving him. "We weren't ready for you, Raven Carver. We weren't fucking ready."

I shift my frown to the city below again, dismissing his words. "Wanna go in now? You can make me a cup of coffee in that fancy machine in there. I'm freezing, in need of caffeine, and I have no idea what to do with all those buttons."

With a light touch to my shoulders, he turns me around to face the room.

Maddoc is in the little kitchen-like area, leaning against the countertop, a hot cup of coffee at his lips and one right in front of him. Eyes on me.

I turn back to Captain.

He smiles, and even though he's still got a lot to work out, I can tell he's lighter right now than he's been in weeks. He winks, and I move toward Maddoc.

Maddoc pushes to stand at his full height as I grow closer, and when I reach him, he nods to my cup, but before I can even make a move to pick it up, he grips my chin between his knuckles and holds my face still.

He drops down, bringing his mouth to my ear. He grazes his lips across the sensitive skin beneath it before whispering, "You keep this up, and I might have to do something real crazy, like lock you in my room and throw away the key."

"Keep what up?" I murmur against his chest.

"Fixing us. Making us better. Making us stronger."

My throat closes, and a frown pulls at my brows.

He keeps going. "You recognize what we need and when,

like you've known us all your life. You're connected to us, and that's not something we'll ever be willing to let go of, Raven. Never. None of us. No matter fucking what."

They'll never let you go. Not now that they have you. My mother's words slam me in the face and I tense.

He feels it and pulls back to look at me, a scowl in place.

"Shut shit down in your head, Raven. Now," he warns, picking up my cup, and handing it to me.

"What if I decide I don't wanna stay?" I ask even though that's the farthest thing from the truth at this point.

A slow smirk stretches across his lips and he pushes against me. "I'll pretend you have a choice, and say it'll be a damn good time convincing you, too."

I glare. "I hope you know if I wanted to leave, you couldn't stop me."

With an airy chuckle, he moves past me, throwing over his shoulder, "Keep believing that if it makes you feel better. Either way, you stay."

Sexy bossy bastard.

As soon as everyone got up and dressed, we took our time, jacked around a bit, before hitting the road and driving through the night.

The sun is only starting to rise when we make it back.

As soon as we pull through the tree line, Maybell steps out the front door of the mansion.

Bitterness fills me.

Even though she owes me nothing, I can't help but feel a sense of betrayal by her.

I'm not stupid, I know she knew what I was walking into at the courthouse. I'd bet she knew the entire story and more. It was in the way her eyes hesitated, all the cryptic things she'd say to me, her allowing me to move in with the boys. Yes, she can't exactly control them, but she was a little too happy to watch it happen.

And I'm pretty damn sure she already knew Ms. Vega, even though the day I was dropped off by my probably not a social worker social worker they acted as if they'd only just met.

She starts toward us, opening her arms for Maddoc to walk into.

He kisses her hair and she pats his back, moving to cup his face when she steps back. "You okay, boy?"

"Yes, ma'am."

She tears up, taps his cheek and moves to hug each of the boys.

Maybell takes a deep breath before she turns to me.

I can't help it, I know I'm wearing a frown of some sort, but I no longer trust the woman in front of me, not that I ever did. I guess what I mean is I wanted to, but now I know I shouldn't.

I can't trust her just because they do. There can be no free pass.

The weight of the boys' stares has me wanting to look to them, but I won't make this easy on her by breaking contact.

"I'd like to talk to, Raven. Alone," she says.

The wrinkles framing her eyes become more profound when all three hesitate a moment before walking in the house.

I waste no time. "You knew and you let me get ambushed."

"I learned along the way," she admits. "Suspected a bit when I saw where you were coming from, and then I pieced it all together. Once I opened my eyes, it was clear."

"You're being real careful with your words right now, Maybell. You're afraid to speak openly because you're not so sure what all we figured out."

She doesn't deny it. "Everything I do or don't do is for those boys."

Right. Because that is where her loyalty lays, as it should. I'm just the outsider, something I need to be sure to remember when others are involved.

"You can't ask me not to tell them you hid this."

She nods earnestly. "I know, and I won't." She steps closer with sad eyes. "Just like you won't tell them because you know I had no vicious intent. I love them and you see that."

"No good will come of lies."

"I know. And tell them if you need to, but I think it's irrelevant at this point. I know it hurt you in the end, but it helped my boys, and that's what I needed to happen. I'm sorry, child." Her eyelids slope. "It won't be fun being caught in the middle of this."

Won't be fun, as in there's still more to come?

"He bought me from her and fed me to his sons."

"And you don't exactly hate the outcome, do you?"

"I—" My mouth clamps shut.

Well, shit. No. I don't. Much prefer it, in fact.

But who the hell knows what Rolland Brayshaw has planned for me.

I look back to Maybell, who reaches up and gently palms my cheek. "Don't let that woman's words play tricks in your mind, child, you're smarter than that. I told you once before, you belonged. I asked you to start believing it and you have. Keep pushing back at the nagging inside telling you it's not right. It is. But, Raven. It's also not over. There's a long road ahead, more to learn, more challenges to face."

"Like what?"

"In time, child." She steps back. "Go on inside, they've been waiting to have you home, but then everything happened with Maddoc and still it wasn't right. You're all here, now. Your man, and his brothers. Go, and try to love them like they love you."

With that, she walks away, and I can't help but wonder what the hell I've gotten myself into.

Or more, what the hell did my mom get me into?

Chapter 18

RAVEN

THE HOLIDAYS PASSED IN A BLUR. I WAS THANKFUL WHEN Christmas morning came and went without mention – seems the boys aren't ones for celebrating either.

I did, however, find a brand new iPod and wireless earbuds sitting under my pillow that night. By the way Maddoc frowned at the items, I knew he wasn't the one who left it. Then, when I pushed play and the first song that hit my ears was "Bad Bitch" by Bebe Rexha, I knew it was Royce.

I should have figured as much right away.

Maddoc would have tossed it at me and told me not to argue but accept, while Cap would have walked in and sat down, placing it in my hands, but Royce? He's the silent little lover type who hides his underlying sweetness with dirty innuendoes and flat out raunchiness. And somehow it totally works for him.

Captain pulls his SUV into the parking lot at Weston High, not one of us moving to step out when he puts it in park.

Both boys shift in the front seats so they can meet Maddoc's eyes.

"If he steps on the court tonight, freeze him out. He doesn't touch our ball, I don't give a fuck what the situation is or who tries to force otherwise. Collins Graven is no Wolf, he won't be treated like one."

They agree and the four of us step out right as a few other cars pull in, parking beside us.

Mac steps out of one with a couple other guys from their team, and Leo steps from the other.

He doesn't spare me a glance, not even a glare, in fact, but moves to the guys for some bullshit bro-shake. He purposely positions himself between me and Captain.

"You missed a couple bangers, man," Leo laughs, shifting a little more right so I'm at his back, now blocked from both Cap and Maddoc's view. "Bunch of gymnasts and shit were in town for some showcase. Helluva time."

Only Mac laughs, entertaining his fake news.

In the same second, Maddoc reaches around him and drags me forward, my shoulder knocking into the dickhead beside me as he does. He spins me around, pulling my ass against him, so I'm face to face with Leo with him now at my back.

Leo falters a second when he sees Maddoc's possessive hands on my abdomen, frowning at his feet a moment when I lean into him even more, but he catches himself quick and takes a half step back.

"Anyway, yeah, man. It was a good time." He quickly looks to them. "You guys ready to go in yet?"

Maddoc drops against the bumper of the SUV. "We've got some business first."

Maddoc gives a sharp tone I wasn't expecting, and I force a straight face when really I'm on the edge of a smirk.

Leo can't hold it in, though, and his scowl is caught.

"You can go inside," Maddoc adds, officially coloring me curious in the shift between boy and master.

Leo licks his lips, glancing from one Brayshaw to the next, and I doubt he realizes it, but there's a hardness tethered in fear staring back.

He's angry, but more, he's a scared little bitch.

"Yeah, all right." He looks to Mac.

"Mac stays," Royce adds, knowing Leo was about to call on him.

Leo gives a tight shrug before walking off, his grip on the strap of his duffle bag real fucking tight.

My eyes follow him and every rigid step he takes, so do Mac's.

Only once Leo is far enough away does he move closer.

"Something I should know?" Mac asks in confusion.

"No." Maddoc's hold on me tightens. "Any word on if Collins talked?"

"Nah, man. He's a dumb fucker, but he's not stupid enough to run his mouth at Brayshaw."

The guys don't say anything, but their silence is enough for me to know they disagree. It isn't something to be spoken out loud for another ear to hear, though.

"Let's get in there," Captain says and he, Mac, and Royce all move to grab their bags.

Maddoc buries his face in my neck and presses his lips right against my pulse there. He makes no other move, but it kicks harder from the simple contact and as if he was waiting for it, his lips stretch into a smile against my skin.

I roll my eyes even though he can't see me and push off him right as the others step back around with his bag also in hand.

We only get a foot through the door before we're rushed by

their coach and shoved through a side door leading to an empty locker room.

Coach Brail grips Maddoc by the collar and shoves him against the cool metal.

I jerk forward but get yanked back by Royce.

"I told you to keep your fucking cool!" he shouts in his face.

Maddoc makes no sound, but quickly dislodges himself and in an instant, he's flipped it, and the coach is slammed against the lockers.

His eyes widen then narrow.

"Watch your fucking hands, and your mouth while you're at it." He jerks him forward, slamming him again, then steps back.

"Your dad—"

"Isn't here," Captain supplies easily.

"Time you realize that." Royce steps forward.

A chill runs down my spine and a smirk finds my lips.

I fucking love this shit, when they power up and the front line grows stronger, their reach further.

"We respect you, Coach," Maddoc tells him. "We work our asses off and listen to what you have to say and perfect what you tell us to. We listen to every fucking word you say ... on the court. Not fucking off it, and not when it messes with my family. We did what you said, what he told you to tell us, and that didn't work out well for any of us. No fucking more. From now on, you will do as we say, when we say it." The coach's features tighten, and concern fills his eyes.

"You won't be seen as going rogue. He's on board," Captain speaks of their dad, letting the man know he can breathe a little easier.

Coach Brail's shoulders relax some and he gives a very reluctant nod.

Maddoc backs away, shrugging. "It's nothing personal. You

know we'd take a hit for you, but Raven will take no more from any-fucking-body. No one gets a pass, it's the only way to fix this mess. The leash needs to be tightened."

The coach looks ready to argue, but instead a tight chuckle leaves him, and I tense when he steps forward. He smacks a hand down on Maddoc's shoulder giving him a little shake and walks out.

What the fuck was that?

"Respect."

I jump when Royce answers what I thought was an inner thought and the guys chuckle around me.

"Let's go, we've got a game to play."

Coincidently, Collins is a no-show to the game, but Perkins is front and center looking far too disappointed when his school's team plays one sick ass game of ball and takes the win in the end.

"You ever gonna talk to me or you forever pissed?" Bass drops down beside me.

"Depends." I tilt my head. "Can you be honest?"

"Ask your questions, Carver." His grin's easy.

"Why'd you come to me over them? Why not go direct to your bosses with the video news or tell them about it the second I went off the wall and tried to fix it?"

"Because you didn't demand it. You earned it."

"You saying they haven't earned it from you?" I grow defensive and he chuckles lightly.

My shoulders relax a little.

"They've earned every fucking bit of my loyalty, but they demanded it first, earned it later. With you though." He shakes his head and looks away. "Man, Rae, you came up in here and threw their order into the shredder. Everyone watched in shock as it quickly went from them wanting to toss you in the grinder to tossing you in a fucking Brayshaw sized bubble."

175

My forehead wrinkles and I look back to the now near empty court, the teams having cleared to change and shit now that the game is over.

"You had no agenda or hidden reason for anything you were doing, unlike most people."

"So a girl you hardly knew does some stupid shit to piss off the guys you say have all your loyalty and you give her info over them?"

He's quiet a minute, so I look his way again, finding him staring.

"I don't do much that feels right, Rae. In fact, not sure I've ever done anything that has, but for whatever reason, putting you first that night did." He looks away. "I'm not even sorry I did, despite all the fucked-up shit that followed."

My eyes are pulled back to the court when I feel him.

Maddoc doesn't bother looking at Bass until he's standing right in front of me.

"All set?" he asks him.

"Always," Bass coolly responds.

"Good. You can go now."

Bass pushes to his feet and walks out, throwing "Later, Rae" over his shoulder as he does.

Maddoc gauges me with unsettled eyes and a deep wrinkle on his forehead.

"What?" I ask.

He licks his lips and looks off. "Let's go."

Okay then.

The boys are extra peppy tonight, which is a solid fuckin' change from the last few days. They're fired up and ready to party.

We make a quick stop at the house to drop off their gear and then go to a small pub on the town strip.

The waitress's eyes light up the second we walk inside, and I want to vomit.

"Long time no see." She grins at each of them, her smile faltering slightly when she spots me in the mix. "You're Raven Carver."

I don't bother responding and move past her – of course my boys follow.

Royce laughs as he takes the seat beside me, Maddoc and Captain opposite of us.

"What?"

"Nothing, you're just a natural, unapproachable bitch. I dig it." He nudges me with his elbow. "Very Brayshaw of you," he laughs lightly when I punch him in the thigh.

I look to Maddoc, finding both him and Captain grinning.

"Can I ask you guys something?" I ask, tearing open a sugar packet for the hell of it.

"If we told you no, would you ask anyway?" Cap teases.

"Yes," I laugh and prop my elbows on the table. "Was that true, about your dad being okay with you guys making moves on your own?"

"We don't run shit by him before we handle business, Raven." Maddoc frowns.

"But you listen to him."

"We trust his judgment. He's been where we are, dealt with shit from the Gravens along the way."

"And now?"

"And now he understands things have gone too far."

I eye them. "Me."

"You," Maddoc confirms, leaning forward. "The second he touched you when he knew you belonged to me, the second he tried to take you from me he sealed his fucking fate. I wanted to ruin him before on principle. Now I'll destroy his entire fucking world and everyone connected to it."

My blood shouldn't warm at his words, yet here I am, growing hot beneath my clothes. The gleam in Maddoc's eyes tells me he knows it too.

"But to answer your question, RaeRae, yeah." Royce motions for the waitress. "He told us to do what we needed, so we will."

"Starting tonight," Maddoc adds, nodding at the chick when she wordlessly sets down four waters.

"Tonight?"

Royce looks away while Maddoc holds his face blank, but Cap, he grins into his cup.

"What's tonight?" I ask again and they chuckle.

The waitress comes back, setting down a couple pizzas.

"Carb up, RaeRae. You're gonna need it."

They get straight to eating so I do the same and twenty minutes later we're back in the leather seats of Captain's SUV.

It only takes a few minutes before I realize where we're going.

I scoot forward in the seat, but Maddoc pulls me back, and this time onto his lap.

"What are we doing?

"Getting excited?" Royce bounces his eyebrows.

My stomach flips. "What are we doing?"

Cap pulls in and drives along the inside of the dirt path, not stopping until he's right at the edge of the entrance.

The hairs on the back of my neck start to tingle when Mac all of a sudden appears and the gate is pulled open.

Captain rolls through and every head turns to watch as the sleek Denali makes its way forward.

"What the hell are you guys doing?" I ask, but it comes out as a bit of a whisper.

"I told you," Maddoc speaks into my ear. "We're done hiding."

"Perkins will cause problems, no? The other families you talked about, they'll know you guys are leading now, aren't you supposed to wait 'til you graduate? Someone will rat."

"Let them," Maddoc mumbles in my ear.

I tense then slowly spin to frown at him. "You want it to happen."

"Someone needs to be the example. Let them challenge us. Never again will we fall at any other's hands. Not us. And not you."

"You're not above the fucking law, Big Man—"

"Yes, Raven." His eyes darken, determination etched across every inch of his face. "We are."

My stomach about bottoms out at his words and I jerk when a hand touches my upper arm.

I look to Captain.

Always with those reassuring eyes.

"We know what we're doing."

"Have you dealt with snakes before, Cap?" I challenge, and a rare smirk that has me pulling back a little finds his lips.

"We are the snakes, Raven."

I gape at him a second before a laugh bubbles out of me. "Well, shit. Let's get the fuck out."

Royce grins and all at once, the boys reach for their handles, but when I reach for mine, Maddoc yanks me toward him.

I frown but he only winks in return, and then the boys are stepping out, all fucking eyes on them.

Maddoc turns his head to look at me and reaches out a hand.

I glare, not missing the teasing gleam in his eye – he knows I hate this shit.

At the same time, though, there's a lot of stray females out here, better they learn quick who they can and can't touch.

I slide across the seat and step out, leaving his hand hanging, but I do take him by surprise when I grip his collar and pull myself up on my toes.

"Real cute, Big Man," I whisper, and the corner of his eyes tighten in humor. "Now finish your little show."

His eyes blaze and a low groan leaves him as he dips his head and kisses my neck a moment.

I drop to my feet and he stands to his full height, one of his hands sliding into my back pocket as the four of us walk toward the wooden crates at the edge of the setup, and my adrenaline starts pumping to the beat of the loud ass music floating through the air.

It's like an instant, natural high no drug could ever give me.

I look around at all the people partying and placing bets, smaller fights already happening in the back corner while the larger circle is kept clear by nothing but a couple barrels and tied ropes.

My fingertips tingle.

This fucked up shit is in my soul.

Bass meets us at the first area.

He nods at the guys, then shifts toward me and a rare smile breaks across his face.

"Ready for some fun?"

I tense, my brows snapping together. "Wait, what?"

He frowns and looks to Maddoc. "You didn't tell her?"

"Tell me what?" I rush out, a little too excited when I could be reading this all wrong.

Maddoc's eyes shift between mine, but his lips stay tightly pressed.

"Maddoc," I prompt.

The boys step closer and Bass steps back.

"All you wanted while you were here was to fight. We took that from you," he says.

"If I wanted to, I would have found a way," I argue, but it's weak from the sudden weight of his eyes.

"And I'd have loved pissing you off when I stopped you."

My lips twitch.

"Now, quiet and listen." He pulls me close. "You were

ready to give up everything for us, so we're giving you something back."

I open my mouth to speak, but nothing comes out. My head pulls back, and I look across at the three of them.

Royce is grinning, Cap looks a bit unsettled and Maddoc wears his usual frown.

"Wait, so..."

"You're on the card tonight if you want it, RaeRae." Royce shakes me.

"Are you for real?" My stomach flips and I frantically glance from one to the next. "You guys are gonna stand back, as in not step in, and watch me fight?"

Maddoc lifts his chin and my mouth clamps shut.

My lips purse. "There's a catch."

"You wanna fight?" He holds his arms out. "You watch me fight."

"Fucking deal." A laugh bubbles out of me, and his glare intensifies. "What, you thought I'd say no? Pass on the chance of seeing you go alpha out here? Hell, no!" I grin. "Go for it, Big Man. Whoop some fucking ass."

That earns me some laughs and then I'm lifted and placed on the nearest crate so he and I are eye to eye.

"Do not move. Do you understand? I don't care what your reason could possibly be, piss your fucking pants if you need to. Your ass – that ass of mine – stays right fucking here."

"Yes, boss."

He stares a moment longer before he steps back and yanks his hoodie and shirt over his head. He throws both in my face and steps under the ropes, gaining the attention all over again.

Damn, he's fine.

Royce and Captain hop up beside me.

"We're in for a real fucking treat tonight, folks! Not only are the Brayshaws here – the motherfuckers that make all this possible for your scoundrel asses – but one is standing in this very ring, not that you needed to be told that," the hype guy yells into his megaphone. "No bets are being taken on this fight, this is for pure entertainment people cause you see, here's what's happened..."

My brows pull in and I glance at Royce, he shoots me a quick wink before turning his malicious smirk on the ring.

The pit of my stomach grows tight.

"Y'all remember our dark-haired queen of the night, right? She popped in like a backward Barbie and out like a west coast warrior?"

What ...

"Well, her name is Raven Carver, and she's back, people!" he shouts, and people start shouting in excitement, eye after eye flying my way and I wanna die.

"I'm gonna fuck you guys up for this," I mumble for only Cap and Royce to hear.

Assholes laugh at me.

"Now, a couple weeks ago, Raven, or Rae as we call her, slipped in here for a minute, and when she left, our warrior got jumped."

Some people laugh, others throw out 'fuck thats' and the like, but my spine shoots straight, and I grip Cap and Royce by the thighs.

"And guess what else?" the guy shouts. "We know one of the guys who done done it." People scream, and I jerk forward but, the boys yank me back down. "Bastards and bitches, welcome to the ring, the dumbass who put his hands on Maddoc Brayshaw's woman."

My pulse spikes as a dark figure makes his way toward the ring, several big ass buff dudes following close by.

He steps in the center, facing away from me.

"Y'all know the drill, they swing 'til they can't. You stay back and out the way, and when this little bitch has thoroughly had his ass handed to him, you can spit on him and walk away." He pauses so the crowd can shout once more before pulling his megaphone back to his mouth. "Game time, motherfuckers. Shirt off, pansy. Let's get it."

The guy hops down and my fingers dig into Royce and Captain's jeans as I watch the dude across from Maddoc start to pull his hoodie over his head.

I squint to try and see better, but I can't make him out.

My eyes lift to Maddoc's and right as they do, his meet mine.

His move prompts his opponent to turn as well and my jaw clenches shut.

Leo.

That little bitch.

"Cap..." I start, but he ignores me, so I snap, "Royce."

"Yes." He covers my hand with his and squeezes. "He fucking helped Collins. He gave him the video, and it was his boot that was marked against your ribs. He— "

"Is a dead man in that ring," I whisper, anxiousness now fighting its way in and pushing out all the excitement and adrenaline because I know Maddoc is fucking foaming out the mouth right now.

His friend. Someone he half trusted, who I thought was sketchy as fuck, fucked them.

Fucked me.

"We have to show these people, Raven," Cap whispers in my ear. "And this is the place to do it. These people are drifters, you know that. Word will spread, and everyone will understand."

"You don't fuck with a Brayshaw," Royce finishes for him, looking to me and I reluctantly pull my eyes from the scene to meet his. "None of us."

The horn blares longer, the crowd gathers closer, and the intensity sparks like an invisible fucking flame.

A thrill runs down my spine and I glance around — wide eyes, baited breaths, and shaky hands surround me.

We all feel it, the power surging from the man in the middle.

My man.

And it's on.

Chapter 19

RAVEN

LEO TRIES, I GIVE HIM THAT, BUT HE'S NO MATCH FOR THE FURY boiling inside every inch of Maddoc. He was played by his boy, and he's letting everyone know what'll happen should they stray.

Punch after punch, kick after fucking kick, and Leo still pushes to his feet, but only after Maddoc steps back to allow it.

And he continues to allow it, waits for it in fact, all to knock him back down with the full force behind his fist.

Leo's cheek is busted open, his brow split just the same. Blood pours into his eyes and he wobbles on his feet, hands barely at his chest when he readies himself.

The crowd is no longer shouting but whispering with wide eyes.

"Cap." I shake his thigh, not taking my eyes off Maddoc. "Should we…"

Leo's legs give and he drops to his knees, his arms flopping to his side.

"No," Cap says calmly. Instantly. "He's got it coming and he knows it."

"Why you think he keeps standing?" Royce whispers in my other ear. "He knows what he did, and he accepts it."

Maddoc glares down at him, blood and sweat covering his body as well. His dark hair is matted and has fallen against his forehead. His chest heaves, his tattoo angrily rising and falling with each breath.

He gets right against him, forcing Leo's head back completely.

Maddoc bends and grips his arm, causing Leo to fall to the side slightly.

My eyes widen as he grips his fingers and snaps the first two back completely.

Leo wails into the sky and I wince.

There goes his shooting hand.

Maddoc spits on him then kicks him over and the crowd flips the fuck out.

Beer is thrown and his back is slapped a solid fifteen times before he can even move from the ring.

Maddoc steps out and moves toward me, Leo's blood splattered across him, his own dripping from the corner of his eye and lip.

"You ready?" he rasps, eyes wild, overtaken with adrenaline and burning with vitality.

I glance to Cap and Royce, both waiting for me to make my move, letting me decide.

It's my turn to fight, that's what they promised me tonight, and I've been dying to let go of some of my frustrations, but Maddoc ... he's completely fucking out of it.

A mad man standing.

I push against him, kissing his sweaty pec, right over his tattoo. I look up into his crazed eyes. "I'm ready to get out of here."

His brows furrow, his tongue slipping out to tap at the cut on his lip. A tremor runs through him right before he dips, gripping me under the thighs and lifts, storming away in the same move.

The crowd parts for him as he charges toward the vehicle.

He slides in the backseat, leaving me on top of him, while the others climb in the front.

I bend, grabbing the sweater from the floorboard, wiping away Leo's blood from his chest and face.

He jerks it from my hand and tosses it behind him, yanking me against him, my knees pushing into the fold of the seats.

He reaches between us and slips his hand in my leggings, tearing a hole in the seams between my legs and I start panting.

The music is suddenly cranked up piercingly loud.

Maddoc's eyes hit mine, dark and dangerous, and fucking burning for me.

He's fucked in his head right now and needs to be brought back, he needs to escape the dark place his mind has taken him.

His free hand slides up my chest until he's got the base of my neck in his hand.

Mine shoot out, instinctively sliding across his torso before pausing at his ribcage, and he shudders against me.

He leans forward sliding his lips across my skin until he's blowing in my ear. "Don't make me wait, baby. I can't wait."

He pulls back, his eyes as black as ever, begging for the first time, as if I could deny him when he looks at me like that.

"Take what you need, Big Man."

He lifts his finger to his lips, telling me to keep quiet, then his hips move off the seat so he can free himself from his joggers.

His dick sticks up straight and he shifts me, lining perfectly with the tear in my pants and my pussy. He pulls me down on him, pushing on my shoulders to make sure he's as far in as he can be.

He growls into my chest, flexing inside me, and my breath hitches.

My head goes to fall back but his hand moves, cupping the back of my neck to hold it up.

"Eyes. On... me," he growls in my ear, a deep guttural moan following and my body quivers against him.

He kisses the hollow of my throat as his free hand grips my hip, showing me how he wants it. I grind into him, my ass playing like a swing, back and forth, back and forth and my legs start to shake.

He tears open my sweater and bites at the flesh of my breasts and I cry against him. His hand flies up to cover my mouth as his teeth clamp over me, tugging until I fall from my bra and he pulls my nipple into his mouth. Scraping his teeth back and forth in opposite directions and I start coming, forcing him still but he growls and knocks my hands away.

Both his hands find my hips now and I drop my face into his chest, squeezing my eyes shut as it becomes too much. I cover my own mouth to keep in my moans as he forces my orgasm longer while fighting for his own.

It only takes a few more seconds before his muscles grow rigid, and his hot cum fills me.

He reaches into my pants and pinches my clit, flexing inside me and I whimper, moving my mouth to his.

"Again," he breathes against me and I meet his eyes. "Squeeze my dick, baby. Drive me crazy the way only you can."

I barely register the sound of the vehicle doors opening and closing, but the second they do, Maddoc is no longer fighting for quiet.

He groans loudly, rips my shirt off the rest of the way and

lays himself flat across the seat, his knees coming up to rest against my back as I still straddle him.

I drop against them and roll my hips, pushing my ass into him, forcing his dick to angle inside me.

My head falls back onto his knees and he lets me this time.

My moans blend with the music and he's right there with me.

When I peek at him, I find his eyes closed just the same, so I close mine again.

We fuck each other with no touches and no words, both completely lost in the fucking feeling of him inside me, stretching me. Filling me.

We come for the second time, and I collapse forward against his chest. He pushes my hair from my face and turns my head so he can run his lips over mine.

"I wanna give you what you need," he whispers. "I'm keeping you."

That's the last thing I hear before my eyes close and sleep takes over.

WHEN ME AND MADDOC WOKE IN THE MIDDLE OF THE NIGHT, we found we were parked outside the party pad, so we snuck in, me with his sweater pulled over my head since he shredded the shit out of my clothes. We quickly passed out in his designated room upstairs.

Thankfully, he was able to grab me some of Royce's old sweats that had a tie string and a random T-shirt of his to throw on before we went downstairs to eat with everyone that was allowed to stay over after their little kick back they apparently had last night.

In the kitchen, Cap has some girl on his jock, who insisted on helping him cook and Royce has a straggler in his lap. I know she wasn't here for him last night, because Maddoc said he was in bed alone when he slipped in there to get me clothes.

I can't help but smile at the ridiculousness of all this.

All this time I've been with them, they've been extra on edge or something, always trippin' on where I was and what I was doing. Things have been tense for them lately.

This scene though, it's like they've jumped back into the roles they filled before me, their minds at total ease while they just let loose and flip off the world in typical Brayshaw fashion – free, horny ass boys.

Well, at least Royce, whose hand keeps mysteriously disappearing under the table.

The girl is feeding him, but every few bites she pauses and starts shaking, her lips clamped shut. After the fourth or fifth time, I laugh, and his eyes bounce to mine.

"Really?" I raise a brow.

He frowns but then winks and moves to whisper in her ear.

Maddoc glares at me, but I laugh and pop a shoulder, right as she fights to hold in her moaning.

I lean closer to Maddoc, speaking for only him to hear. "We could make this a competition, Big Man? Go right here on the table where they can watch this time?"

He glares harder and I laugh loudly.

Obviously, I was joking, and he knows it.

After an hour or so, everyone is kicked out and the cleaning crew arrives.

We move to the porch to wait for them to finish up.

"Hey, what ever happened to those guards from the warehouses? The ones from the night you guys first followed me?" I ask.

"The ones who tried to take advantage of you?" Cap lifts a brow.

"Yeah, those ones."

"Put 'em on a bus to nowhere the next day." He eyes me.

"As in..." I slide my finger across my throat, and he tips his head.

"No. As in, never again allowed here or in any of the other towns our people run. Forced to go with nothing but the clothes on their backs. We always try the easy way first."

I look to the other two who nod, agreeing.

"And if they fight you on your choice?"

Royce mimics my move, running his finger across his neck and I laugh.

Right.

"Come on you guys, let's go home, they can lock up when they're done," Cap stands and we all follow, climbing into the vehicle.

Royce tosses me my shredded hoodie and I open my mouth to speak, only nothing comes out, so I shrug.

All three laugh, Maddoc pulls me close to him, and then we're moving.

His lips find my neck and slide across before he tilts back and closes his eyes. We didn't sleep that much last night.

I glance from his swollen lips to his long, dark lashes, and then shift to look at the other two. Cap meets my eyes in the mirror and gives a soft wink and Royce bops around in his seat.

A deep sigh leaves me, and I look away.

My mother was right, I do wanna stay.

Maybe even permanently.

The realization isn't as scary as I thought it would be.

Chapter 20

RAVEN

"Fuck no." Maddoc glares.

"Hell to the no," Royce laughs.

Cap frowns.

"Uh..." My head pulls back slightly. "I'm sorry, did you miss the part where I said, 'I'm going'? Pretty sure there was no question in my sentence."

Maddoc crowds my space. "Heard it just fucking fine. Fuck no, is my response."

I roll my eyes but don't step back. "I owe her one, we haven't talked since she helped me out that night. I only need an hour."

"No."

I look to Captain, the freaking logical one for help, but he lifts his hands and steps back.

"Traitor," I spit, and he cracks a grin, so I flip him off and turn back to Maddoc. "I'll be back before you have to leave for practice."

His jaw clenches and his eyes snap to Royce who shakes his head no, then Captain who gives nothing but a shrug. He groans, then levels me with a glare. "One fucking hour."

"Dude!" Royce shouts through an adorable pout. "Are you getting pussy whipped or what? Tell her no!"

I grin and head out front, but when I step out and reach behind me for the handle, I'm shoved out of the way and Maddoc joins me on the porch, closing the door before the others step through.

I look from it to him with a frown.

He moves toward the railing and pulls me to him, so I'm standing between his legs. His frown morphs into something different, and he drops his forehead to mine, closing his eyes before he speaks.

"Do you understand me like I think you do?" he whispers and the pit of my stomach heats.

"I like to think so, yeah."

"Why do I demand things from you?" His eyes pop open. "Why do I make decisions for you?"

"You mean why do you try to make decisions for me?" I whisper.

He chuckles against me, his hands moving to my belt loops. "Do you?"

I nod and his eyes heat.

"Say it."

I take a deep breath. "Because you can't handle not knowing where I am, but it's not in an aggressive way. It's possessive and carnal and all a part of your need to protect me – even if I don't think it's necessary."

His grip finds my hips and squeezes. "Keep going."

"You want me safe, and you can't think straight if you don't know for sure that I am. It fucks with your head, which fucks with your concentration and throws off everything you've taught yourself to control..." I trail off.

He buries his face in my neck, rumbling, "It's the most frustrating fucking thing I have ever felt."

"I bet you hate I have that power over you, just as much as you don't."

"You bet right."

I laugh lightly.

"Do you hate it?"

"I love it." My grin is slow.

He nods, running his fingers through my hair. "Well, I'm pretty fuckin' sure I love you, so I'm glad you're on board."

I freeze in his arms and his other hand slides up my side. He kisses my cheek then steps around me. Without another word or looking me in the eyes again, he disappears inside.

And I stand on the porch still frozen with my hands in the air for several minutes until the front door closing snaps me out of it.

I glance back to find Captain looking all fresh with his keys in his hands.

"You good?" he asks me, and I shake my head.

"Yeah, fine." I swallow, running my tongue over my teeth. "Can you drop me at the house on your way out?"

He raises a brow. "Promise to get out?" he teases, and I laugh, shoving him and get in the passenger seat.

"Do you meet her at the same park every visit?" I ask him, and his features tighten.

"Yeah."

One word is all I get until I'm climbing out.

"Raven," he calls. "You could come, if you want..." He trails off, not meeting my eyes.

I walk around to the driver side, forcing him to look at me. "I will go with you each and every single time you go. Always. But only if you ask me."

His eyes tighten around the edges and he reaches out.

Gripping my neck in his hand, he gives a curt nod and slowly releases me.

Captain's phone dings right then and he laughs quietly, lifting the screen for me to see.

MADDOC: 47 MINUTES, RAVEN...

WITH A PLAYFUL GROAN, I WALK BACKWARD AND CAP WINKS, but then his eyes lift over my shoulder and his face is wiped of all emotion.

The blank look of a Brayshaw takes over and he rolls forward.

I turn to find Victoria leaning against the porch.

Her eyes follow the black SUV until it pulls away, then slowly slide back to mine. "You're a few solid weeks past 'tomorrow,' Rae."

The night I was jumped, she and her friend scared them away and she brought me back here. I promised her the money I won in betting that night, but I took off the next day before I could make it right with her.

I hold out the cash and she frowns. "A deal is a deal."

Her features tighten. I know she wants to turn it down, but she's a poor girl living in a group home.

Free money isn't something she'd be smart to walk away from and she knows it.

Seeming a little embarrassed, she takes it, her eyes thanking me when her pride won't allow her words to.

"Now, let's go for a walk. I could use some air and you can buy me a snack or something," I ease her.

She scoffs, disappears inside and comes out wearing her blue leather coat, and we start walking.

Victoria has that typical beach girl thing going on.

She's tan even though it's winter, and has long blonde hair with a little darker roots, but it's natural, like the sun bleached it, and deep brown eyes. She's short compared to me, but she's fierce.

And when she sparks a joint and cuts her eyes to mine, she's my new best friend.

Not really, but I'm with it.

She passes it my way, laughing when I sigh.

"You out?"

"Yeah, but I'm working on it," I tell her, and she grins. "Sorry it took me a minute to get over here. Shit didn't ..." I grimace. "Go as planned."

She scoffs. "Yeah, no shit. Just because I'm not seen, don't forget I go to the same school." She cuts her eyes my way. "That was ballsy of you."

I look away, shaking my head. "Trust me. Balls had nothing to do with it."

"So, what was it, then?"

It's sort of like what Bass had said to me the other night, so I try to explain it to her.

"Because they deserved me to. There's not a whole lot of people like us can do to handle a situation, not with where we're at in our lives right now." I take the joint when she passes it back. "So..."

"So, when you have the ability to do something, you do it, fuck the consequences?"

I nod, sliding my eyes her way.

She's not judging. Something tells me she understands what I'm saying.

"What about after you did it?" she wonders. "Once you saw how it affected them, did you regret it?"

I lick my lips and look forward. "I wanted to."

But I didn't.

"That's big of you, Rae." She gives a tight grin and looks away. "Born in hell, yet your conscience didn't burn."

"When I first got here, all the shit you heard floating through the house and at school, that was all because I could. But this last time, maybe even a move or two before if I'm real, was different."

"Because you care about them."

I look her way. "I didn't need a minute to think. The decision was made the second I understood what had happened."

"Guessing you're not about to tell me what did happen?" She lifts a blonde brow.

I laugh, shaking my head. "Hell no. I'm only talking to you now because it seems you took the stick out of your ass."

She rolls her eyes and looks away. "I've got issues. When they nag at me, I take it out on everyone else."

Unapologetic.

I appreciate it.

"How's the house, by the way?"

"Same shit, different day. Maybell's a little more on edge lately, so we haven't been able to sneak off as much. Vienna hasn't been there much this week, not sure what's up with that since her shit's still there. All in all, I could use a drunken night."

"And your man?"

She shrugs. "Gone. He was a drifter and I helped pass the time."

"You sound so broken up about it," I joke.

She laughs, looking at me. "He was good for passing my time too."

I chuckle, glancing her way, seeing something in the shop window and focus straight again.

"Don't look, but that car has been following us for the last three blocks."

She scoffs. "Do you really think you're the only one who watches their back?"

My eyes cut to hers.

"If it wasn't tailing us, it would have passed a long time ago." She smirks.

"You spotted him in the window at the stop light back there?"

"Duh." She grins. "What do we do?"

I shrug, a zing of excitement hitting me. "Ask him what the fuck his problem is?"

Victoria's mouth opens but then closes and then opens again. "He has a car and could have a gun on his seat just waiting or something."

"Okay, Boyz in the Hood, we'll play naïve little dolls for a minute. The ice cream shop is a few stores up, we go inside."

Nothing else is spoken until we step in.

Victoria spins in front of me so she can discreetly look into the street.

"They parked across the street. What do we do?"

"You buy me ice cream and we take our time."

"Because that makes creepy cars leave," she deadpans.

"No ... but it does make pissed-off Maddoc appear."

Her frown is instant and then a laugh bubbles out of her.

We order something small, and like clockwork, not ten minutes after my 'allotted time,' a familiar SUV is rolling slowly down the street.

"There they are." I burst from the booth and building, not waiting for Victoria to catch up, and dash into the middle of the road.

A car going the opposite way, swerves around me, honking its horn while Maddoc slams on his brakes and the doors fly open. Both him and Royce practically jump out, glares in place.

"Get his keys!" I shout, nodding my chin at the car quickly

trying to pull from the curb at the side of them – they've unknowingly blocked him in.

Royce spins, and darts forward, attempting to knock the guy across the jaw, but the seat drops back, and he misses.

He goes for the keys and the guy grips his arm, but he's able to elbow him from that position and his head snaps back slightly. Royce yanks the keys from the ignition.

He steps back and Maddoc wrenches the door open, pulling the guy out and throwing him against the side.

He shifts and dips away, ready to charge in again but Maddoc and Royce come at him from both sides, and he's fucked.

He tries to swing at one then the other, but the move leaves him open to be gripped by both.

"Get your fucking—" the guy shouts, but they cut him off with a grip to the throat and a knee to the ribs.

Both pair of eyes hit mine.

"He was following us."

Maddoc's eyes tighten and travel over me.

"I'm fine." I can't help but grin. "We went into the ice cream shop and waited."

"Wait." Victoria steps beside me, gaping at them. "They just went caveman and they had no idea why they were doing it?"

They sure did, didn't they?

Maddoc glares, looking from me to her.

He shifts, kneeing the guy in the nuts, and he tries to collapse, but Royce moves to hold him up as Maddoc releases him.

People start to gather outside the business, but with one look at who's out here, they turn blind eyes and head back in.

"Wow," Victoria bites and I glare at her.

She lifts her hands, her mouth clamping shut in amusement.

Maddoc reaches into the guy's pocket, but before he can pull out his wallet, tires screech behind them and they jerk around to look, a truck has stopped and another guy rushes forward.

"What the fuck," Royce yells.

Maddoc moves just in time to meet the dude's blow.

They start swinging like crazy, and then Royce and this guy start full-on fighting again.

"Damn it!" I shout and rush for the vehicle.

"Is this shit normal?" Victoria shouts after me.

"Get over here!" I yell at her and throw the trunk door open, pulling out two bats.

I toss one to her and her eyes pop open.

"Basketball players just happen to have two bats in their trunk?"

"No." I glare. "They have four. Now shut up and help!"

But right as we round the back, we're bulldozed by two newcomers.

The bat falls from my hand and the blonde chick who bum-rushed me kicks it away.

With a growl, I look to her.

"Oh shit," she mumbles, bracing herself, and I spin away kicking her in the stomach, making her fall to the ground, but she grips my foot and yanks, taking me with her and rolls on top. I'm able to throw her tiny ass off just as fast.

I scramble for the bat, but right as I lift it, it's ripped from my hand and I'm gripped from behind, the guy who had Victoria stopping me from slamming it across this chick's fucking face.

"Captain's here!" Victoria shouts and the guy holding onto me curses, pushing the girl behind him when she stands to try and shield her.

Victoria lifts the bat and aims it at her while keeping her eyes on the guy at my back. "Let go of her or blondie takes a hit to the head!" she shouts, and he instantly lets go, stepping back.

To my fucking surprise, Victoria pulls back, ready to slam her with it regardless, but Captain appears and yanks it from her hand doing a double take when he sees who it is.

He grips my wrists and yanks me behind him, but I move to stand beside him.

Cap holds the bat with both hands, speaking to the tatted-up guy.

"Tell them to stop," he says of the others still boxing Maddoc and Royce.

"Fuck you, tell them to stop," dude throws back.

"You're not from around here." Cap takes a step forward. "Here, you do what we say. Tell them to stop, or we'll have half the town here in minutes to take all four of you out, not that we need the help." He eyes him suspiciously. "But something tells me you don't wanna be seen. You've already got one on the ground and the other won't be far behind. Your fucking call how bad of shape they are when you try and leave."

The guy's glare intensifies, but a whistle leaves him in the next second, so Cap calls out to Maddoc and Royce and all the grunting stops.

"Who are you?" he asks.

"Fuck—"

An arm snakes around my neck and I'm dragged a few feet to the right.

"Maddoc!" Cap shouts and Victoria picks up the other bat.

The grip tightens, so I lift my legs and drop all my weight, while pulling on the arm and the guy is forced to bend his back.

Maddoc comes rushing, but I swing my leg forward, then back, kicking him square in the dick and he collapses behind me, his grip falling so I spin, but I'm shoved away in the next second and Maddoc starts pummeling him.

His opponent is quick and spins, jumping to his feet and steps back in the next second.

I glance behind me and see the rest are in a standoff, except Royce. Seems he refused to let go and has got his guy's arms lifted from behind, his knee in his back.

"Raven?" the guy who just attacked me whispers, looking from Maddoc to me.

Maddoc's eyes cut to mine.

I step forward, but Maddoc yanks me back in the same second.

"G?" I ask, my eyes widening when I realize it's him.

He nods, blood in his teeth when he grins.

"What the fuck are you doing here? And what the fuck is this?" I throw my hands toward the rest of us.

"Raven," Maddoc growls behind me.

I lift my hand over my head, and slide it along Maddoc's neck, leaving it there in an attempt to soothe him. It works and he shifts, breathing against my palm a second, so I lean farther into him.

"Tell your people to get away from mine," I tell him and his eyes pinch, but he nods.

He looks over, and Maddoc takes advantage of his eyes being elsewhere and puts some distance between us and them.

"We good?" the tattooed guy calls over – he must be the boss – and G nods.

He looks to me. "I need you to tell the other one to release mine."

His?

"RaeRae?" Royce calls, having heard him.

"Down boy," I tease to be an asshole and laugh.

"Mama said you're free, little bitch," Royce jokes, pushing off him and coming to stand beside us.

I look back to G and his jaw ticks, his eyes locked on Royce.

"Hey," I snap, and his attention comes back to me. "What the fuck is this? Why was he tailing us?"

"Can you have her put that down," the tattooed guy looks to Victoria.

Captain rolls his eyes at her, tearing the bat from her hand, and she growls, crossing her arms.

"We need to talk to you guys, but not here," tattoo says.

"And you fucking are?" Royce glares stepping toward him.

The guy stands tall, a lazy tip of his head that almost reminds me of my boys cocksure attitude. "Name's Alec."

"Pansy ass fucking name," Royce goads him and I fight a grin.

I look up at Maddoc. "Where can we talk?"

"Here," he forces through clenched teeth, glaring at me for suggesting we let them decide.

"Brother," Cap calls, his eyes sliding to mine.

Maddoc's features tighten, but after a moment he agrees.

"Fine." He steps back but keeps me at his side.

He lets his eyes travel to Gio then move to Alec. He gets in his face and Alec stands against him. "You get in one vehicle. Pull out behind my brother, I'll be behind you. You think about taking off, I'll run you into a fucking canal."

Alec eyes him, but the blonde at his side tugs on his arm and when he looks down at her, his entire demeanor seems to soften and he nods, reluctantly agreeing.

They start to walk toward their vehicle, but Royce pops off again.

"Pussy whipped fucker."

Alec spins, but Gio steps in front of him.

"Just go, man. We're here for a reason." Gio looks back at me and winks.

Instantly my eyes fly to Maddoc's finding his jaw set tight, angry eyes on G.

"Maddoc," I call, and he shakes his head no, moving for his SUV.

"All you in Captain's, group home girl, too."

What the fuck?

Yeah, right!

I dart forward, but Royce wraps his arms around mine and lifts me off the floor.

"Royce—"

"Nope. Not this time, RaeRae. You're in trooouble."

"I'm not going," Victoria snaps.

Royce spins around, his laugh obnoxious and right in my ear.

Yeah, I know how this goes...

Captain frowns as he steps toward her, and her back straightens.

In one swift move, she's over his shoulder.

"Are you fucking joking me right now?" she shouts, banging on his back.

When Captain moves along like nothing, she growls, lifting her head to look at me being carted away a few feet in front of her, my back flat against Royce's chest, arms stuck beneath his hold.

"Really?" she says flatly. "This is how things happen when you fight them?"

I don't bother responding, dropping my head against Royce's shoulder instead.

He kisses my temple and I roll my eyes. "Yeah, blondie, it is. Now quiet, 'less you wanna show my bro there what else that mouth can do."

"Oh, how original."

"Damn right I am, one of a fucking kind, baby."

"Shut up, and get in," Captain gripes and then we're on the road.

Victoria glowers in the back seat but doesn't try to escape like I did the first time they threw me in.

She's handling it better than me.

Captain drives past the Bray houses, rounding the opposite side of the property and pulls onto a small dirt road, parking mid-way down.

Everyone jumps out at once, still cautious of each other.

Maddoc's eyes lock with mine as I make my way to him, satisfaction flashing in his eyes when I move to stand right beside him.

"Giovanni Acri," Maddoc says, eyes still on me, quickly cutting them to Gio. "Born in Stockton, California. Graduated three years ago, and no record since."

When they frown, Royce laughs.

"You really drove a truck registered to you to fuck with people like us?" Maddoc speaks slowly. "What kind of fucking amateurs show up with a clear job without doing research? Or at least a fucking rental car if not a stolen one?"

"Excuse me—" the girl talks, so I dart forward, but Gio slips an arm between us and my three step forward.

A frown takes over all their faces and they relent.

"Fine. All right, relax." Alec wraps his arms around the girl. "My name is Alec Daniels. This is my wife, Oakley, my brother Rowan, and Gio is one of my men."

"Why are you here?" Captain asks, frowning at Victoria when she hops up on his hood looking bored.

"You're Brayshaw," Alec says.

"And?" Royce growls.

"And we're part of the Rivera family. We never meant to fucking fight with you today, but your girl—"

"My fucking girl," Maddoc cuts Alec off and I'd swear his lip twitches slightly.

His hand on his wife tightens.

"Right, your girl is smart and spotted us while we were

trying to find out who all was in your crew so we could approach you. We haven't been able to reach Rolland and he's kept you three under wraps. We weren't supposed to meet until you graduated."

"The Riveras?" Royce's eyes widen and he looks over the four of them.

He nods. "Oakley is Rivera by blood, we were brought in, like you. We run the Riverside district."

Cap nods, stepping forward. "You have the fire academy as your cover," he says, having heard of them it seems.

Alec nods. "That's how we find and train our men. We're the guys people call when the judicial system fails them. We step in and make it look ... natural."

"You're arsonists." Royce frowns.

"No more than you're anarchists. You take the law into your own hands where it's needed in your community. We do the same thing, just not too close to home. Imagine our surprise when someone came to us to take down one of our own."

"You were hired to burn our shit down?" Captain asks him, and Alec nods.

"Your home, your school, your warehouses," Oakley supplies.

"By who?"

"That's the tricky part." His eyes cut to mine. "It was a female."

All their eyes fall on mine and I jerk. "You thought I did it?"

Alec lifts his hands as if to say 'you're the only girl around.'

"Well, I'm poor so... obviously not me."

"Yeah, Raven, how the hell—" Gio is cut off when Maddoc steps in his face.

"How do you know her?" he demands, disregarding every-thing being said in search of the answers he wants more.

Gio glares. "Ask her."

"I'm asking you."

I look at the blonde when she fights a grin. She sees me looking and winks, so I glare at her.

"We grew up together," he tells Maddoc.

The vein in Maddoc's neck is throbbing against his skin, but he stays in Gio's face.

"Good for fucking you." Maddoc's hand flexes at his side. "That was then. Stay away from her, do you understand?"

"What are you worried about?" Gio goads him and my eyes widen.

I step forward, but Royce yanks me back while Captain squeezes between them.

"Shut your mouth, dumbass, or I'll let him flip the fuck out. You're big, too, I get it, but nothing would stop him when it comes to her, so quit trying to be a smart ass and know your fucking place, and here you don't have one. She's his and she loves it. Period."

"Wow." All eyes fly to Victoria when she pops off and she widens her eyes like an asshole.

"Look, it was our duty to notify you—"

"You could have just called, no?" I cut Oakley off.

She looks to me. "Yes, our duty was only to make sure you were aware, that's how these top rank families work, but we came out of respect. Rolland's helped out my father many times, I hear, and we wanted to make sure the loyalty was passed to you guys." The blonde smiles and damn if she isn't perfectly sweet looking.

"Anyway, we've been here two days, and we have to get home to our daughter now," she says, stepping forward to shake my hand.

She moves down the line and then her husband steps up to shake the boys' hands.

"I'll email you the recording of the girl. She clearly didn't know about all the family ties."

"An outsider. Thanks, man," Maddoc grumbles and returns Alec's gesture.

Gio and the other guy hold back. "So, uh, we're gonna stick around another night or two. Catch up on some sleep," he announces, his eyes sliding my way briefly.

A deep crease takes over Maddoc's forehead, and his stare shifts to me. When his eyes narrow, I turn to G.

"They have a place on third where people are allowed. Come over around seven. The boys are playing ball, I'm getting drunk." I shrug.

Gio grins, looking to the guy beside him, Rowan as they called him, who glares at me. Gio catches it and drops his smirk at the dirt. He goes to step forward, like he's about to hug me but Maddoc is suddenly at my back, making him laugh.

"Later, Raven."

Maddoc's chest leaves my back and I turn around.

Victoria shakes her head, her eyes wide. "Wow." She gapes at me. "I know I already said that, but really though, that's all I got. Just ... wow."

Then the horn blares and she squeals, slipping off the hood.

Captain and Royce stand outside their doors laughing and she fake laughs back, flipping them off.

"Assholes."

"Yeah...you have to ride with those assholes," I tell her, and she glares at me.

"Seriously? After all that?"

"I need to ride with Maddoc alone."

She crosses her arms. "Ride with or ride in general?"

I waggle my brows, and she rolls her eyes, but a grin is on her lips. "Fine. Whatever."

"If they take you home, come to the party pad later. You can bring Vienna or whoever if you want."

"Why, so you can beat her ass, away from anyone who will care to stop you, for touching lips with your man?"

I pause, thinking about it. "Actually, yeah, sounds like a good plan, now that you mention it."

Victoria laughs, shaking her head. "I told you, Maybell is acting weird. I won't be able to get out."

"I'll handle it."

"Oh, you've got it like that now?" she teases.

"I just might," I admit and move past her, toward the very pissy, very sexy, and angry big man waiting at my door.

"Raven, huh?" He licks his lips. "Thought nobody got to call you that?"

"You guys don't call me Rae."

"We're not everyone else."

I step in front of him and he grips my hips, depositing me in my seat.

"You're right, you're not," I confirm.

"Has he ever touched my body?"

"Your body?" I raise a brow and he frowns.

"Yeah, my body. Has he ever touched it?"

I shake my head.

"Don't lie."

"I'm not. Just wait, you'll understand."

"Understand what?"

"I said wait."

He glares, but it goes away when I slide my hands down his pants.

"Now, take me home, wear me out, and then wake me up to party."

He leans forward, sliding his lips across mine before nipping on my bottom one. "I can do that," he whispers.

Chapter 21

RAVEN

"Wow," Vienna whispers, looking around the court from where we sit.

Victoria nods. "Now I get why Rae hangs with them." Her eyes scanning the group just the same. "Basketball shorts."

"Hmm..." I muse. "God's gift to women."

We all start laughing.

"The fuck?" comes from Maddoc.

My eyes jerk from his junk to his eyes and his tighten.

I grin, and he stalks toward me, raising a brow. "It's true. I've been watching the way you bounce around for months now."

A slow smirk pulls at his lips and he leans over me. "Yeah, and how do I bounce?"

"Long and to the left, Big Man," I whisper with a smile, making him chuckle.

His green eyes darken, demanding I meet his lips, so I push up and give him what he wants.

Gio steps up beside us in the next second and whips his shirt off his body.

Man, he's grown up and filled out the lanky boy body I remember.

Tattoos and weighted muscles cover his soft brown chest. With dark hair and dark eyes, he's definitely got that 'keep away' look going for him. The kind that makes you want to do the opposite.

Maddoc grips my head and brings my eyes back to his with a frown.

I wink and his jaw clenches.

"Look at your boy, G," I say under my breath and Gio takes a drink from his water bottle, peeking over at Rowan leaning against the hoop post.

His eyes are locked on Gio.

"He looks like he wants to take a serious bite out of you."

"Raven," Captain scolds. "Stop."

I hold in my grin. "What?"

"You can't just say that shit."

"He does." I tip my chin and they all look, seeing the struggle in Rowan's eyes from across the court just the same. "Damn, he's turned on right now."

Maddoc yanks me up, running his hand over my ass as he scowls at me.

"Yeah, if only he'd get out of his own fucking head. He's good at playing hot and cold," Gio mumbles, then jerks his head calling Rowan over.

"Wait." Victoria leans forward and Gio grins at her. She eyes him a minute and her brows jump. "You're gay?"

"What?" Royce's attention is caught, and his eyes cut to Gio. "No..."

Gio holds his hands out, eyeing him.

"Really?" Royce gapes.

He tips his head back. "Why you look so surprised?

"Guess I'm a stereotyping prick, 'cause you don't look gay." Royce sizes him up.

"Yeah, and how do I look?" Gio goads him.

I laugh, knowing exactly where this is going. Doubt Gio's met someone like Royce – honest, blunt, and completely fucking unashamed.

Not to mention run by his dick.

Maddoc shakes his head and moves for the cooler – he too knows his brother well.

"Fucking, good, my man. You look good. Strong and capable." He laughs at himself, making us laugh. He tilts his head and I shake mine. "You play three?

"What?"

"Three-way."

"I have." Gio shrugs.

"Well, the chicks around here love a solid sandwich, so if you're up for it." He shrugs. "I mean I'm not gay, but I like to share my toys." He grins like a dumbass. "And I'm great at multiples, just ask RaeRae."

"Royce!" me and Maddoc shout at the same time and he laughs.

"I ain't lying." He keeps laughing, dodging Maddoc when he whips a towel at him.

Rowan is suddenly standing there and steps forward with a frown. "That's not gonna happen."

"Why not?" I spur him on.

"Stay the fuck out of it!" Maddoc bites out from where he stands, and I waggle my brows.

Royce eyes Rowan, sliding his stare to Gio, and then back.

He's too perceptive for his own good and reads them both right.

Rowan hasn't claimed his spot yet, and poor pretty boy, Royce is about to force his hand.

"Yeah? And why not?" He licks his lips enticingly, slowly

sliding his eyes to Gio. "I'm not a selfish bastard, I'll make sure our frosty filling handles him good, even help her out if I need to."

Rowan steps close to Royce. "You want him in your party?"

"Yeah, man." He smirks, eyes flashing with amusement. "I do."

I look to Gio whose eyes are about black from watching.

"Then I'm the one in the center," Rowan says.

"Guess he's hot today," I mutter under my breath and Royce winks at me.

At Rowan's words, Gio goes from drooling to frowning in two seconds flat.

"Uh, clearly they haven't labeled whatever it is they're doing or not doing."

Again, all glares cut to Victoria.

"What?" she snaps with a shrug. "Tell me I'm wrong?" she dares, looking straight at Rowan.

Both guys tense a minute, but then everyone laughs, and they do their little back slaps. Fresh beers are passed around and we all move for the patio chairs on the side of the yard.

Maddoc switches on the fire pit and everyone kicks back, getting comfortable.

"How the fuck did you end up here, Raven?" Gio asks.

Maddoc tenses behind me, and I laugh. "Long story, G."

He nods – he's never been one to pry. "Been here long?"

"Few months now."

His eyes tighten. "Were you at your mom's all the time before?"

I nod., looking away.

"Damn, girl." He reaches forward, pinching my knee and Maddoc knocks his hand off.

Gio lets out an easy laugh, and eyes Maddoc, before looking to the others and back to me. "Seems you found your place, huh?" he asks with a soft smile and my chest constricts.

Maddoc's arms tighten around me and Royce and Cap watch me intently.

I don't want to answer, it's my business, but I don't wanna insult my boys either, so I nod.

"Yeah," I rasp. "I did."

He grins. "Who would have thought two troublemaking punks like us would make it out in the end."

I force a grin, because did I make it out, for real? I mean, I was only brought here because my man's dad needed me to get out of prison so ... who knows what happens if it doesn't work.

Yeah, can't really follow with that.

"We should go," Rowan stands.

Gio nods, his eyes on me. "It's ... damn good to see you like this, Raven."

"Like what?" I tease.

"Happy." He shrugs. "Content enough to sit still, not out hustlin' every second to stay ahead."

I tense and Maddoc's lips move to my ear.

"You're good, baby," he whispers.

"Thanks, G," I say, a little raspier than I'd have liked, sinking into Maddoc more.

I don't look across the group, I don't want to see their faces.

Thank hell the girls went inside to make a call.

Gio stands and moves to grab my hand, squeezing.

He whispers where only me and Maddoc can hear. "You deserve this, Raven. Keep reminding yourself of that."

I nod.

He shakes Maddoc's hand and then the rest of them, Rowan's next.

"Your family is welcome back, anytime," Maddoc tells him. "But maybe next time, don't fucking tail us."

They laugh lightly, waving bye on their way out.

And suddenly I feel heavy.

Maddoc senses it and moves us both to stand. He looks to his brothers.

"You guys coming?"

Royce looks to Cap who shrugs, and he cuts a grin back to us. "Nope. We're gonna find us a cream filling."

I laugh and Maddoc drags me away.

"We'll drop the girls at the home," he shouts behind us and the four of us are in the truck and headed back in the next minute.

"So are you sure you're not mad at me anymore, Rae?" Vienna asks and I push my head against the seat.

"I'll fuck you up if you so much as wave at him again," I say instantly, and completely fucking serious. "But no, and only because he planned it. Still think you're shit for suggesting it. Still don't like it. Still wanna smack you a bit for it."

I look to her when a tight laugh leaves her.

"But I understand it's what he needed" —I glare— "the move not the kiss. I can be pissed about it because I say so, but I decided not to knock you out."

Maddoc's chest shakes with silent laughter.

Vienna blinks a second and then laughs again. "And I thought it was because I talk too much."

"And ask too many questions," I add.

"Yet, you had this freaking jaded ass chick with you today."

The three of us girls laugh at that and Maddoc shakes his head.

When we pull up at the house, the girls hesitate.

I wink at Maddoc. "Go through the front door," I tell them.

Vienna nods but Victoria gives me a mocking frown, before a grin slips and she steps out.

Once we get back to the house, we take quick showers then move for the media room.

Maddoc climbs over me on the couch and drops down,

holding his weight up with his elbows. His eyes shift between mine, a rawness written in them. "I don't like to think others knew you before me."

"I know." I run my hand through his wet hair.

"Was he right?" he asks, and I look away, but he forces my eyes back. His hand moves from my chin to run across my cheek. "Was he right?" His eyes tighten at the corners. "Or is this still about convenience for you and fun while you're at it?"

I consider his words. "What does it mean, to be happy?"

"Come on, Raven. Don't play dumb."

Unease seeps into my chest. I don't like to think about these things, it's better to leave this stuff unsaid than to understand it. All that does is make the hit harder when the shoe falls. "Maddoc, I'm not normal."

"I don't like normal."

"Well, I don't know how to do this."

"Me either."

Damn him.

I shake my head, taking in a deep breath.

"I told you," I whisper. "I told you not to try and keep me."

He drops his lips to mine, and his eyes close. "Too late, baby." He kisses me, pushing his knee between my legs. "Way too fucking late."

I kiss him back, falling further into the cushions as his weight comes down on me. Like I told him, I'm not normal. I wouldn't know happy if it slapped me in the face.

All I know is my chest is constantly tight when his eyes are on me, I'm on edge more than normal, and extra needy when it comes to him − it's new and I don't understand it. It's also annoying.

But even so, I don't hate it.

And I have no intentions of leaving.

Chapter 22

RAVEN

"Excuse me," the teacher snaps when I push on the door to walk out.

I look at her over my shoulder, raising a brow. "Yeah?"

"You need permission to exit this class."

"She needs permission for nothing," Captain says from his seat, not bothering to pull his eyes off his notebook – he's been writing in that thing a lot lately.

The teacher looks from me to him and turns back to her lesson.

My lips press together, and I push through the door, headed for the bathroom.

As I round the corner in the hall, voices catch my attention and my steps slow.

"Stop jerking me around, asshole. I want the damn document. Now."

I peek, finding Principal Perkins in Collins' face.

What the hell? I can't believe he'd show his face here!

"I told you, it's safe," he growls, jerking his backpack from Perkins' hands. "It hasn't moved from the cabin—"

"Quiet," Perkins cuts him off, gaping at him.

The cabin?

My eyes narrow in thought.

What the boys stole...

They have what Perkins wants back!

"I want you to bring it to me. I never should have trusted you with it in the first place," Perkins says.

Collins pushes back, inching into his face now. "Why the sudden need for it, huh?" he goads, tipping his head like he's onto whatever Perkins is freaking out about. "You were all for me locking it away before. What, does her going back to them cause you problems?"

"It's you and your inability to keep the trash around for longer," Perkins snaps back instantly. "Apparently, you're inept at charming even the lowest of low." That'd be me. "This won't happen the way we hoped, so I need to speed things up to protect my own."

Wait, what the hell are they talking about?

"You're a damn fool," Collins spits. "Why are you even doing this? He'll never fucking forgive—"

"This is not about forgiveness!" Perkins shouts, quickly looking down the hall and I jerk back. "I don't need to explain myself to you. All I know is, if Donley finds that paper before all is said and done, I will end you myself," he hisses. "You're turning out to be as worthless as your father claimed."

Who the fuck is Donley?

I peek again, right as Collins moves to grip him by the suit jacket, shoving him against the lockers. "Watch your fucking mouth, Uncle."

My eyes shoot wide.

Uncle?! Holy shit!

"You're lucky I fixed it for you before it blew up in your

damn face, trying to hide this was stupid on your part!" Collins shouts.

"But it works out fucking lovely for you, doesn't it? You end up with what you want! You should be thanking me!" Perkins jeers back.

An evil chuckle leaves Collins and he says, "You might have clued me in where I was left out, but you need to stop trying to squeeze your way back. You were nixed from the name and plans eighteen years ago when you went after the trash's mom and ruined a bulletproof plan of business, that had already been solidly fucking agreed to!"

"It was supposed to be—"

Collins cuts Perkins off, "And it wasn't! And now my life is fucked, we're the underdogs when we were supposed to become equals. You fucked that up! I'd be standing strong beside them if it wasn't for you!"

Become equals? With the boys? How?

Perkins laughs lightly, and Collins draws back. "Yeah, you could have had that. You could have had all that leading up to this point. But don't stand here and cry about it, kid. We both know your eye is on a new prize now. It's not about what you want anymore, but who, and I'm the one making sure this happens."

"Yeah, to protect someone you shouldn't care to."

"Don't start your shit with me again," Perkins fires back.

"I don't know how you expect this to work!" Collins shakes his head. "They'll never allow it."

"They won't have a choice," Perkins counters. "Rolland Brayshaw will make it right. Why do you think she's here?"

"And if he doesn't?" Collins questions him. "If for some reason his plan is different from what you've assumed?"

Perkins smirks, complete confidence seeping through. "She will make the choice herself, once she learns the alternative."

What. The. Fuck.

My heart starts hammering in my chest as I try to make sense of what they're saying. I have to be the "she" they're talking about.

So, Rolland does have a plan for me?

Collins steps away, his frown deepening.

I shoot back around the corner, pushing against the wall.

What the hell is going on? Does Perkins seriously think I'd choose Collins over my boys?

And why would he think that?

Fuck Collins, fuck Perkins, and fuck Rolland Brayshaw!

"You need to go before they get wind you're here, Rolland pulled your transfer the minute his son went to jail. Guarantee one of their watchers spotted you the second you stepped from your car," Perkins warns him.

Collins says nothing back, but what can only be described as a fist hitting a locker echoes through the empty hall, followed by retreating footsteps and the slam of a door.

I wait a minute or two to be sure they're long gone and continue for the girl's bathroom.

As soon as I push inside, I'm gripped by the wrist, swung around, and slammed against the long mirror.

I try to push off, but Collins is ready for it, grips me harder and slams me back a second time, my head rebounding against the broken glass.

"Ah!" I yelp.

He does it again, and my muscles begin to give – I force my feet as steady as I can.

My eyes start to flutter, but I squeeze them shut a moment and attempt to refocus.

Warmth trickles down my neck and spine, soaking into my shirt, creating wetness across the back of my shirt with each bit of blood spilled.

"Not so fucking tough right now, are you?" Collins pushes his forehead against mine, forcing my head to grind against every shard. "Face it, Rae, no matter how hard you act, no matter how many fights you get into, you're still just a damn girl. Forever weaker than a man."

"I see no man," I rasp.

I'm slammed again, and my eyes close, but he shakes me, and they peel back open.

"What did you hear?" His bloodshot eyes bore into mine.

"Everything," I lie, knowing they could have been talking there long before I listened in.

His eyes strain. "If you so much as breathe a word about this, I'll make sure the next batch of shit your mom buys is the last."

A laugh bubbles out of me and his lip curls.

"Like I fucking care, she's dead to me, might as well be dead to the world, not that I believe you have it in you." I choke slightly and attempt to swallow past the blood dripping down the back of my throat. "You're nothing but a pussy."

He backhands me across the face, and I growl.

I lift my knee, going for his groin, but I'm sluggish and he shifts before I can even attempt, knocking it back down.

He tsks at me, and a smirk plays across his lips.

I lick the blood from the corner of my mouth and spit it in his face. "Fuck you."

He grips my shirt, keeping me steady. "I could right now, and no fucking body would be able to stop me, Rae. Nobody."

"You sure about that?" comes from behind us.

Collins jerks around, just in time to take a fire extinguisher to the face.

He's knocked back and slams against the marble sink.

With a deep growl, he charges Victoria, but I push off the mirror, whimpering when a few pieces of hair are ripped from my scalp from the glass woven in it.

I trip him, and on his way down he grips Victoria's shirt,

trying to yank her to the floor with him, but I shove her back and she flies into the door, her shirt tearing across her chest.

I push off his back and move past him, but he grips my pant leg and I slam back to the ground.

I hiss from the pain, my hands flying to my head as I try to kick him in the face with my other foot, but he knocks it out of the way and climbs up my body.

Victoria runs out the door, and he starts laughing, blood spilling from his mouth, like I'm sure it is mine.

"Why the fuck did you fall for him?" he growls in my face, but there's a helplessness in his eyes that has me frowning. "It wasn't ..." A tortured laugh leaves him, and his features tighten. "It wasn't supposed to be this way, Rae. Not for us."

He has my hands pinned beneath me, and his darts up to grip my neck, but he doesn't squeeze.

With his elbow pushing against my sternum, I couldn't break this if I tried. "This is a real fucking stupid move, Collins," I rasp. "Let me go while you still have the chance."

Footsteps pound in the hall and his eyes darken, gone is the feebleness he just showed.

His hand clenches tight while his jaw trembles. "Too late, huh?"

I try to gasp for air but get nothing.

And then the door bursts open and in they come – one, two, three.

Collins is tackled by Maddoc while Captain and Royce drop beside me.

Cap reaches out, pushing my hair from my face.

I cry out when his hand scrapes across the glass matted in it, and he freezes a second before yanking it back. His eyes widen when he finds it covered in blood. "Oh, fuck!"

"Oh shit..." Royce drags out, gripping my hand.

"Royce." My eyes start to roll, and things grow foggy. "I..."

"Raven," Cap calls, but I can't see him anymore. "Maddoc ... shit, Raven!"

Everything goes black.

MADDOC

It's crazy, how a drop of blood expands when it touches a cotton shirt. Even more when it's a continuous flow. It spreads like a silent explosion until all surfaces are covered, then it starts to drip.

I was covered. My brothers were covered, and still she bled.

Through the towel we held while waiting for the ambulance. Through the bandage they temporarily wrapped around her head. Through the bedding on the stretcher.

It didn't stop.

We've seen this shit before at the warehouses, we know the head bleeds more than anything and gauging the seriousness of the injury is not always as cut and dry as it appears.

It's never been the blood of someone we love before, though, so staring at the shit someone else made spill from her body to the point she lost consciousness, has me teetering on the edge of insanity.

If Perkins and half the fucking school hadn't followed us into that bathroom, pretty sure all the blood in Collins' body would have been running across that tile floor.

I wanted to keep beating him, but when Captain freaks out, I know it's serious.

I'll never forget the look in his eyes when he lifted his hands, both smeared with her blood as she laid there, lifeless.

We weren't there in the seconds before, we had no fucking

clue what had happened, so to us, she was fucking dying right then and there.

I'd never felt so helpless in my life.

My fists couldn't fix it, my money couldn't help her. My name meant jack shit. In that moment, I was nothing but a scared fucking boy who thought his girl was dying right before his eyes.

She didn't.

She woke up on the drive to the hospital, told the nurse who stuck the IV in her to fuck off and passed back out.

All three of us about fucking fell over in relief.

She was busted up, bleeding out for all we knew, but she was still her – fire and sass.

As soon as we got to the hospital, they had to put her under to remove the glass from her skull and run some test to make sure she didn't have any swelling in her brain, but that was two hours ago and she's still sleeping.

I dart from my seat, and Royce yanks me right back down, growling in my face.

"Do not fucking wake her up." He glares, glancing at Raven in the hospital bed.

"Fuck you!" I hiss. "She's mine, I do what I want."

The nurse scoffs and cuts me a glance, before walking out.

Fuck her, too.

Maybell walks in the second the lady is gone. "All's taken care of. Signed what needed signing."

"And her mom won't find out?" I ask.

"Her mama won't care." She shakes her head.

"Will she find out?" I ask again.

Maybell darts her eyes to where Victoria is sitting, pretending not to listen.

"Call me when you leave," she tells me. "Come on now, Tor."

Captain stops pacing long enough to plant his feet in front

of Victoria who is lying across the little couch, tucked under a hospital blanket she snagged off Raven's bed.

"She stays." He glares down at her and she doesn't acknowledge anyone has even spoken.

Maybell scoffs, mumbles something under her breath and walks out, but Cap makes no move to step away.

As soon as Maybell's gone, Captain's stance widens, and Victoria's eyes lift. "What?"

"Tell us what the hell happened in there," he demands.

She rolls her eyes and drops them back to the stupid fucking magazine she's acting like she's reading.

He slaps his hand over it, bending to get in her face. "I asked you a question."

She sighs and pushes up a bit, getting even closer. "I don't know what you take me for, and I don't care to hear it, but spare me your 'holier than thou' bullshit. Raven will wake up and she'll tell you what she wants to tell you, be it the truth, or a lie. And you'll be none the wiser because I'll agree and go right along with it, just like I did the night she said she fought but was jumped." She yanks the magazine from under his hand and he slips forward more, now even closer to her. "Because it's her story to tell or lie to cover, and the answer she gives doesn't affect me. But my answer? It could affect her now, couldn't it?" She gives a bitchy grin. "And who am I to dictate the outcome of her mess?"

"She's kinda growing on me..."

All eyes dart to Raven as she gives a weak grin toward Victoria.

Victoria snorts. "Yeah well, you're all right, I guess, when I'm not having to save your ass."

"Bitch please, you're weak compared to me."

"Says the busted-up chick in the raggedy gown."

Raven grins, shifting her eyes around the room, pausing when they land on me. "Guess I'm in the hospital."

We rush to her side.

She rolls her eyes, then winces. "Fuck, my head."

"Yeah, your fucking head," I snap, waiting for her to come back at me, but her brows smooth out when she looks my way again.

I have to use all my fucking concentration to force my body not to shake right now.

"I'm good, Big Man," she rasps and sits up.

Good. Right. She got attacked on our grounds, again.

"Doc said soon as you woke up you could go. You wanna?" Royce asks gently.

She nods. "Why would they even put me in a room if they were letting me leave?"

"Because the caveman demanded it, threw their name out there real big and loud like," Victoria offers and Raven laughs, looking to her.

Our eyes go with her, and now that Victoria is standing and the blankets fallen, we see her torn shirt and the dozens of scars across her stomach.

Her eyes hit Raven's, who pointedly looks down and Victoria's eyes snap wide as she spins away, clearing her throat.

"Well, you're awake, so I'm gonna head back." She rushes for the door, freezing when Captain's bloody sweatshirt lands on her head.

She stands there facing the door a minute, before pulling it off and over her head. She slowly steps from the room without a backward glance.

Raven shrugs off our questioning glares while reaching out to touch Cap's arm in thanks.

"Raven," I regain her attention. "The fuck happened today?"

"What did you steal from the Graven cabin the night we broke in?" she asks, frowning when all three of us hesitate.

She pulls her hands away from us, looking off to the side.

"Why are you asking this now?" I eye her.

A humorless laugh leaves her, and she tenses from the pain it causes.

Her eyes slide back to mine, and she does nothing to hide her irritation.

She opens her mouth to speak right as the nurse walks in with a smile. "Oh good, you're awake!"

"Get out," she tells her.

When the woman makes no move and just fucking stands there like a damn statue, Raven slowly drags her glare from mine. "I said out."

The nurse rushes from the room and Raven looks back to me, eyes cold as fucking ice.

"I'm only gonna do this once, so listen and understand what I'm really trying to say," she forces past clenched teeth. "Stop whispering in my fucking ear how much I 'belong' if you're gonna treat me like the outsider I already know I am when it's convenient for you. I get it. You want answers and you expect them the second you demand and not a moment later." Her eyes narrow and she leans forward. "But look at me, Maddoc. Look where I'm sitting, look at my face. Have I not earned them, like a good fucking girl" – she purposely makes a mockery of herself – "just as much, or should I drop to my knees and beg like the peasant would for her king?"

My jaw ticks at her bullshit and I shoot from the seat to crowd her space, but I get no time to respond because Captain beats me to it.

"It was Zoey's birth certificate," he rushes out, and while Raven's eyes fly to his, I feel his glare burning into the side of my head. "And, no, you didn't earn shit, and you'll never have to beg. You fucking deserve to know. I don't wanna hide anything from you."

I meet my brother's eyes and finally, he pulls them off me to look to her.

"Ask whatever you want," he whispers ruefully.

Royce drops his eyes to his lap, and I keep mine locked on Raven's face.

"Why would he have that?" she asks him. "Collins, I mean?"

"We think he was the money behind the move," he answers.

She considers what he says a second, then her brows furrow. "Zoey's mom. The transfer?"

He nods. "Bet he was the one behind what Perkins offered you to leave, too."

"That little bitch is working with Perkins for some reason, but that's all we know," Royce adds, looking up at her. He moves to grip her hand and squeezes. "And for the record, I wanted to tell you that a long time ago." His glare flies my way.

"Uncle," she says, and our frowns meet.

"What?" I ask.

"I heard them in the hall. That's why he waited for me in the girl's bathroom, he knew I was listening, saw me maybe, I don't know. He called him Uncle." Her eyes bounce between ours. "Said something about cleaning up his messes."

Captain darts to his feet while Royce scoots closer to Raven on the hospital bed.

"What do you mean?" he prompts, but she ignores him and fires off a question of her own.

"Who is Donley?" she asks.

"Donley is the head Graven, Collins' grandfather."

"He wants the birth certificate back, he's afraid Donley will find it." Her eyes fly to mine. "He has no fucking clue we broke in and stole it weeks ago."

"So, Perkins is making moves, and Collins is coming in to sweep them under the rug when he leaves loose ends?" I ask.

"I'm not exactly sure. It sounded like Perkins was the one in charge, but then maybe needed help with something and

Collins was who he went to for it. He didn't seem like he trusted Collins much, though."

When she flicks her eyes away a moment, mine narrow.

"Raven."

Her lips pinch together before she says. "He acted like I was the center of the problem, said I'd see things their way in the end." Her eyes bounce between ours. "He mentioned your dad, and how he'd have to make it right."

"Make what right?" I push to my feet.

She shrugs. "Don't know. He said, 'why do you think she's here.' Why am I here, you guys?"

"This makes no fucking sense," Royce grumbles, sliding his hands down his face.

"Wait." Cap freezes a minute, then speaks low, almost as if he's talking to himself. "How could the birth certificate possibly make any noise in the Graven world? She's my kid. Brayshaw." He looks to me. "How could that affect them? Why would Perkins wanna hide this, hide her, from them?"

"That's not all," Raven adds. "Collins said Perkins was washed from their hands, I assume he means Graven's, years ago."

"Did he say why?" I ask.

She licks her lips and looks to me. "When he went after the 'trashes' mom, aka Ravina."

"What the hell does all this mean?" Cap shakes his head.

"Did he say when?"

She nods. "Eighteen years ago."

"What ... not long before you were born."

She eyes me a minute before hers grow tight. "Oh my god..."

"What?" Cap barks.

"Your mom." Royce slowly stands, eyes on her. "She's from here."

Chapter 23

RAVEN

I DROP BACK ON MY ASS, LETTING OUT A DEEP BREATH.

Royce tosses the stack of papers he was going through and falls beside me. "There's nothing fucking here about your mom." His head hits the wall. "Shit's useless."

"This is everything from the binder I stole from Maybell?"

Cap nods, but the deep frown taking over his forehead as he stares at the papers in front of him, has me curious.

"Cap."

He takes a second, then lifts his eyes to mine.

"What is it?"

"Huh? Oh." He drops it between his legs, looking over the next. "Just an old hospital visit of my dad's. My ... biological dad." As he says it, his frown deepens even more, but he wipes it away and looks back to us.

"What?"

"Nothing," he sighs. "It's just this is everything. Staff records, bank accounts, contracts, deeds to the docks and

Brayshaw blacklists. Affidavits, copy of the Brayshaw will, our adoption papers, even a list of all the other families' names and locations."

"Okay..." I prompt him to continue.

"What if everything around his arrest and trial aren't the only things he hid?"

"Perkins," Royce guesses.

Cap nods, looking to him. "He's in the fucking picture in the yearbook, but his name is nowhere in it, and then nothing else. It's odd. Why is he nowhere in any of this, but then in one forgotten and maybe accidental photo, and now the principal at our fucking school. That was decided by Dad. He knew he was in our business before then. He was a teacher at our elementary school. He's always fucking around. Why has he not been sent away? Or at least, why is there no paper trail to him?"

I bend forward picking up the yearbook and turning to the page they had folded over. A young Rolland stands there, right beside Perkins with both Cap and Royce's dad and another man, all their arms tethered around each other's necks.

"We need to ask Dad about this," Royce says before leaning over to point out their fathers, and I grin.

"You look just like your dad." I laugh, trailing my fingers over the man's dark and daring eyes. He even has Royce's playful smirk.

"I'm way better looking than him," he teases, winking when I glance his way.

He tries to hide it, but there's a tinge of dejection in his eyes.

"And the last guy?" I ask, focusing back on the image. My eyes travel over the blond in the blue blazer and crisp white button-up.

"Don't know," Royce says.

I read the headline beneath it. "Says Brayshaw High's Finest and Faculty. Could he be a teacher?"

"He doesn't look much older, RaeRae."

I nod, frowning. "Yeah."

Royce pushes to stand. "I'm going downstairs to see what's up with dinner."

He offers me a hand, but I shake my head.

"You avoiding him?" He raises a brow, but worry pulls at his eyes.

It's sad how stressed he gets when he thinks there's an issue between any of us. It's kind of like how he hated riding in the back, alone. He needs his family to be solid.

"I'm not avoiding him. He just happens to be down there and I'm up here."

He eyes me. "Right."

After he walks out and down the hall, I look back to the photo. There's something familiar about the nameless man, but I can't put my finger on it.

"Raven, you know Maddoc didn't purposefully hide shit from you, right?"

I shrug, flipping through some more pages. "He has every right to, Cap. Nobody ever said you guys had to spill your secrets. It's whatever."

Cap bends in front of me, pulling the yearbook from my hands, and I look up.

"I'm serious, and it's not whatever if it made you feel put out. When we broke in and took the birth certificate, you weren't living with us yet, we were all still getting to know each other, so it wasn't something we were ready to share. Maddoc's not the type to stop and think later about filling you in on missing pieces."

"I know what type he is." My eyes bounce between his. "You don't need to level things out for him."

"I want to make sure he doesn't fuck this up. You say this is new to you and you don't know how to do this, well it's new for him too, and neither does he. He's not always gonna say the right thing, and he'll probably forever make the wrong move first." I laugh lightly and he grins, but his eyes hold a gentle seriousness. "You have to know he will always feel the kick in his gut when he disappoints you, even when he doesn't show it."

My chest grows warm and I look away a second before meeting his gaze. "Yeah, and how do you know that?" I tease with an easy grin.

He watches me. "Because I feel it, and you're not mine."

Cap stands, and my eyes follow.

I take the hand he offers and let him pull me up.

"I told you," he whispers, squeezing my palm. "You're good for us."

The truth to his words stares back through those light eyes of his.

"It's real inconvenient, you know," I tell him.

"What is?"

"Caring," I whisper. "I'm not really a fan."

He laughs lightly, and I fight a smile.

"Food's ready."

I turn to find Maddoc standing in the hall just outside the door, hands in his jogger pockets.

I nod, let go of Cap's hand and we both slide past Maddoc, but he gently grips my elbow, holding me back.

His eyes tighten as he searches mine, and he sighs, dropping back against the wall. He pulls me closer and I willingly lean into him.

Maddoc's hand comes up to slide across my cheek, his thumb brushing over the cut on my lip.

His internal struggle takes me by surprise when it seeps through his cautious touch. "Soon as one wound heals, another appears." His eyes lift to mine, tortured and trying to hide it.

"It's pretty much how things work in my world."

"But your world is our world now," he corrects, moving his lips to my forehead before dropping them back to mine. "And in our world, this is unacceptable."

"Really?" I tease, and his hand slips up the back of my shirt, pushing against my spine to bring me closer. "So, you'll share your world, but not your mind?"

"My mind is dark, baby."

"And?"

His mouth comes down, sliding across mine before he steps back, releasing me. "And you're afraid of the dark."

I LOOK TO CAP WHO SITS BESIDE ME ON THE COUCH WHILE Royce and Maddoc finish cleaning the kitchen. "What am I missing, about Zoey's mom?"

He doesn't hesitate. "Perkins was engaged to her mom."

I jerk upright, shifting to face him full on. "I'm sorry...what?"

"He's had it out for us for years, always lurking in the corners, always trying to fuck our takedowns by tipping people off, and we wanted to know why." His forehead creases and he looks away. "The only way we saw to get to him, was to get to her." He lifts his eyes to mine. "We knew it would only be believable if it were me pretending."

"And then it became real," I guess, eyeing him. "Do you love her?"

Angry eyes slice to mine. "She hid my fucking kid."

"Yeah," I nod lightly. "I know, but that's not what I asked."

He shakes his head, looking up at the ceiling. "I will never forgive her. Ever. Way too much has happened now. It wouldn't matter if she was sick and dying or claimed to be forced into it. Nothing could ever make me forget or forgive how she gave away the innocent baby who grew inside her for nine fucking months, without telling me. Nothing."

I drop back against the cushion. "I get that. When Collins threatened my mom's life, I didn't even care. I wouldn't even care." I roll my neck to look at him and he copies my move. "Not even a little bit."

"Considering everything I know, I'd say there's nothing wrong with that, Raven."

"Yeah. It's funny, though. I spent my whole life with her and I don't give a shit where she ends up, but I've only known you guys for a hot minute and when Collins breathes your names the wrong way, I lose it. I see red and I want to strangle him with his stupid alligator skin belt."

Cap laughs, lightly hitting my knee with his.

I consider what I said a moment, then ask, "Everyone says you love your parents despite the fucked-up shit they do, how at the end of the day, you love them even if you don't want to, but I don't. Does that make me sick, not caring if my own mom dies but livid at the thought of someone messing with you guys?"

"No." Maddoc's voice flows over my shoulder. I look, following him as he and Royce step into the room to join us. He drops on the ottoman in front of me. "It doesn't make you weak. It makes you Brayshaw," he whispers, and my chest grows tight.

Family runs deeper than blood.

Damn.

"When we demanded answers from Zoey's mom," Cap continues. "All we could squeeze from her was she left the birth certificate blank, claiming not to know who the father was."

"That's how she was able to sign over all rights to Zoey without you."

He nods, looks to Maddoc, then back to me.

"We checked with the registry department and found out

the paperwork for the birth certificate was filed thirty-seven days after delivery. It only takes five days to file when done at the hospital."

"She lied."

"She fucking lied. She did put my name on it, and Collins Graven was the one hiding the original." Cap leans forward. "Whether he hid it to clean up after someone else or not, he knew, and I almost lost my daughter because of it."

Son of a bitch.

I push to my feet and move for the cabinet, pulling out a bottle of some fucking dark whiskey I can't pronounce, and take a swig from the bottle.

I cough, wiping my mouth with the back of my hand and slam the bottle against the counter.

My hands start shaking so I clench my fists to stop it.

I let them think I betrayed them with a guy who literally had some kind of hand in fucking their entire world in one way or another. Not to mention I floated around their school with him while everyone sat back to watch the train wreck that was me force their hands still. Somehow, Collins fucking knew their dad would ask them to play it cool. Or shit, as cool as three hotheads can play it.

Collins knows something they don't and he's proving to be a reckless bastard.

I look back to the guys, finding all their eyes on me.

I take another drink, carrying the bottle with me out the back door to the patio.

It only takes a few seconds before they're out there with me.

Maddoc moves behind me, caging me in against the railing while Cap shifts to one ukside, and Royce the other.

I lean back, closing my eyes when his arms wrap around me.

The bottle is passed down the line without a word spoken.

Collins, the piece of shit, he had a hand in taking Zoey away.

He did what he needed to make them think he took me.

And he wants to take their place and power.

"We should take his life."

"We will."

Chapter 24

RAVEN

It's Saturday night, and the boys are having one of their bigger parties, so like the one I first came to with Vienna, it's at some random house they found, and only those who got the cards, then followed the driver from school came. There's a solid fifty people here, all Brayshaw and a few I even recognize from the warehouses.

Speaking of the warehouses...

I lean back in my seat when Bass walks up with two unopened beer bottles as a peace offering.

"What do you say, Carver?" he holds one out for me. "Can the help sit with the queen?" he teases, but there's a softness in his stare he chooses to share, letting me know he's standing here with genuine intent.

With a playful roll of my eyes, I snatch one from him and he grins, dropping his onto the coffee table in front of me.

He pulls out his lighter, popping the tops off both of our

drinks. Leaning forward with his elbows on his knees he speaks low, "I fucked up. I'm sorry."

I eye him. "For what exactly?"

"For putting the video shit on you and you alone. I should have come to you all, as a group." His eyes bounce between mine, and I frown.

"Why do I feel like you've got more to say?"

He chuckles. "Because you're smart and can read people."

I smirk, taking a quick drink of my beer. "So out with it, Bishop."

He nods, considering his next words carefully. "I've been around a minute now. I've seen what these people call Bray Girls – senseless girls who want a piece of power, even if it's only on a bed for an hour once or twice. Those girls?" His brows jump. "They come and go, most of the time every few days. It was always expected. They knew they were on a temporary schedule. There was no respect, they were never included. They were just around so when it was time to hit the sack, they were near."

My nose scrunches, and he smirks.

"Don't like hearing that, huh?"

"I'm aware of how each of them plays." I glance at Maddoc, who openly watches us from his spot against the wall on the opposite side of the room, arms crossed, biceps bulging, glare intact.

Heat spreads through my abdomen and as if he senses it, his lip twitches. "He's mine now, so I don't give a shit about what he used to do."

I look back to Bass.

"Just him?" he asks bluntly.

"Just him, though, the other two are real close to catching up," I joke and he knocks my knee with his, making me laugh. "Nah, Maddoc is..."

"You," he says. "Maybe a little crazier."

"Only a little?" I lift a brow.

He chuckles. "I'd bet you're pretty fucking even."

"He likes my crazy, and I want his madness. It's pretty fucking simple."

Bass nods. "Looks simple, natural-like, from the outside, too. I think that's why people are trippin'."

"What do you mean?"

He lets his tongue touch his lip ring before continuing. "The guys haven't had a single Bray Girl since you came in. Not even the two free Brayshaws."

"They fuck all the time."

"Yeah," he nods. "They fuck, but they don't allow anyone extra time around. Not since you got here."

"They would if there was someone they wanted to keep." I grow protective.

"They want to keep you." He dips his head. "They don't want you to think you're like the others. They've been trying to show you what you mean to them, the only way they know how."

"This isn't some big gang bang, Bass."

He gives me a pointed look. "Trust me, I know. Maddoc is real fucking clear on who belongs to who, feel me?" He lifts a brow and I laugh. "All right, look. Everyone around here knows, without a doubt, nobody could stand with them, so nobody has dared to try. Behind, yeah. In the same circle, sure, but never beside." He licks his lips and looks off. "You, though, Rae. You might just be able to stand a solid foot in front." He meets my stare. "I think I saw that before they did. Maybe I even acted like a bitch about it."

"What are you trying to say, Bass?"

"I'm telling you there is no one like you, Raven Carver, and we all know it. We see it and feel it and that's some powerful shit, girl."

I try to look away, but he shifts, keeping me in his line of sight.

"What, you thought not?" he asks.

"I'm tired of people saying that like it's what I was looking for here. I mean, who fucking cares—"

"I care," he cuts me off. "I care because you doubt your power over this place and I want you to find it."

I eye him a minute and he frowns, his lips pinching together.

Huh.

Pulling my feet up, I sit Indian style on the couch and lean my forearms on my knees, dropping closer to him. "Why?"

He starts to sit back, but I tilt my head and lift a brow in challenge.

"Why do you want that for me? Why's it so important?"

He curses under his breath, running a hand over his face quickly. "Because I need to know a girl who lived like me, fucked up mentally and cut off emotionally – to most, anyway – can fight her way from the bottom and come out with sharper claws, not broken ones."

I slowly drop against the cushion. "Who is she?

This time he tenses. "Who?"

"Don't play dumb. Who's the girl you're worried about making it or not?"

His eyes strain. "They didn't tell you..." he wonders. "I almost thought they'd brag."

"They're not the type." I study him. "Well, maybe Royce but..." I trail, trying to ease some of the tension.

Bass gives a half grin, dropping his stare to his feet a minute before looking back up with a squint. "My sister."

"Sister."

He swallows and looks away. "Yup. Your boys, they stepped in when the people around us failed. Got us out before worse could happen." He absentmindedly runs his fingers over the back of his hand.

"Got you out..." I trail off, glancing at Maddoc once more. "Like they saved you?"

When he doesn't answer I ask, "So where is she? One of the girls in the home?"

"Nah." He shakes his head. "She's away from here, as she should be."

"Bass—"

He shakes his head, so I clamp my mouth shut. He doesn't want to talk about it, and who am I to pry.

I glance away, doing a double take as I do, and a smirk takes over my lips.

Change of subject. Perfect.

"And uh ... how about the chick who looks ready to castrate you while also looking like someone pissed in her Pradas?"

He scoffs. "You even know what Prada is?"

"Fancy shit, Collins told me all about it." I grin and he laughs.

He looks the way I did, and his features harden. He downs his beer with his eyes on her. "She is the opposite of you – a follower. A rich bitch who only dates rich boys." He looks back to me, his features blank.

"Wanna make her jealous?" I joke and an instant laugh breaks through his cool covered face.

"Nah, I'm not in the mood to fight your boy tonight." He chuckles.

"Ah come on, you can hold your own." I smile. "I mean, at first."

He smirks goodheartedly and pushes to stand so I stand with him.

"You're good people, Bass Bishop."

I lift my fist and he knocks his into mine, puts a cigarette between his lips, slides his DJ headphones back in place, and nods his goodbye.

And just like that, the poor boy with swag for days has the rich bitch panting in her silk panties as she watches him stalk on by, ignoring the shit out of her.

Good for him.

Before I can even step from my spot, Royce is gripping me by the thighs and lifting me in the air.

I yelp and smack him in the back of the head, but he only laughs harder. We pass Maddoc and Royce spins me, letting Maddoc get in a good ass slap.

"Brother, stealing your woman, a'ight?"

"Careful, asshole, she's still sore!"

"Ha!" Royce laughs. "I bet I know where, brother!"

I roll my eyes and hang on best I can, while he snags the two bottles in Cap's hand and runs out.

"Those were ours, dick!"

"Raven thanks you, Cap!" he shouts back and runs into the back yard where he finally lets me slide down.

We both laugh at his silliness, and I grab the beer he hands me.

There are several little groups spread all around the grass area, so he leads me to the side of the house, out of prying eyes.

I pull back, frowning at the dark orchards. "Royce—"

"Shit," he cuts me off. "Hang on, sorry." He pulls his phone out and turns on the flashlight, propping it up beside an old air conditioner unit. He drops down against the side of the house, so I move with him.

"I was trying to entice you into some freaky shit, RaeRae," he jokes, tossing a sandwich baggy full of weed in my lap.

My mouth drops open.

"That's for you." He pulls out an already rolled blunt. "This is for us." He grins.

"How much did this cost?"

"Didn't cost me shit." He takes it back and stuffs it in his pocket. "I better hold it and give it to you at home since your jeans are tighter than virgin pussy."

I start laughing and he flashes me a smile, sticking his tongue out.

"Been in many of those, Royce?"

He frowns at that. "Nah, actually. Haven't."

He's quiet a minute, so I take another hit.

"How old were you when you lost your virginity, RaeRae?" he asks, and I tense.

He looks my way when I don't answer, and he runs a hand through his hair. "Shit, I ...fuck."

I shrug, looking out at the darkness that surrounds us. "I was twelve when it was stolen. Fifteen when I gave it away."

He runs his hand up his arm, flipping it over to study the tatts there. He won't look up. "Wanna talk about it, RaeRae?" he whispers and my chest warms.

Such a softy at heart, this playboy.

"Not really, he was fifteen, too. Had no clue what he was doing." I glance his way. "Couldn't get the job done, not like you probably could," I joke, and his head snaps my way.

His lip tips, and it only takes a second for his shoulders to pep back up.

"Oh, I'd have rocked your world, baby." He grips my knee shaking me.

"No doubt." My eyes widen as my brows lift and he flips me off. "But only if I wasn't a virgin, yeah?"

"Exactly." He snatches the blunt from my hand and takes a hit.

"That like your one rule of thumb?" I tease. "Don't wanna get 'em sprung?"

He follows the ashes as they fall to the grass.

"I don't wanna ruin it for anyone, and knowing me,

RaeRae, they'd regret it later." He licks his lips and looks back to me. "Least I can do is make sure it won't be the one time they're sure to never forget that they wish they could, yeah?"

My eyes soften and I tilt my head.

"That right there makes me think you'd be a solid first fuck, Royce," I speak low.

He stares a second, trying to fight it but we both bust up laughing.

"Reason number two hundred seventy-five why I like having you around, RaeRae. You make me feel good, even when I'm feeling like a piece of shit." He gives a soft grin. "You make me feel normal."

"You're not a piece of shit."

He lifts his hands, beer in one, blunt in the other. "But I'm a bad guy."

"No, you do stupid shit. You're an awesome guy."

He scoffs, his head facing forward while he looks at me out of the corner of his eye. "Would you let your daughter near me, if she was different than us?"

I wince, but thankfully it's dark and he misses it. I swallow subtly. "Different how?"

"If she was good."

I glower, shifting toward him. "I'd wish she could find someone like you."

"Why?" he whispers.

"Because, you'd love her. Hard, raw, probably a little too possessively, and definitely beyond anything a normal guy could."

"How do you know?" he rasps.

A deep crease forms on my forehead. "I just do."

His eyes flick between mine, and finally, a small grin comes out. "So, I'm a catch, then?"

A laugh spits from me and he joins in.

I exhale and drop my head back. "You're a catch, for sure."

"And Maddoc?"

My lip tips up. "He's the shark, ready to eat up all the others to stay on the tip of my tongue, like he wouldn't be there regardless."

Royce laughs. "You tell him yet?"

"Tell him what?"

"You love him."

My stomach tightens and I take a sip of my beer. "Do I?" I ask, quietly.

"Damn, RaeRae. Never thought it would be one of us feelin' it and having to shake it out the female."

"I've never loved anyone, not even my mom, to be honest. Not even when I was young and dumb."

"You mean innocent?"

I shake my head. "I was never that. I was a thief, and some would say a bully."

I wasn't, not really. I just didn't let people run all over me, couldn't if I tried. And I tried. It was so much easier to leave things alone and move along, a lot less messy and troublesome for me, but I've never been good at restraint.

"You were a natural born survivalist, a fighter."

"I was a bebe ass kid nobody wanted around because I knew and saw too much or because they didn't want to chance my mom slipping into their husband's – sometimes wive's – beds. She had no dignity. No hard limit. Just a sick bitch through and through."

"Raven," he calls, but I don't look. "You're nothing like her."

At that, I roll my head against the house and I finally meet his stare. "I almost became her for him, for you. Is that what love is? Venom in your veins driving you to throw out all morals and self-respect for the sake of someone else? Without hesitation, and little to no remorse?"

His eyes tighten as he studies me.

"If it is, then how could loving him be a good thing?" I ask.

"I think it's necessary."

"I think it's pathetic."

"I think you're wrong." Both our heads snap right to find Maddoc and Captain standing there.

Shit.

His jaw clenches as he tries to keep his cool when I can tell all he really wants to do is flip the fuck out right now. He sure as fuck won't do it here.

He kicks the beer bottle beside me and shifts his glare to Royce.

Royce holds up one hand while putting out the blunt with the other.

He hops up, pulling me with him.

I dust off my jeans and move to stand right in front of Maddoc, but he turns on his heels and starts walking. "Let's go."

Silently, the four of us exit around the side of the yard and head for Cap's SUV.

Captain and Royce bullshit about nothing on the drive, but neither of us says a damn thing, and in a few short minutes we're pulling in front of the house.

Cap and Royce step out and I dart just as quick, but he's quicker and jumps out behind me. Gripping my elbow, he pulls me back, pushing me against the inside of the door frame.

His eyes flick between mine, defiance lining every inch of me, I'm sure.

"Raven—"

"Stop," I tell him. "I'm not doing this."

"Why not?"

"Because ..." My eyes widen. "I don't want to, okay?" I grow defensive and his hands jerk away from me. I swallow the bile fighting its way up. "Just because you decided to say what you did doesn't mean I'm going to say it back. It

247

doesn't mean I'm going to try to ... love. I told you I'm not normal."

"Neither am I," he snaps.

"Then stop pretending we can be!" I shout. "Stop feeding into the thought of being—" I cut myself off and look away, but he forces my eyes back.

"What, happy?" He gets in my face. "No. I won't stop, Raven. Everything around us is fucked up and influenced by one thing or another, one person or another. We don't have anything for ourselves at this point, not completely anyway. But you? I want you, for me. Only fucking me. I don't see anything wrong with that."

"Well you should, because—"

"Cut the shit, Raven!" His hand hits against the window beside my head. "You feel like I do, but you're fighting it. Why?"

"I said I'm not doing this."

"Doing what?" he shouts, creeping even closer. "Why, pick a fight when we have no reason for one? Why not let it happen? Would loving me be so bad?!"

"Yes!" I shout right back, pushing on his chest but he doesn't budge. "Yes, it would be so bad. So fucking bad!"

"Why?!"

A humorless laugh leaves me. "Seriously?" I gape at him. "I was ready to fuck someone else to protect you. Someone who touched me without permission. I wasn't talking out my fucking ass when I said love is weak, because if what I'm feeling is love, Maddoc, I don't want it! I hate it!"

"Why?"

"Because! It's like you're in my fucking head, dictating moves I used to control, fighting against my every step." I shake my head. "You're like weight beneath my skin, pressure against my chest, a fog inside my damn mind I can't get rid of!"

"Raven—"

"To love you would mean to let go of a part of me, the part that I worked damn hard to get – understanding and accepting I need no one to survive, knowing I can do this all on my own without a helping hand or dropping to my knees."

His shoulders fall. "Baby..."

I swallow. "To need someone is weak, because what happens when they leave, and you fall flat on your face? I don't want to be weak, Big Man, not even for someone strong enough to carry us both."

The vein in his neck throbs against his skin, and his throat bobs with a deep swallow, but what has me holding my breath is the way the creases at the edge of his eyes smooth out.

His hand wraps around my neck and I welcome it, gripping his wrist to keep it there.

He moves in, running his nose along my jawline, pausing to whisper in my ear. "I make you weak?"

"Yes."

He growls against me, his grip tightening. "That's good, baby. Real good."

I frown, and he pulls back, a smirk in place.

He rolls his hips against me, lifting my chin up so his lips can touch mine.

I fight the urge to lick his, but he has even less control and slides his tongue between the crease of my lips in a second, tasting me.

Another groan leaves him.

His hand glides up my side, pausing at the edge of my breast. "You said love makes you weak." He nips at the corner of my mouth. "You said I make you weak." He nips my jaw. "If love makes you weak, and I make you weak, then baby," he breathes against my skin, pulling the lobe of my ear between his teeth. "What's that mean?"

I pant, my body going slack against the door. "I...mmm," I

moan when he runs the tip of his nose up my throat. "Fuck off."

He laughs against me, his grip tightening, his chuckles quickly turning into a moan.

His mouth flies to mine and while his kiss is hard and possessive, crazed for more, his hands on my neck and face are gentle, almost feather light. It's like he's afraid to grip me fully, knowing the small wounds on the back of my head aren't fully healed.

He pulls back just as quick and lifts me.

With a husky chuckle, I jump up in his arms and he jogs for the door, running up the steps and inside.

Right when we make it through the threshold of the doorway, my back hits something and Maddoc stumbles slightly, catching himself and me before we tumble.

His eyes fly over my shoulder and his body turns to stone.

His hands release me, and I frown, slowly sliding down, but when I shift to look over my shoulder as well, my muscles lock just the same.

"Good. You're all home."

Chapter 25

MADDOC

"Dad."

Holy shit.

I stand there frozen, my hands still stuck on Raven's side.

Captain glances back at me, shifting the smallest bit in front of Raven, a move that would be subtle to others, but not Rolland Brayshaw.

The edges of his eyes tighten, and he looks from Captain to Raven, and then me.

"Well." He glances at Royce who stands a few steps in front of us. "This isn't quite the way I thought this would go."

We all hesitate another second, but then light laughs leave us, and we move for him.

He grins as we step closer, reaching out to hug each of us.

"This is a fucking surprise," Royce laughs. "Thought it took thirty days for a decision to be made?"

"The decision was made before I even got there. It was out

of the judge's hands, the hearing was simply semantics. Two weeks was as quick as I could get all the Ts crossed."

"Why didn't you tell us?" Royce asks.

"We've kept it quiet for now. I wanted to avoid it getting back to the Gravens until I had a chance to come home, and ... evaluate."

"Evaluate?" I ask. "Evaluate what? And why didn't you respond to any of my messages? I've been trying to reach you for weeks."

Our dad grins and clasps my shoulder. "I'm sorry, son. I would have, but I had a lot to get a handle on."

"Evaluate what?" I ask again, hating the unease creeping up my spine. I have no fucking idea why I suddenly feel on edge.

"It's just business, we'll talk about that tomorrow." He smiles at each of us, hitting his hand against Cap's chest. "Damn boy, you've grown."

He scratches the back of his head, shrugging with a small grin.

"Yeah, them shoulders came outta nowhere," Royce teases. "He was a puny ass white boy one day then boom, fuckin' wingspan for the books."

"And you're still a skinny asshole." Cap shoves him.

Royce flips him off with a grin. "Please, I'm just a silent killer. They have to use their imagination to wonder what's under these clothes, then boom. Sculpted masterpiece. Five percent body fat, baby." He lifts his shirt, hitting his abs.

Our dad laughs then runs a hand down his suit jacket. He nods, his features softening as he looks between us. "This is ..." He nods again.

The front door clicks open and all our heads jerk to see Maybell rushing in, tears in her eyes as she steps forward.

Her hand shakes as she steps in front of my dad, placing her hands on his cheeks.

"Good to see you standing here, boy."

"Good to be standing here, Ms. Maybell." He pats her hand on his cheek. "I owe you so much." He grips her hand, holding it in his.

"You owe me nothing." She smiles softly. "They're my boys, too, but if you're in a giving mood, I could use a day or two off."

Our dad laughs. "We'll make that happen, Ms. Maybell."

RAVEN

HOLY SHIT.

He's really fucking standing there, not fifteen feet away.

Ten seconds in and I stand on one side of the room while they stand on the other, their father at their side – the man who "owns" me.

I guess I didn't really stop to think about what would actually happen once he arrived – sure as shit didn't expect it to be this quickly.

It's safe to say I'm a little more than unsure.

I'm ready to run.

Apparently, my feet agree, because I don't realize I'm backing up for the door, one silent step at a time, until my foot catches a rogue basketball on the floor and I slip, falling right on my ass with a hard thud.

My hair falls into my face, but my eyes pop up, right as five sets of eyes hit me.

Fuck.

Cap rushes over, like I need help up or something, but I stand quickly before he can reach me and take a step away.

He frowns, but I keep my eyes on the man across the room.

His eyes, I should have recognized them – they're identical to the ones I've been staring into for weeks now.

His casual gaze runs the length of me quickly, before settling on my face.

"You must be, Raven."

"Don't play that." I shake my head, and the creases of his eyes tighten subtly. "I already told them what you supposedly failed to."

All three of the boys' heads jerk toward me, likely from my use of the word supposedly but I don't look away.

"Ah." He nods, crossing his arms. "I see."

I tilt my head, glaring. "You were really gonna stand there and lie to their faces, hoping I would have taken your little hint to keep quiet?"

"Raven," Maddoc warns and I cut my glare his way.

"No," Rolland responds. "Well, yes, I suppose, but only until I had a chance to speak with you first."

"And why would you do that?" Tension swims in my stomach at the query in his eyes. "These are your sons, I'm nobody. They deserve your honesty."

His eyes drop to my hands and I freeze, yanking them from my hoodie pocket.

"You still have it," he muses.

Perceptive son of a bitch.

When I say nothing, he asks, "May I see it?"

"No."

"But I'm the one who gave it to you."

"You also bought me from my mother, so forgive me if I'm not ready to hand over the only thing in reach to kill you with should you give me a reason to."

His eyes widen slightly before he can stop them.

"Raven!" Captain snaps, but I ignore him.

"Seems someone has grown up a little wary —"

"Don't pretend to know or care how I grew up," I cut

Rolland off. "And just ... stop. What are you even doing?" I glance at Cap who watches me, Royce whose brows are lined with tension, and then Maddoc, who frowns at us both.

Rolland tilts his head slightly like he doesn't understand what I'm saying.

"Your sons have missed you. Focus on them, not me."

"But they have you to thank for getting me here, even if you did cause some problems along the way." He tries to smile, but when he doesn't get one in return, he nods instead.

"Ms. Maybell, would you please step upstairs with Raven. I'd like to speak with my sons a moment."

Maybell's features tighten and she waves me over. "Come on, child."

I scoff, shake my head and spin around. I yank the front door open, but I only get a step out before Maddoc is gripping my arm.

My eyes snap to his, and his jaw clenches. I yank away and step onto the porch, Maybell right behind me and the door slams.

I lean my head against the wall a second, then spin to face her.

"Can I come back to the house?"

Her forehead crinkles, but her lip twitches. "Not gonna run, huh?"

I glare, and she laughs, a sigh falling shortly after.

She reaches for my hand and slowly drops to sit, her feet dangling over the edge of the porch, laughing lightly when I pull from her grip.

She pats the space at her side, so I plant my ass beside her. She blows my damn mind when she pulls an old school metal pipe from her pocket, packed and ready to go.

I gape at her, a laugh escaping me, and she shrugs.

"I'm an old, achy woman who deals with a good dozen females on a daily basis. These nerves are shot."

I laugh and watch her hit it, taking it when she passes it my way.

"You knew I was smoking the whole time?" I ask her.

"I know everything, child. I've been a mother to many." She looks my way. "I also knew you stole the binder from me."

"Why not confront me, or take it back?"

"I wanted to see what would happen next."

My mouth opens then closes. "What?"

"I wanted to see what would happen next," she repeats. "I knew you'd do no harm to them. I could feel it in my gut."

"You shouldn't have trusted in your gut. You don't know me."

"I know you're a fighter, like them. I knew right away you'd love him, and I was waiting to watch it happen."

I frown at the orchards. "Maybe I don't."

She scoffs, and my eyes fall to my feet.

"Maybe ... I don't want to."

"Raven," she starts but pauses for a long moment. Finally, she shifts to face me. "Child," she whispers, something sounding a lot like devastation making her voice crack. "Things are gonna get real complicated, but I need you—"

The door is thrown open and a crazy-eyed Maddoc storms out, his feet screeching to a halt when he spots us off to the side.

His shoulders visibly drop.

Maybell smiles meekly from me to him. "Yes, boy, she's still here."

Maddoc nods, his frown not leaving me.

"What?" I ask a little more bitchy than necessary.

"Come inside."

"I'm talking to Maybell." Anything to prolong this.

"We're done, child."

My stare slices back to her and she offers a tight smile.

"Go on, girl," she whispers, her hand reaching out to

squeeze mine. "Boy," she calls and Maddoc comes over, helping her stand.

He kisses her temple and she makes her way down the steps.

I stand and Maddoc steps against me.

"You good?" he rasps, his voice tense.

"Are you?" I counter, and he frowns.

I step past him and into the house.

Cap and Royce are on the couch, so I drop between them, not missing the frown that comes from Rolland as I do.

Maddoc moves to sit on the arm of it, on the other side of Royce.

"So," Rolland starts.

"So..." I let my eyes trail him this time. "You look like the man I used to see once a week ... but at the same time, you don't." My eyes lift to his. "You played the trucker role well, never would have guessed you owned a suit, let alone wore one like a king."

His lip tips slightly.

Fool.

"I'll take that as a compliment."

"Don't. You're fake. What's the point of being you, the supposed man to beat, if you can't even be real?"

"I have a lot of enemies."

"A lot of people do. Only the weak hide from theirs."

His eyes harden slightly. "Are you weak or are you smart, Raven?"

"I'm not the one who got sucked in by the she-devil and landed my ass in prison for eleven years over beat up pussy."

"Raven," Royce draws, but Rolland lifts his hand.

"It's okay, son," he says, and I grind my teeth together.

"I don't need you to pacify them for me. I can handle them on my own."

He eyes me, then slowly stands. "Perhaps we should speak

257

tomorrow. It's late. Let's all try our best to get some sleep." His eyes bounce between the four of us then tighten. "I'll take the pool house for the night. Ms. Maybell set it up for me. Tomorrow, I have some calls to make, but soon." He looks back to me. "We'll speak."

I don't respond, but trail every movement of each of them as they walk him out back, hugging him as he exits.

I take the steps two at a time and rush into my room.

I pull my knife out, flipping it open and closed several times.

He's home.

He's fucking home.

Son of a bitch, what's this mean? And what the hell was Maybell trying to tell me with her cryptic ass bullshit?

I groan, dropping my head into my hands as it starts to pound. I reach into my side drawer and swallow two ibuprofen, jumping when my door is thrown open and Maddoc steps through the door.

He closes and locks it behind him, lifting his eyes to mine.

My features tighten right along with his, but when my shoulders drop his follow and he rushes me.

I toss the knife to the floor and he scoops me up and drops me on to my mattress in the same second.

He pulls my jeans off while losing his and my legs fall open, welcoming him in. He takes up every inch of the space, pushing his dick against my clit over my underwear.

His rough hands run up my sides until he's pulling my shirt over my head, but he doesn't pull it all the way off. He leaves it tangled there, covering my face, my arms both up.

His lips drag across the edge of my breasts, his chin pushing my bra down so he can bite on my nipple.

He licks it, blowing his warm breath over the wet spot, making me shiver.

"Maddoc..." I whisper, and he grinds against me.

"Almost, baby." He kisses his way to my left breast and does the same, before making his way up my neck, and finally he pulls the shirt off the rest of the way.

I grip his face and pull his mouth to mine, kissing him fiercely.

Hungrily.

Fucking needy.

I shift my lower half, gasping when the heat of his head slides past my underwear.

He groans against my mouth and reaches down to shove them aside the rest of the way. He aligns himself and I lift my hips, forcing him inside me when he tries to take his time.

When I sigh, he grins and nips at my lips, but when he catches my eyes, his features shift.

His hand comes up to run down my temple, slowly sinking into my hair.

His hips move leisurely, deep full strokes that are driving me mad, but it's such a good kind of torture.

I moan softly, and he drops his forehead to mine.

"Wrap your arms around me, baby."

I do as he asks, and he buries his face into the crook of my neck, sighing against my skin and he fucks me slow.

"I love the feel of your pussy, baby," he whispers. "So tight, so wet."

I throb around him and he twitches inside me.

"So fucking good." He grinds deeper and my head tips back. "And mine."

My fingers twitch, and I slide them up his back, gripping the tops of his shoulders, using his body as a barrier and forcing him deeper.

"Come for me, baby." He bites against my neck and I start to shiver. He lifts my knee, pushing it out and he hits deeper. "Come with me."

And I do. I come as he does, both our bodies jolting against each other.

He pulls out and once we clean-up we drop back onto the bed, moving under the covers this time.

We both lie there silent for a few minutes when he finally speaks.

"I meant what I said to you," he tells me. "His being here changes nothing between us. You're mine, Raven Carver. No matter what."

"And are you mine, Big Man?" I ask despite myself.

"Yes." His answer is instant and should settle me.

Unfortunately, it doesn't.

Chapter 26

RAVEN

I DIDN'T SLEEP.

Not even a little all weekend, and now the sun is almost up as the smell of bacon wafts through the bottom of the door, but it's when the rich aroma of freshly brewed coffee hits my nostrils that I tense.

Yesterday, thankfully, Rolland spent the day in his office going over Brayshaw business and we stayed up in the media room, watching crappy movies Royce picked out.

Today seems we won't be so lucky.

Never thought I'd be excited for school.

I slip from the bed, leaving Maddoc laying there, pull on some sweats and a hoodie and make my way downstairs.

Sure as shit, there he stands, slacks and all, dressed up already.

He doesn't look up but says, "Good morning, Raven."

I frown and drop on the bar stool. "How'd you know it was me?"

This time he does turn, a grin on his lips. "My sons weigh twice what you do. I would have heard them coming the second their feet hit the hall."

I hold his eyes. "Cap likes to do the cooking in the mornings, so you should have asked him to join you or waited, and they let Maddoc make the coffee so he can decide how strong he wants it. Now it won't be what he needs for the day."

He rolls his shoulders to hide that they grew tense and he turns back to his task at hand − flipping bacon in a fucking crisp white dress shirt.

He clears his throat. "And Royce?" he asks quietly.

I watch his back intently. "Royce likes hot chocolate. Usually Cap makes it for him so it's ready when he wakes up. He helps set the table. They all clean up."

Why am I talking?

Rolland pours a cup of coffee and reaches into the fridge, producing a bottle of creamer.

He sets both in front of me. "And you?" He crosses his arms. "What is your role, exactly?"

Ha! Please.

I shrug, not up for his little game − whatever the hell it might be. "No role. I'm just some girl sleeping in your house, Mr. Brayshaw."

He nods. "Right. Because my sons would allow some girl into their world as they clearly have you. I was afraid this might happen."

"Well." I lean forward. "They weren't exactly given the choice, now were they?"

"I see you think you understand the situation." His eyes narrow. "What exactly did your mother tell you, Raven, you know, when you convinced my sons to take you to speak with her?"

Bastard was watching from a cell.

"Plenty. And my mother's a whore, not much of a liar, you

should know this after your many hours spent with her, so I don't doubt too much of what she shared. Oh, but don't worry, she made sure to close her lips when she felt her cash flow would be affected. Safe to say your real intent" —I widen my eyes like an asshole— "will rot with her corpse should she croak before you spill ... so long as she gets what she wants, but I'm sure you know all about that." I pick up the cup and creamer, lift a brow and add, "They don't like a big breakfast before school."

I give a shitty smile and move to the other side of the house, leaving him standing there with the smell of burnt bacon.

I end up in the weight room, and drop onto the mat, fix my cup and watch the wind beat on the trees through the window. It angrily swishes at the branches, but not to be deemed weaker, they fight back, lashing in both directions, defying their demand to fall in line.

I lift my cup to my mouth and blow, but as soon as it hits my lips, I freeze, deciding better of it and set the cup down.

A light laugh comes from behind me and I jerk to find Royce.

He leans against the frame. "'Fraid he spiked your shit, RaeRae?"

I shrug and his smile grows.

"Smart." He chuckles, jerking his chin. "Come on, girl. Let's go."

"Do I have to?"

"You want fresh coffee or not?"

"Are we leaving?"

He laughs, walking over to pull me up. He wraps his arms around me, staring. "You good?"

"No reason not to be yet, right?" My eyes bounce between his.

"Right," he says but the corners of his eyes deceive him.

"Level with me, Royce. Am I about to be blindsided?"

"I have no idea, RaeRae," he whispers. "I like to think not, but I won't be okay with it if you are."

There's a knock on the door frame and we both shift to look.

Rolland's stare bounces between both of ours and his forehead creases further. "Join us."

Royce releases me, and Rolland turns, heading back toward the kitchen.

Royce chuckles and picks up my coffee mug and the creamer.

"What?" I ask, following him out.

"He's royally confused." He hits me with a grin. "He has no idea which one of us – if any – you're fuckin' and he's too damn proud to ask."

A laugh bubbles out of me before I can stop it. "But I was playing joyrider on Maddoc when we walked in last night."

"Yeah, then Cap ran to your rescue when you fell, and now I had you hidden away in the farthest room in the house, wrapped in my naked arms while you felt up my strong, tattooed chest with your rough little hands."

My face soothes out as I blink at him, making him laugh loudly.

"Kidding." He lifts a brow. "But pretty sure it might look that way to a man who has no fucking clue what he came home to."

"I'm betting he's more aware of things than you guys realize."

"Maybe." Royce bends to whisper in my ear since we're entering the kitchen. "But he don't know how we feel, only what he's told, RaeRae. Power? It's always in the pussy."

I laugh loudly and all eyes jump to me.

Maddoc glares but turns back to the coffee pot – the empty coffee pot.

Stove is cleared off, too.

I glance to Rolland and he winks, but I don't acknowledge it, and head over to Maddoc.

He turns his head, running his lips across my temple mindlessly as he pulls down a few cups. "Why'd I wake up alone?"

"Couldn't sleep."

"That doesn't answer my question." He frowns.

I don't get to respond because Rolland speaks next.

"We have much to talk about, but later." His eyes zero in on me. "If you boys want to head out, I'll get Raven dropped off."

Silence.

Not one of them moves, not one of them speaks.

Rolland's eyes bounce across the four of us, swinging my way when I snap.

"No."

His brows jump. "No."

"Hell no." I cross my arms. "They go, I go."

He crosses his arms now, leaning back against the table. "It wasn't a question. I need to speak with you, privately."

"About what?" Maddoc asks but gets ignored.

"You need to speak, speak here. I have nothing to hide, so unless you do, why hold your tongue?" I challenge, and his eyes intensify.

"I'm afraid, it doesn't work that way," he speaks slow. "I must speak with you, alone."

"Too fucking bad," I snap, and he glares.

Maddoc shifts. "She rides—"

"Listen, little girl—" his dad cuts him off, but Maddoc pushes forward, stepping in between us.

"I said she rides with us," he affirms, and my stomach muscles tighten.

Yes, baby.

"We're not changing that right now." He then slowly

glances at me over his shoulder. "We'll be out front." He holds my eyes, cutting them to my pocket and back, making sure I understand what he's telling me without words.

They can't hear me out there like they did at my mom's, but they'll hear it if I whip my knife out and throw it at the fucking window.

He doesn't think I'll need it. If he did, last night would have gone a lot differently.

He and I, we're laced together with a tight needle and thread.

When I tear, it's him who bleeds.

My apprehension has overrun me and seeped into him.

When Royce hesitates on the bar stool, I look his way.

He nods through his frown, they grab their shit and walk out the door.

I don't pause but spin back to Rolland who, of course, is attempting to read my every movement.

"Your sons are impatient, so..." I roll my hand to get him speaking.

Rolland only leans back farther.

"Okay, fine. Clearly you're waiting to feel me out. I'll start. Did you plan this?" I ask.

"Yes."

"Which part?"

"All of it," he admits with ease.

My pulse kicks a little higher. "Why?"

"It was necessary, and to answer the question you won't allow yourself to ask, my sons had no idea."

My head pulls back slightly, and I step closer, bracing my hands on the bar. "Don't stand there and pretend to know me. And don't put words in my mouth. They told me they weren't aware, I chose to believe that. But, hey, since we're talking about it, what's the purpose of all this? Why am I here?" I challenge, not expecting him to give any real reason.

But Daddy Brayshaw is a smart man and gives me absolutely nothing while giving something at the same time. "Because I need you." He tilts his head. "Also, I never slept with Ravina, not a single time."

My brows draw in and he stands.

"All those times I was there, I was simply paying her for the time to speak ."

"About?"

He eyes me. "Things. You."

"Couldn't have been a very beneficial conversation. She knew nothing about what I did or where I went. Why not hire a PI? Clearly, money was no object."

"I couldn't have people asking questions that I could not answer, and you're right. Our talks weren't always good ones, but you belonged to me at that point, so she made sure she found something to share when she knew I was coming."

"You in the business of buying little girls, Rolland?"

His features tighten, and he sticks his hand in his pocket, producing a piece of paper. He holds it up but not out, simply trying to taunt me. "I have to tell you something."

"What is it?"

"In a minute, but first, you have to give me your word you won't tell my sons."

My head snaps back. "Hell no."

"It's the only way."

"It's the wrong way." I push off the counter and go to exit the kitchen, but he stands and blocks my path.

"I'm afraid we're past what we all want at this point," he says.

I scoff and shove past him. "You didn't do your research if you thought for a second I was capable of being manipulated like this. Whatever she was that you were used to, don't expect the same from me. People around here may see you as one man, but I see another. I owe you no loyalty, and your sons have mine. You don't get a free pass. I don't give a shit what you like to pretend your last name is." I let my eyes run over his form before bringing them back to his. "I hope you spend some time with your boys, Mr. Brayshaw, like real time. It won't take you long to realize they won't put up with lies. Not even yours. You wanted fierce, strong, determined men? You've got them." I shrug. "Time will tell if it was the wrong move on your part or not."

"I'm not done talking."

"Well, I'm done listening."

His expression remains blank as I turn and walk out the front door, leaving it open so he hears the words I know will leave Maddoc next.

"Good?" he asks.

I nod. "Just another day in the life of rich and crazy, twisted bullshit."

"What does that mean?" Maddoc glares.

"Apparently, your daddy has a secret he doesn't want me to share with you."

Every muscle in their faces goes slack.

I look at Rolland over my shoulder, who, shocker, has moved closer to the door.

"Fuck you and your ultimatum. You may have had her in your pocket, but you'll never have me."

My brows snap together when an instant grin splits his lips and he claps.

He fucking claps.

My mouth drops open.

"Thank you, Raven."

"For?"

"For being everything they believed. They trust you with all they are, and it seems they were right to."

"So what, this was a test you all agreed to?" I spin to glare at the boys.

"No, no." Rolland regains my attention, shaking his head. "I told them I wasn't sure you could be trusted, but they were quick to defend you. The four of you building loyalty without the pressure of having to is exactly what I had hoped for."

"Other than getting out of prison?" I sass.

Royce laughs and Rolland's lip twitches.

"Other than that."

Rolland looks to his sons. "As much as I'd love to watch you boys play, I need you guys to keep my homecoming quiet until after the championship game. Donley Graven will be there, and I'm hoping to catch him off guard in a few days."

"Why?" Maddoc pushes.

"I have some things to get in order before I go to him."

"What things?" Royce questions.

Rolland grins. "We'll discuss everything soon, boys."

"I have a daughter," Captain rushes out, out of fucking nowhere.

Everyone freezes and dead silence surrounds us.

My eyes slice from Cap to Rolland in complete shock.

Shoulders wide and strong, held high with his chin, Captain stares into the eyes of the man he loves like a father but hid his deepest secret from in order to protect his baby girl.

All thoughts melt from Rolland's face and his shoulders fall. His eyes grow soft as the corner of his mouth lifts into a sad smile.

He nods, speaking low, "I know, son."

Both Royce and Maddoc tense while Captain's frown grows sharper.

"What do you mean, you know?" Cap asks him. "You never once asked about her."

"And you never once mentioned her," he says quietly and Captain drops his eyes to the floor, looking back up while Rolland steps closer. "The first call I made on my way home was to our attorneys. The papers are being drafted as we speak."

"Papers?" Cap's voice cracks and I move to grip his forearm.

His free hand comes up to rest on my side.

"It's time she comes home, son."

Cap's grip tightens and I imagine his face is stricken with an overwhelming sense of uncertainty, but I don't look. Something tells me he wouldn't want me to see.

"Can it really happen?" Royce asks quietly, stepping toward his dad. "She can come home?"

There is nothing worse than false hope.

"It can and it will." Rolland makes his way down, clapping Royce's shoulders on his way but stopping beside Captain and me.

He glances at me a moment before turning to Cap. "It will take a little bit of time, few weeks maybe, but she will be here soon. I promise you."

Cap starts shaking and his head drops to rest against mine.

"I have a designer ready as well, she's simply waiting for your call to discuss setting up a room fit for her. I was hoping to talk to you about this tonight."

Cap releases me, shifting to hug his dad, and his brothers move, patting his back.

They stand like that a minute, before stepping away.

Maddoc quickly grabs me and pulls me against him while Cap moves for the SUV.

Rolland nods at the four of us and heads back inside.

Together, we leave for school, the three of them seemingly a little lighter than before while I'm growing more heavy by the second.

THE LUNCH BELL RINGS AND I STAND FROM MY SEAT BUT DROP back down when Cap looks up at me with troubled eyes.

"What's wrong?"

"Got a call from Dad's lawyers already," he tells us.

"When?"

"About an hour ago."

"And?"

"They want me to come down and do another paternity test for Zo." He looks between us. "Says some shit about it needing to be done the legal way."

"So do it." I frown.

"Where the fuck was this guy when we needed him for this shit?" Royce mumbles.

Cap scoffs. "Maybe if I wasn't such a scared bitch about it and talked to Dad from the get-go, he'd have helped me, and she'd have been here all along."

"Cap—" Maddoc starts but he raises a hand.

"I know, I'm just ... can't not think it, you know?" He looks away. "Perkins went through a shit ton of trouble to try and keep her a fucking secret. He was dead set on keeping her away from me, from us, called me out and cornered me on every little thing. It wasn't easy to be Brayshaw with him lurking around." He meets our eyes again. "Why go through the trouble and risk us putting him in a ditch? He knows if it wasn't so risky at that point, we wouldn't have hesitated to get rid of him."

"Maybe it was because he cared about the mom?" I ask.

Cap shakes his head. "We hoped he did, but he kicked them both out the second he caught us fucking. He never cared about either of them."

"I wanna know why Dad allowed Perkins to fucking stay at the school when he's a slimy ass bitch," Royce says.

"Exactly!" Cap throws his hands out, anger etched across his face. "What's the fucking deal, man?"

What has him so edgy?

"Packman." I wait until he looks my way. "Are you worried about the test?" I ask point blank.

He reaches out gripping my hand. "Not in the slightest, but it makes me feel like a piece of shit," he admits.

Are you sure?

He squeezes my hand.

"We'll do some digging on Perkins, but stay sane, man. One thing at a time. Let's focus on getting her fucking home," Maddoc tells him and he nods. "You want us to come with you for the paternity test?"

He swallows, dropping his eyes. "Yeah." He looks to me. "I want you all to come with me."

"Then we will," I tell him.

Chapter 27

MADDOC

I wrap my arms around Raven as my brothers slip past us.

"Town's news crew will be here later, they get first dibs on interviews after the champ game."

"Interviews?" She frowns. "How long will that take?"

"'Bout a half hour, they know to come to the three of us first if they want time from us, but they'll wait until after Coach's speech, let us get showered and changed, and then meet us in the locker room. We don't talk with the school reporters and shit."

"So what you're saying is it's gonna be a good minute before we get out of here tonight?"

I chuckle, sliding my lips across hers, and nip lightly. "Yup. You good with that?"

"I'm good with that." Never one to surrender, she nips back.

"Now, Brayshaw!" Coach calls, and I growl against her lips, pulling away.

"Sit by our bench."

"Yes, boss."

After she slips into the gym, I enter the locker room and head right for my locker. I start stripping down right away, my brothers and the rest of the team already halfway dressed.

"You good, brothaman?" Royce asks Cap quietly, pulling his jersey over his head. "You been zoning out all day."

I quickly pull my game jersey on and turn, leaning my shoulder against the locker to block us off from the others.

Cap laughs lightly, his eyes tightening. "Yeah. Hard to fucking focus right now." He looks at us. "I was gonna wait, say something once we got out of here and Raven was with us, but fuck it." He glances behind us seeing nobody near. "I couldn't handle it, so I called that designer lady Dad mentioned, just to see if it was true, and she really did talk to him already."

"That's ... good news, right?" Royce asks warily, noticing the same brittle expression on Cap's face.

"Cap?"

He tilts his head slightly. "I don't know. She was talking ideas and I just sort of sat back and listened, in shock and shit, but then she started saying how she could run a wire across the hall that would allow us to talk with each other at night, some fun little kid toy thing or something."

"And?"

Cap's eyes lift to mine. "And across the hall is Raven's room. Turns out she's under the impression the room across from mine is the one she's decorating."

"It makes sense she'd need to be closest to you. She doesn't know us yet and that's where she'd be most comfortable." Royce shrugs, looking my way. "Maybe he figures RaeRae will move into your room?"

My face tightens.

"Maybe he didn't stop to consider it?" Cap asks, hopeful.

"Maybe he plans on her not being there," I say, and they

frown. "That just means we need to set him straight. She's an area we won't budge on. He'll understand."

"Yeah, you're right." Cap sighs, his shoulders relaxing. "So, do I trust that all this won't make it worse with Zo? I mean all the shit Perkins threatened, the group home assholes being on the property, all the shit we've pulled ... I can't lose the little time I have with her."

"With him home, things are different, the threat is higher," I tell him.

We all know it's true, that's why he says, "That's what I'm afraid of."

Coach comes in right then, smacking his hand against the row of lockers as he makes his way to the center, and everyone faces forward.

"This is it, gentlemen. Last fucking game of your high school careers. Some of you will move on to play in college, some of you will never play again, so make tonight count. Go out there, give every ounce of yourself, and walk away tonight as district champions." Everyone cheers, and he nods. "Graven Prep will not make this easy on you, make them wish they had."

He lifts his hand and it starts, wolf calls surround us until each and every one are in sync. He starts clapping and everyone follows. "Let's go boys!" more howls. "Let's fucking go boys!"

We jog from the locker room, through the hall and burst into the gym.

The crowd stands and starts screaming, my baby right there, front and fucking center just behind our bench as we take our lap around the gym, stopping once we make it back to our court.

"No sign of Collins or Donley," Cap whispers, and I nod.

I'd looked, too.

"This is our game, brothers." Royce smacks both our backs as he jogs past, moving in to his warm-up drills.

Damn fucking straight it is.

There's nothing like home court advantage for a champ game.

This is our school, our fucking people.

They will not beat us in our own house tonight.

RAVEN

THEY MIGHT JUST FUCKING LOSE.

Down by eleven, they can't get their shit together. For every shot they make, Graven Prep makes a three-pointer. For every three-pointer Maddoc makes, they get free shots from a fucking bullshit foul.

I'd like to know what's up the referees' asses tonight again, they've only called on us, even when Cap clearly took an elbow to the chin.

He held back, knowing what it would cost if he reacted, but too bad for the dude, Royce saw and has no chill, so the guy caught one back to the spine in the next move. He's whining on the bench now.

Maddoc charges across the court and into position in perfect time for Mac to pass him the ball for a perfect shot.

It's neck and neck, every person in this gym is on their feet, but all that can be heard is the squeak of sneakers across freshly polished flooring and the dribble of the ball.

They rally, and suddenly we're only down by two, and everyone knows the ball is going to Big Man. The defenders flock him.

He manages to jump up and catch the pass, but when he

pops up to shoot, he's shoved by a Graven asshole and he falls to the ground, sliding across the floor.

Royce rushes forward, ready to lay him out, but Cap blocks him chest to chest while Mac helps Maddoc stand.

And now this is it, the refs can't avoid it or turn a blind eye this time, and three free throws are given to Brayshaw's all-star.

A slow smirk stretches across my lips and the crowd starts flipping out in excitement. They know their boy won't miss.

Like nothing, one, two, three, Brayshaw now leads by a point with two seconds left on the game clock.

The ball is turned over and a lame attempt at a full court shot is thrown and missed right after the buzzer sounds, signaling the end of the final game, Brayshaw High now district champs for the first time.

They jump up giving bro hugs and chest bumps, and each of my boys' eyes flies to mine with pride shining through their game faces.

Good job, guys.

Maddoc winks and the three turn back around.

Refusing to shake hands with Graven Prep, the Wolves trample, with heads held high, toward their locker room. Graven slowly exits after them.

The stands quickly thin, everyone from Brayshaw ready to get their party on, the rest not wanting to be in here when the losing team re-emerges.

Vienna pops over to me with a grin. "Hey."

"Hey."

"Miss me?" she asks.

I frown. "You been gone?"

She shrugs, her lips thinning. "Went home for a bit, came back, went home again, thought maybe you noticed."

"You know what, Victoria did mention it." I nod.

Her nose scrunches a bit. "Yeah, so my dad fucked up his liver real good and was looking bad. Surprisingly, he asked for me and social services thought it would be good. Said I'd benefit from spending some time with him sober and in case he croaked." She rolls her eyes, speaking a little too quickly. "Little did they know he got his skanky girlfriend to bring those mini shots here and there when they docs weren't watching. But whatever, he's pathetic." She glances around.

I eye her. "You good? You seem a little on edge."

"Huh?" She looks back then smiles. "Oh, yeah, I'm good. Hey, you wanna take a quick smoke break? I've got one rolled."

I glance at the locker room doors. The coach for sure will give a solid you fucking rock speech and Maddoc said they had to do interviews.

"They'll be a while." She laughs lightly.

I shrug. "Sure, why not."

I rise from my seat, nodding at Bass on my way out.

He frowns, looking from me to Vienna but I keep walking.

"It's crazy how you and Victoria are cool now."

"Why do you say that?" I glance around, following her lead and stepping around the corner where no one can see.

She doesn't respond, instead pulling out a joint and lighter, but fumbles with it. She drops the joint twice, her thumb slipping from the clip of the lighter.

I study her, taking in the way she keeps fidgeting. "Are you on one?"

Her head pops up, eyes widening. "What?"

"You know what, I'm good." I change my mind, lifting my hands in my jacket pockets while backing up. "I'm going to wait inside."

I turn and walk back, but she shouts out.

"I'm sorry!"

I let out a deep sigh.

This is why having friends is low on my list!

I turn back but she's right there, and when my arm burns

with a prick, my eyes fall to the spot just in time to see her jerk a needle away.

My other arm shoots up, gripping her neck and tears instantly fall from her eyes. "What the hell was that?!"

"I'm sorry," she gasps, her hand shooting up to grip mine.

I squeeze, but my hold doesn't grow tighter.

I shove, but she remains standing.

I move to swing, but nothing happens.

My knees give, and I fall forward, a fog taking over my vision as dark shadows bounce in and out of focus. Feet pounding against pavement echoes in my ears and I try to speak, but nothing comes out.

I squeeze my eyes shut, and when I open them, a flash of blue appears before darkness takes over.

"It's okay, Rae," Vienna whispers. "It's just a little Special K. And he promised not to hurt you."

"She's stirring, should I inject her again?"

I frown, my eyes slowly fluttering open. It takes a few moments for me to regain focus and when I do, my eyes land on a window at first.

I blink a few times, but it doesn't do much to help.

My head starts pounding and I move to lift my hand to it in reflex, but it doesn't budge.

Right then, a deep chuckle hits my ears, and my eyes dart around, spotting a silver-haired man sitting opposite of me, a Stepford wife look-alike at his side, but when I blink she becomes clearer.

Collins' maid?

I try to tilt my head, that's when I realize I'm lying flat, my back parallel with the seat as they sit right side up.

I move to shoot upward, but my limbs won't work.

"Where the hell am I? Who the hell are you?"

The man grins, his age showing in the crow's feet framing his eyes. He tips his head. "Well, hello to you, too."

"Sir, shall I inject her again?"

That has my eyes snapping down, looking over my body I spot someone sitting by my feet – another man.

"Was I unclear?" the silver-haired man asks in a firm voice. "I told you, bare minimum, I need her speaking."

"Where the hell am I?!" I shout, but it comes out muffled and sluggish.

He speaks to the man again but keeps his eyes on me. "Continue, Doc." He grins, folding his hands in front of him. "You're in the back of my limo, of course. A bit cliché, if you ask me, I prefer a town car, but I needed the space for today's adventure."

The man, who's maybe mid-fifties, leans closer. "Do you know who I am?"

"A piece of shit."

He lifts his hands as if he agrees. "My name is Donley Graven, and this is the less than spectacular and of no importance or strength, Estella Graven." He motions to the woman at his side who doesn't speak. He sits back in his seat and lights a cigar while the man pulls the needle from my arm and situates himself.

"Collins' maid," I rasp.

Donley nods. "Yes, and his mother."

"He got less than he deserved."

The woman says nothing but Donley chuckles. "I bet."

"What do you ..." I swallow past the dryness in my throat. "What do you want from me?"

"Confirmation," he says flatly.

The thin man by my feet drops down to his knees beside me and I stare as he pushes up my sleeve, ties a knot just above my elbow, and slides a needle into my arm with ease.

My breathing speeds up as blood spills into the tube at the end.

"Don't panic," Donley tells me. "It's just a little blood, Brayshaw. If what I heard is correct, you are quite fond of it on a normal day."

I don't take my eyes off the man's movements. "What kind of confirmation are you looking for?" I ask, knowing he won't answer me.

"I must say." My eyes fly to his when the squish of leather sounds. He moves closer. "You are quite beautiful. Exquisite, really, though you don't seem to know it." His voice lowers. "Perhaps that's the key though, hm? A quiet beauty so loud it seizes every soul on sight. That is what's happened here, isn't it? All those around you have fallen for the allure." His eyes trace over me and my stomach turns. "I bet she hates you for it, your beauty..." He trails off and I frown. "Likely even told you otherwise your entire life?"

"You know her."

He ignores me again. "Shame really, when you could have been loved and fawned over, reminded of your perfection every day. Raised like the princess you were meant to be."

I frown at the fascination he boldly shows.

"Tell me, sweet Raven. Has he told you yet?" He tilts his head. "Rolland, I mean."

Shit. He knows.

"Last night." Donley's eyes harden. "When he got home, did he tell you I'd be paying you a visit?"

I open my mouth but nothing comes out and he clicks his tongue, sitting back.

"Shame, I told him patience wasn't on the menu."

Wait. What?

"You talked to him?"

"Had lunch with him even, before he went home."

Rolland lied.

"Tell me, are you a virgin?" Donley asks.

Panic fights its way up my throat, but I force it back. "Fuck you."

He sighs, lifting a hand to the man at my feet. "Defiant, just like her," he muses to himself.

The man at my feet moves to the floorboard. Propped up on his knees, he scoops his arms under me and pulls until my back hits the carpet beside him.

I try to scream, but it comes out as a rough whisper at best, and I watch, horrified, as the man unbuttons my jeans and yanks them down, freeing one of my legs. He pulls at my underwear next.

"Don't touch me!" I hiss, but I'm ignored as he positions my feet so they're planted flat against the floor, my knees up. "I'm not—"

"Stop speaking," Donley cuts me off. "You had a chance."

I grind my teeth together.

This asshole, he thinks I'm some dumb girl because he caught me slipping – never again.

Collins' mom, Estella, looks out the window as I'm spread open right here at her heels.

"Don't fight and it shall be quick." Donley turns to Estella, who passes him a fresh drink without turning his way. "Doc?"

My eyes squeeze shut, and I think I feel moisture build at my lashes as pressure hits in my pelvic area, but I feel nothing other than disgust.

Only the weak cry.

"Doc," Donley barks.

The doctor clears his throat, but even still, there is a slight hesitation before he speaks. "Hymen has been broken, sir. She is debased. And ... swollen, so recently active." He clears his throat again, his troubled frown shifting away from the three of us.

Donley sighs, and I force my eyes to meet his. "I guess it's to be expected with a mother like yours." He downs his shot, not looking away. "The blood sample will confirm what I already know, which is I'm staring at the very last of the Brayshaw bloodline." He blinks. "Well, besides Ravina, of course, but she's not much use to anyone, now is she?"

"I ... huh?"

"That's right." He studies me. "Your mother is none other than Ravina Brayshaw, one and only child of Raymond Brayshaw. You, dear girl, are Brayshaw born, Brayshaw blood." He slips on his suit jacket and reaches for the handle. "Fix her clothes and get the hell out of here. Won't be long before her fight's back and she puts you on your ass, Doc."

And then he's gone.

The doctor quickly slips my underwear, jeans, and shoes back on.

When his hand comes up to touch my cheek, I croak, "No!"

I jerk, managing to move my shoulders slightly, but he quickly pulls back, looking down at me.

Distress lines his aged eyes. "I'm not going to hurt you, Ms. Brayshaw. In fact, I find myself in quite a predicament at the moment."

"Yeah?" I rasp, trying with everything I have to push from the floor, but I only manage to scoot an inch left. "And what's that? You realize you're now a dead man walking?"

"No, miss." He shakes his head. "I find an impossible decision in front of my eyes, one that, if the wrong move is made, will be the end of my life. But the other ... will lead to the loss of another's. An innocent," he whispers. His eyes implore mine, an urgency in his that has sweat building at my hairline. "Tell me, miss, what shall I do?"

I clamp my teeth together, speaking through them, "Leave."

With a grim smile, he sets an envelope near my head,

patting it lightly. "You're proof, Ms. Brayshaw. And once you've figured out the secret we now share, you may seek me out, should you wish. You'll know where to find me."

And then he too leaves.

The second the door slams, there's no longer any question if I'm crying. Tears roll into my ears as I stare at the black felt roof.

I wiggle my fingers and toes, but that's as far as I can get.

I lie there, vulnerable, weak ... worthless.

And angry.

I refuse to lie here thinking of the helpless little girl I swore I'd never be again, so I count to one hundred over and over, until finally, I'm sitting, and then standing. I step from the vehicle, seeing we're only blocks up from the school, parked in front of a church of all places.

There're a few men standing at the entrance, both glance over but refocus their attention elsewhere just as quick.

I open the driver door, finding the cab empty and slip into the seat, instantly digging through the console and glovebox. A business card for Brayshaw High catches my eye and I freeze, pulling it out. Printed on the back, the contact information for their proud leader, Principal Connor E. Perkins.

"What the fuck," I whisper to myself.

I fall against the seat, my eyes closing as wooziness hits, then with a deep breath, I force it away and step back out. I grab the envelope from the back, make a left and keep walking. With each few steps, my strength returns. It won't take long until all my muscles are once again mine to control.

I keep forward, not stopping until I get to where I need to be.

Chapter 28

MADDOC

AFTER OUR TEAM MEETING AND SHOWERING, IT TAKES A GOOD half hour for us to walk back into the gym, all three of us pausing when we find Raven's seat is empty. Only a few stragglers waiting for some of our other teammates are left, but not my girl.

"Where is she?" Cap sighs.

"There's that group home chick." Royce nods his chin. "Let's ask her."

We make our way to Vienna and she turns with a smile. "Oh, hey."

"You see Raven?"

Her shoulders fall a little, but she nods. "Oh, yeah, actually, she asked me to tell you."

"Tell us what?" I step closer to her.

"She took some shots with a few of the girls at half time and got pretty wasted, but she wanted to stay and watch you guys play. She walked home, said she'd see you guys later." She shrugs.

"She's at home?"

"Yeah." She looks between the three of us. "Why, should she not be there without you? Alone, I mean?"

"She lives there, girl, she can be there whenever the fuck she wants," Royce snaps and we move past her.

"Someone's lying," Royce whispers. "Raven wouldn't want to be there alone with Dad. She doesn't trust him yet."

"I know."

"Fuck," leaves Captain.

We only make it to the edge of the walkway before none other than Donley fucking Graven steps from the parking lot.

"Well, if it isn't the three degenerates, the bastards of Brayshaw." His eyes move over the three of us. "Interesting game, huh?"

Why is he here? He wasn't even at the game.

"Fuck you," Royce growls. "You pay off the refs to call in your favor, Grandpa?"

Donley chuckles. "Even if I did, you boys were off yours tonight. Almost gave us another win."

"And without your precious grandson," Royce goads him. "Tell me, Graven, how's physical therapy going for the boy?"

Donley glares. "I will take great pleasure in what comes next. There was a clear miscalculation on his part," he muses.

His part...

My eyes narrow and his eyes gleam.

Fuck, he knows.

"Tell me." He clasps his arms across his front. "Does Rolland know which one of you she's fucking? He'll pay a high price for that."

I jerk forward, but Donley's security appears from all corners and just like that the three of us are surrounded.

"Maddoc..." Cap speaks, slipping his hand into his pockets, a move that doesn't go unnoticed.

"No need for the knuckles, son." Donley grins. "I was just leaving anyway. I was only waiting for verification the car I came here in was ..." He tilts his head back and forth slowly, a slight grin pulling at his lips. "Vacated. You tell your principal I said thanks for an interesting night, will you?"

His driver pulls up and he slides in, but before he can take off, he rolls the window down, his silver hair a deep contrast against the black paint.

"Make yourselves useful and get this to Ms. Brayshaw." He smirks, tossing an envelope from the window before he's gone.

"The fuck?" Royce's head pulls back.

Captain moves for the envelope, quickly tearing open the seal.

His eyes scan over the paper, widening as his jaw goes slack.

"Cap?" I ask, but he doesn't say anything. "Cap!" I snap.

His eyes cut left, his forehead tightening.

I rip the paper from his hand, tilting it so Royce can read as I do, but when I get a better look at the document, taking in the large state seal at the bottom edge, my muscles grow tight.

My head fucking swims, making no sense of what I'm seeing.

"Ravina Brayshaw?" Royce says, then cuts his disbelieving eyes to mine. "Ravina fucking Brayshaw? Does that ... so is..."

"Raven Brayshaw," I think I say out loud.

"Holy shit." Cap runs a hand over his face, looking at me. "Something's happening."

My phone rings and I pull it out, seeing Bishop's name flash.

I don't even get a word in before he says, "Get here. Now."

"Raven?" I guess, meeting my brothers' frowns.

"Hurry."

The line goes dead.

"She's not at fucking home," Royce growls and right as he says it there's laughter behind us.

We spin, finding the group of girls coming out behind us, Vienna in the middle. She freezes when she spots us, then slowly starts walking again.

"Uh, hey. Still here?" She smiles tightly.

Without a word, Royce moves for her.

Her eyes widen and instantly tears form as she shakes her head, but Royce pulls a bandana from his back pocket, gagging her with it.

The girls at her side yelp and scream, running off as Cap pulls his hoodie off and over her head backward, tying the strings loose enough so she can still breathe but tight enough to keep it from falling off her head.

We toss her in the bed of the SUV and head straight for the fucking warehouses, ignoring her kicks and muffled screams.

Cap makes it in record time.

It's funny to think we were worried about being seen out here only weeks ago, knowing word would get back to our dad or worse, Zoey's social worker. It was a bitch to slip in unseen just to pull Raven's ass out that night.

Now here we are again, coming after my girl who doesn't know how to fucking listen, but now we don't hide. We won't handle this quietly and behind closed doors.

Everyone gets to see who the fuck we are, like they did the night I made a statement out of Leo.

Freedom to do as we please, it's the worst kind of addiction. A poison that wraps around every bone. A sickness that fuels our every step.

"Leave the girl?" Cap asks, reaching for the door handle.

"For now."

We step out, and people turn, glancing our way and

nodding before turning back to the games holding their attention.

We face forward, moving past everyone and following the sound of roaring onlookers.

Bass spots us and runs, literally, to our sides.

His eyes are wide. "I couldn't fucking stop her. And you took too long."

"What are you talking about?" I growl getting in his face.

"Maddoc!" Royce shouts, running forward.

I shift to see, spotting Raven in the center of the fucking ring, with a dude.

I grip Bishop's shirt and push into his face, but Captain jerks me away.

"Her first, him next," Captain yells.

"You're fucking dead."

"You think I want her in there?" he shouts, keeping up with me. "I work for the Brayshaw name! And apparently, that's her. I had no fucking choice."

I stop glaring at him.

"How—"

He slams a paper into my chest, and I glance at it. My eyes snap to Bishop's. "She had this?"

He nods, eyeing me.

Son of a fucking bitch! Donley knew she already knew!

Did he get to her first?

"Maddoc," Cap bites out.

With a growl, I stuff the paper in my pocket and charge forward. I shove through the few people in my way and yank her off him by the waist.

Her head flies back, nailing me in the fucking nose and I growl, "Stop."

She tenses in my arms, her eyes flying over her shoulder.

As soon as they hit mine, her body loses all its fight.

She spits on the guy as we step over his bloodied frame.

I set her down and spin her to face me, frowning when I find a blankness to her I haven't seen in a long time.

"Who is he?" I demand.

"Random asshole. Grabbed my ass my first night here. Without permission," she says numbly, and glances at Captain.

"RaeRae." Royce steps closer, reaching out to touch her arm and she flinches.

What the hell?

"I need to shower," she tells us. "Now."

I lick my lips and look to Royce, jerking my chin at the SUV.

He nods and jogs off.

She flexes her knuckles, inspecting the blood there, but before she can wipe it away, I stop her hand.

Her eyes lift to mine, then she hears her. The mumbles, followed by shrieks, then clear begging straight from Vienna's mouth.

Raven's grin is slow as she turns, locking eyes with Vienna.

Vienna's widen and instantly she starts to cry. "Please, I'm sorry. I had no choice! Please!" she wails, and my brows pull in.

Raven calmly walks over to her and Vienna's mouth clamps shut, her nostrils flaring with each labored breath.

Raven reaches out, chuckling when the girl balks as she runs her knuckles across her jaw, rubbing someone else's blood across her face. She pulls back and taps her cheek lightly, shaking her head.

Right when Vienna's shoulders relax some, Raven takes her by surprise, pushing on her head, until it slams into the crate at her side, just missing her temple.

She's out before she can even scream, her body instantly flopping over and crashing to the ground.

Raven lifts her foot, ready to kick her but instead bends, whispering something in her ear.

She isn't hearing what she's saying, girl is knocked out, but nobody points it out.

Raven stands and looks to Bass. "Leave her there. No one helps her up, out, or home...not that she has one to go to anymore. Tell her if she sets foot in the Bray house, she won't make it out."

She starts walking and we follow, not a word spoken on the entire ride back, but when we turn onto the property, Raven says, "Get Victoria."

Cap slows to a roll, meeting my eyes in the mirror.

"Tomorrow—" I start, but she cuts me off.

"I said ... get Victoria." Her bloodshot eyes lift to mine.

I grind my teeth together, ready to flip the fuck out, but I know Raven. She'll only talk if I make her think the decision is hers.

It's not, but I'll play along. For now.

I climb out and up the front porch.

Maybell steps out right as I reach the door. "Boy?" she asks worriedly.

I place my hand on her arm and slip past her into the house.

All the girls are sitting around the living room and look up when I enter, gawking.

All but Victoria, she sits in the corner, frowning at the TV, doing a double take when I step right in front of her.

She slowly sits up, cutting a glance at the others.

"What?"

"Get up, let's go."

"I ... what?"

I stare at her and after a minute she stands and follows me to the door. We walk out without another word.

Victoria slides into the backseat, her eyes bouncing all around, finally landing on a blood-splattered Raven.

Victoria doesn't ask and we don't explain, all climbing out once Cap puts the SUV in park in front of our house.

Raven starts up the steps and Victoria glances to me with a what now expression.

"Follow her."

She frowns but does, and the two disappear into the house.

"What the fuck is happening?" Royce asks.

"She shouldn't be in there," Cap says, glaring at the front door.

"I have no fucking idea what's going on. We need to talk to Dad, I'm over these fucking surprises."

"Fuck man, Raven a Brayshaw?" Royce whistles. "Crazy ass shit, but fuck if it wouldn't make sense."

"Nothing makes sense."

Me and Royce head up the stairs but Cap opens the back door and fishes around inside.

"Cap?"

"I'm coming." He pauses a second, stuffs something in his pocket, then lifts her sweater in the air, and we head inside.

"I don't think he's here," Royce says.

"He's not." Cap frowns at his phone. "Guess he texted me, says he's at the Empire tonight, he'll be back in the morning."

"Great, now fucking what?" Royce asks.

Captain moves for the bar, pulling down a few shot glasses and a bottle.

"Long fucking day, man."

I nod, moving for an empty stool.

Cap pours us shots and we take them one right after another.

Chapter 29

RAVEN

"Raven," Victoria calls and I blink, looking around. "You've been standing still for the last five minutes."

I clear my throat and dig through my shit, pulling out some weed and papers and slap them in Victoria's chest, then turn back to yank some clothes from the drawer then dart across the hall. When she doesn't move with me, I look back.

She frowns and follows, shutting and locking the door behind her.

I turn up the water, hot as I can get it and strip down completely.

I step inside, hissing at the water, but forcing myself under it.

I lather the soap between my fingers and scrub across my body, but the filth won't wash away. It grows heavier and heavier, and before I know it, I'm frantically breathing, my hands flying over every inch of me.

"Are you a virgin?" Donley's words echo in my head,

growing louder and louder until, until it wraps around my organs and squeezes.

Why did he need to know this? What does he want with me? If I'm Brayshaw, why would he dare touch me?

I gasp, trying to breathe, but my lungs refuse to allow it. My vision clouds, the water beating into my eyes.

Or maybe it's tears?

Slamming my palm into the wall, I growl, but it comes out broken and sharp, and my knees give way, sending me crashing against the tile beneath me.

With my knees bent, I drop my forehead to the floor.

My body shakes with what must be my own tremors, and I again gasp for air.

Two arms wrap around me and suddenly my back is covered, arms locked around my knees.

Victoria lays across my back, clothes on and all, whispering in my ear like I imagine a mother would a child and eventually my lungs expand and I close my eyes.

The irony, though, is closing our eyes is what puts us at risk.

Demons love to play in the dark.

VICTORIA ROLLS A JOINT WHILE I BRUSH MY HAIR, STARING OUT the window.

Raven Brayshaw.

What the fuck.

Donley, the bastard he is, worded himself real careful, purposely slipping in that he'd spoken to Rolland. Rolland, who just today asked his sons not to say anything, told them he couldn't be at their game, because he didn't want Graven to know he'd been released.

The sick fucking part? I believe Donley. I think he really did speak to Rolland.

So, what's that say about Daddy Bray?

I frown. The boys won't understand.

The flick of the lighter catches my attention and I turn around to find Victoria watching me.

"It's ready."

"Light it."

She scowls but does it, and I drop beside her.

"Remember all that Brayshaw knowledge you dropped on me?"

"Don't say it, Raven."

"It was true. They're like Robin Hood without the thieving. Dark knights in Dior."

She scoffs, and I laugh.

"I read the name on Royce's cologne."

We both laugh.

"Do you like it here?" she asks, passing me the joint.

I take a long hit, coughing as I blow it out. I clear my throat. "I like them," I tell her. "But ..."

"But it's scary, too?"

I glare at the vaulted ceiling. "I don't understand it. They make me stronger, but at the same time that strength wears like weakness."

For every burden lifted, a new weight falls.

"It's not easy to trust people when you've learned not to," Victoria mutters.

"Yeah, but how can someone bigger and bolder than me, feel like a slip-up?"

"Because, Rae, you said it since the beginning, you wanted to run away from the world, hide in your own corner when the time came." We turn our heads on the mattress to look at each other. "I'm guessing that would be damn near impossible now, yeah?"

"I could never leave him. I could never leave any of them."

"And what about him? Do you think he'd ever give you up?"

"No," I answer honestly, maybe a little too sure.

She gives a grim smile. "Then accept his world for what it is."

"And what is it, exactly?"

"It's a man's world, we're just the dolls they prep along the way..." She trails off, so much conviction in her voice it makes me think she, too, is conflicted.

I look back to the ceiling, watching the smoke she blows float up until it disappears.

My mind flashes to earlier in the limo – me, laid out and positioned at their will, legs spread, vag out for all to see.

I was the doll tonight, all right.

But again, why? And what did the doctor mean when he said he now found himself in an impossible predicament? He knew what he was set to do before I was even dropped in that limo. He had to have or he wouldn't have had his little tools on hand. So, what was it that suddenly caused him to question his move?

With a deep breath, I tell her, "Rolland Brayshaw is home."

When she doesn't say anything, I look her way.

She glowers. "Why'd you just tell me that? I told you, I don't want confirmation on anything related to them. It's better ... safer not to know."

I shrug. "You'd have found out soon enough."

She hesitates a minute, and then asks, "Have you met him?"

I scoff, looking away. "Yeah, I met him." Thirteen years ago...

"That's crazy."

"It gets crazier." I stand and grab my jeans off the floor, digging into the pocket.

I toss the crunched-up paper at her.

She eyes it, then slowly starts to shake her head.

"Just open it."

"Tell me what it is, I don't need to see it."

"Stop being such a pussy," I snap. "You won't believe it unless you see it."

Her eyes narrow. "Try me."

"Apparently my mom is Brayshaw by blood."

Her jaw drops but nothing comes out.

My brows lift. "Told you."

She opens the envelope.

MADDOC

"WE SHOULD GO UP THERE." I LOOK BETWEEN MY BROTHERS.

"We should not go up there." Cap frowns.

"We should go up there ... naked." Royce grins drunkenly.

The three of us laugh, falling back against our seats.

The second we do, Victoria comes down the stairs, slowing when she spots the three of us laid out on the furniture, eyes on her.

"What's she doing?" Royce asks.

"Waiting for me," she tells him, walking straight over to where we are.

She picks up our half-empty bottle and moves back for the stairs.

"That's it, we get no love?" Royce laughs, and Cap smacks him. "You at least want the shot glasses?"

"Nope!" she shouts just before she's out of view.

"We just got jacked?" I look to my brothers. "We really gonna let that happen?"

Cap and Royce both give goofy ass grins then we're stumbling to our feet and charging up the steps. Once at the landing, we pause, and Cap reaches back so Royce doesn't fall back down.

Victoria laughs at us and rolls her hand out with a smirk. "She knew you'd be right behind."

I glare and step past her, finding Raven sitting up against her headboard, pajamas, wet hair, and all.

"Come, take your spot, Big Man." She pats the seat beside her.

Royce rushes past me jumping on the bed first and she laughs, shoving him away.

He smiles and kisses her temple, then moves to sit against the wall.

Victoria takes Raven's left side while I take the right, and Cap sits in the chair near the window.

Raven pulls out the iPod Royce bought her and sets it on the little doc I moved in here for her, letting music blare through the speaker.

We pass the bottle around until it's gone, no shot glasses needed.

Fuck of a Monday.

Chapter 30

MADDOC

RAVEN'S ALARM GOES OFF AND MY EYES PEEL OPEN, SPOTTING everyone still sitting in the same positions as last night.

One by one, they groan and stretch, their eyes slowly opening.

Raven grunts, dropping her head to my shoulder. "For the first time, I wish I'd listened to you and shut the damn curtains," she whines. "Fuck the sun."

I grin, pulling her tighter against me and she peeks up, smiling.

"Hey, Big Man."

"Hey, baby." I lower to kiss her, but Victoria's fake gag has my glare jumping up.

Royce and Cap chuckle lightly and I look to them, moving Raven off me.

"Come on, we have to leave in thirty."

"Thirty," Royce whines. "What? It takes longer than that to look this good."

Cap rolls his eyes. "You know Raven sets her alarm for the latest time possible."

"Just enough time to wash my face, brush my teeth, and get dressed," she mumbles into her pillow, pulling the blanket over her head. "No need for anything else."

Cap winks at me, nodding his head. "Well, we could stop for coffee—"

"I'm up!" She throws the comforter back, throwing herself up.

"That's what I thought," he teases, walking from the room.

I wait, looking to Victoria who stands and slips her shoes on.

"I'm leaving right now," she says, not looking up, but sensing eyes on her.

Raven kicks me, and I glare.

No.

She lifts a brow.

I give her a look that says you owe me, baby and she winks.

"Victoria, you can ride—"

"I said I'm leaving." She stands, grabs her jacket and nods at Raven, before slipping past me. I follow her to the front and lock the door behind her.

It takes us twenty minutes of throwing ourselves together to get out the door.

Raven's hair is dripping wet and I'm pretty sure she's wearing Royce's sweats and my hoodie, but she doesn't give a fuck.

She steals Cap's glasses off his head and slips them on, dropping against the seat.

Cap stops on the way, and everyone gets their usual, but Raven hardly touches her maple bar, instead passing it up to Royce, and we head for school.

Not until the engine is killed and we're sitting in the parking lot does Raven start talking, acknowledging what we learned for the first time. "Some people will know. They'll have heard from the warehouses."

"They'll be too afraid to spread the word too loud," Royce tells her.

"Who told you?" I ask Raven. "Was it our dad?"

The corner of her lip tips up slightly, and she shakes her head no. "Same person who told you, I'm betting."

"Oh shit," Royce whispers, while Cap spins in his seat.

"Donley came to you." I glare, growling, "When?"

"After the game."

I pull the glasses from her head and she hesitates before lifting her eyes to mine. Her stare hardens, but she keeps them locked firmly on mine, and my nerves are triggered.

She wigged the fuck out last night, went off the wall...

"Raven, what the fuck happened?"

"I feel like shit and this conversation won't be a quick one."

"Baby."

One of her hands slips into mine while she uses the other to guide my face closer.

"Be right back," Cap suddenly announces, and so Royce follows him out.

Raven keeps her stare on me and her eyes gloss over, but she blinks it away just as quick.

Was she about to fucking cry?

"I'm good, Big Man. We'll talk tonight, I promise."

"No. And stop fucking telling me you're good. I need to know now." I glare, unable to hold it in. "Did he hurt you? Did he fucking touch you?"

She gives a sad smile. "There was nothing sexual about his visit," she says and my head snaps back.

"The fuck does that mean?"

"Vienna helped him. She tricked me, got me outside and drugged me."

"You fucking kidding me?" He pushes forward in his seat,

shifting to look at me. "And you didn't fill us in on this shit last night?"

"It gets worse—"

"Worse?!" he cuts me off with a shout.

"He had a doctor with him." She pauses a moment before saying, "He needed to know if I was a virgin."

"The fuck—"

The door flies open, interrupting us, and a wide-eyed Royce pops his head in before she has a chance to respond. "Cap's 'bout to wail on Perkins!"

"Shit!"

We both rush from the vehicle, running behind Royce until we spot them.

Mac and Jason, another teammate of ours, are blocking the halls, making sure nobody gets through, nodding as we rush into the student body office where Captain has Perkins against the wall.

Raven darts forward, but I grip her by the hood and hold her back.

"You think you're so fucking smart, but you flipped your cards one by one without even knowing it, you piece of fucking shit."

"Get your hands off me," Perkins growls.

Captain slams him against the pegboard and it smacks them both in the head as it falls to the floor.

They're about the same build, same height, but Cap is stronger, not that Perkins is fighting back.

"What are you gonna do if I don't, huh? Threaten my baby girl again?" he spits in his face and Perkins' jaw ticks. "Because I'm done with it. One more fucking thing and I'll break your jaw, then every rib, one by fucking one." Captain starts shaking.

"I'm helping you!" Perkins insists, and my eyes slice to meet Royce's.

"By hiding my fucking kid?!" Cap bellows in his face. "By working with Graven? And I found your fucking card last night, motherfucker. Did you send Donley after her?"

"Captain," I snap, needing to know what the fuck is going on, but he only grows angrier, no sign of letting up to be found.

I let Raven go, and knowing what to do, like she always does, she steps closer. "Cap," she says softly, and just the sound of her voice is enough for him.

He freezes, his eyes cutting over his shoulder and zooming right in on her.

Perkins frowns, his stare bouncing between Raven and Captain before flying to me.

My eyes tighten at the concern in his.

He's troubled to see the effect she has on Cap? Why?

Captain drops his chin to his neck and jerks away from Perkins, but just as quick he spins, nailing him clear across the jaw, sending him flying to the floor. He follows and gets in a few more solid punches before we pull him off, and not once does Perkins try and fight back.

Captain yanks free, his hand dripping with Perkins' blood. He walks from the office and we follow him to the empty locker room.

"His blood's all over you," Raven points out and he nods, looking away.

"You good, man?" Royce asks.

"Yeah." He nods, not looking at us. "Can you guys give me a minute?"

Raven grabs both our hands and drags us out where we lean against the frame.

"He's fucked up right now," Royce says quietly.

"He'll be fine when she's home."

"Will she come home?" he challenges.

"She has to."

Raven closes her eyes, her hand coming up to her temple.

I frown, moving closer. "You look like shit."

"I think I'm gonna be sick."

Royce's brows jump and he shoots across the hall, quickly coming back with a garbage can from the closest classroom.

She takes it as sweat starts to form at her hairline. "Shit, I need some air."

"Come on." I start toward the back exit, turning back to Royce. "Wait for Cap."

We get outside, and she runs her hands down her face, taking deep breaths before dropping against the wall.

"No way I'll make it through the damn day." Her forehead scrunches, her hand flying to her stomach, and she starts to gag.

"Fuck, all right, we'll go."

"Go where?" Cap and Royce step out.

"She's hungover as hell. Needs to go back home."

"Just drop me off."

"Yeah, fucking right."

She rolls her eyes. "You guys have your championship pep rally bull, I'll be fine."

"Watch her." I look to Royce who drops beside her while Cap follows me inside.

I head for my first period, the class I happen to share with Victoria.

The teacher cuts herself off when I walk in and all heads raise.

Victoria glares.

"Come on."

She looks around. "What?"

"I said come on."

"What are you doing?" she hisses. "People are staring."

"So."

"So, go away."

Captain groans and moves to pick her up, but she darts from her seat.

"Okay," she rushes out, lifting her hands. "Fucking fine. I'm going."

We follow behind her into the hall then lead her to the back.

"I'm dropping you off with Raven. Don't leave her side."

"I'm not leaving school. I actually want to graduate."

"I'll pay you to sit with her, all right? I'll get your workload and make sure you have no late marks on your assignments. Now, shut the fuck up and everyone to the truck."

RAVEN

I WAKE UP TO THE PADDING FOOTSTEPS IN THE HALL. GLANCING over, I find Victoria passed out right beside me, so I quietly sneak from the room.

I freeze when I spot Rolland coming out of Maddoc's room.

He too pauses, but he recovers quicker than me.

"You're home."

"Surprise."

He nods, slipping his hands into his pockets. "I assume now is a better time than later, hm?"

"Sure." I glare, then turn and walk down the stairs.

I drop onto the recliner and he chooses the ottoman.

"So, you must—"

"Just be blunt," I tell him.

"All right. First, know that I will deal with Donley Graven. He was specifically instructed to stay away until the time came."

"What time would that be?" I eye him.

"There is much you'll need to learn. This world is bigger than our town, but we'll get to that."

"So, it's true then, what he said?"

He holds my stare a moment before nodding slowly. "You are of Brayshaw blood, yes."

"And you've known this entire time? Since I was young."

"Why do you think I came for you?"

I scoff, calling him out. "Not because I'm Brayshaw."

He tilts his head, regarding me. "Why do you say that?"

"Because if that were the case, you wouldn't have taken no for an answer. I'd have been in your car regardless."

"Yes and no," he answers. "It's more complicated than you realize."

I nod. "An easy, clean answer. I should've expected that."

"What makes you say that?"

"You know, you've trained Maybell real good in the act of ambiguity, too." I eye him. "I'm a good judge of bullshit and that's all you've given me."

"That is something you learned from where I left you."

"Thanks?" I snap.

He changes the subject. "Your mother was raised in this very house, you know. It's quite fitting you being here now."

"Yeah, about that." I look around. "My money hungry mother would never stay away from a bankroll like this."

"She's the one who ran away," he says.

"Call me crazy, but the Brays I know wouldn't allow such a move." I watch him closely and the muscle in his cheek twitches.

"What is it you're trying to say, Raven?"

"Someone – maybe even you – was well aware of where she was the entire time. Maybe she never really ran. Maybe, she was hidden."

He tips his chin slightly. "And what reason would one have to do such a thing?"

"Come on, it's basic math, yeah? I'll be eighteen in a few months, which means she was pregnant with me when she 'ran.' So, tell me, who's my father, Rolland?" I ask him point blank.

He hesitates a moment and then lifts his hands slightly. "I don't know."

"You can stick with that, for now, but you have to know the truth will come out eventually. If I know my mom, it'll be when she's ready to claim what she thinks she's owed."

"She relinquished her rights to everything related to the Brayshaw name when she left."

"That's not how her brain works."

"That's how we work," he says. "We do not bend for those who break loyalty."

"Yet you spent eleven years in prison and paid her all through that time. Weird."

"I did what I had to do." He glares. "I could have easily been free, but there was a bigger role that needed filled."

"So, you admit to a crime you didn't commit, to what?" I use air quotes like an asshole. "Protect me?"

"I had to keep your existence a secret. It was the only way to fix what she ruined. It was my sacrifice."

"And they were your chosen sons."

His jaw ticks. "They had a good life."

A humorless laugh bubbles out of me. "A parentless life."

"I did what needed done," he reiterates.

"In order to what?" I sit forward. "What is your goal exactly?"

"My goal remains the same," he states calmly. "To see the Brayshaw name stay on top, continue to be the strongest and best there is. To stop Graven from trying to overthrow what no longer belongs to them."

"You were doing all that just fine, Rolland. If all that is true, you had no reason to bring me here."

"It was my duty."

"So was being a father to the three boys you left behind to keep a name on top and stay the strongest. You're nothing but a power-hungry, selfish prick." I push to my feet, looking down at him. "Make sure you tighten up your responses before your sons come looking for answers. They happen to be full of questions."

I start to walk away, and he snaps, "I am not done speaking."

"Well, I'm done listening."

"Raven," he booms. "Do not move."

I pause and slowly spin around.

Is he fucking serious?

He stands, walking toward me so he can be the one to look down. He eyes me for a long moment, the edges of his eyes tightening with each passing second.

"Have I underestimated your hold on my boys?" he asks, and I'd swear there's a tinge of anxiousness in his words.

Before I can stop it, my smirk grows and his eyes narrow.

"No, Rolland. You underestimated them. They're not the boys you left behind anymore. They're the boys with the ability to bring a grown man down with a snap of a finger."

He inches closer. "Are you threatening me, with my own sons?"

"Do you feel threatened?"

His jaw tics. "Be careful, Raven. Your place in our world is in my hands."

"You act like anything I do will change your plans."

"You can't run from your duties. If you want to blame someone, blame your mother for her inability to keep her legs closed until her wedding night."

"Wedding night..." I trail off.

"She is debased." The doctor's words ring in my ears.

A virgin. My mother was supposed to be a virgin on ...

When my confused expression lands on Rolland's, his smirk grows. A smirk that has the muscles in my stomach tightening, but I don't show it.

"Is it starting to make sense now?" he mocks me. "I think I'll take your advice on this and ... speak to my sons first. If you'll excuse me."

My eyes trail his retreating figure until he rounds the corner, but my feet don't move.

Whatever his plan is for me, no good will come of it.

Question is, when it comes down to me versus him, who will his sons choose?

Chapter 31

MADDOC

"Raven's gonna be pissed." Royce's knee keeps bouncing as he glances around the labs waiting room.

Cap went back not ten minutes ago.

"She wanted to be here. She's gonna wring our necks." He sighs.

"Something's going on, Royce."

His eyes slice to mine. "What do you mean?"

"You don't see it?" I ask him and he frowns. "First off, where the fuck is Collins? Second, Dad shows up but has been avoiding us for the most part, he lied and said he wanted to keep Donley in the dark when it turns out he knew all a-fuck-ing-long he was home. The bastard went after Raven, on Bray grounds and managed to pull in the chick from our group home to help him. Now Cap is wigging out over Zoey and obsessing over Perkins. I get it, but all this shit feels like the timer to the bomb that's about to drop."

Royce considers what I say but waits for me to continue.

"Why would Donley, who never comes near us, make such a bold move?"

Royce frowns. "He wouldn't unless he benefited from it."

"Exactly."

"You thinking Cap knows something we don't?"

"He suspects."

"But he'll tell us." Royce's eyes bounce between mine. "Right?"

I nod. "Even if he doesn't want to."

"Why wouldn't he want to, Madman?"

"When does he ever not tell us when something's bothering him?"

"Fuck." Royce runs his hands down his face, falling back against the chair. "Can't be coincidence he chose today to make Perkins bleed either, can it?"

Nope.

THE RIDE HOME IS A QUIET ONE, AND WHEN WE PULL UP, WE find Dad's town car parked right in the middle of the driveway.

Cap turns off the engine and Royce immediately jumps out, rushing up the steps.

I reach for my handle, but Cap's hand on my arm has me pausing.

I look to him and his eyes fall to the steering wheel.

"Cap."

"Can I ask you something?"

I pause, tension lining my brows. "Since when would you ask?"

He lets out a small laugh. His features tighten, and my muscles follow the move. "Would you do what she did?"

When I don't respond, he looks my way.

"Raven. Would you protect her, no matter the cost like she was ready to do for us, even if that meant losing her?"

"Why you asking me that, Cap?"

"Answer the question, brother." A wretched expression takes over his features. "I need you to."

"Yes. Without a second thought."

He stares a moment before blinking and looking away. "So would I."

"I know you would, just like I would Zoey."

He slowly meets my eyes again, a lost look in his. "You always have my back."

"No matter what."

"You trust me?"

My pulse kicks at his question.

Captain doesn't ask useless questions. "With my life."

"Good." He nods, looking away. "Let's go inside."

Together, we make our way in the front door, finding Royce coming down the stairs with Victoria.

She gives a tight grin. "She's asleep."

"I'll drive you back," I offer but she shakes her head.

"I'm good, but make sure you clear things up with my teachers, like you said."

I pull out my wallet, but she lifts her hands, shakes her head and walks out, closing the door behind her.

Royce frowns from Cap to me. "Dad wants us in his office."

"Fuck," Captain hisses, then quickly shifts toward us. "Guys, look I have to tell—"

"Boys." We turn, finding our dad standing in the hall. "Come."

With one last look at each other, we head his way.

He steps in before us, moving to sit against the edge of his desk.

When Royce doesn't shut the door behind us, he motions toward it.

"It's fine," he tells him. "The girl's gone. It's just us."

"And Raven," he corrects.

"Exactly." Royce eyes him. "It's fine."

He nods, mumbling to himself, "I was afraid of this."

"Afraid of what? What's going on?" I ask.

With a deep breath, he meets each of our eyes. "You know she's of Brayshaw blood."

"Just learned," Royce glares.

Our dad nods. "I'm sorry I wasn't forthcoming right away and you had to hear it from someone else."

"Why would you hide this from us to begin with?" Captain asks almost as if he's baiting him.

My eyes tighten.

"All these years, I had a plan," our dad says. "But it seems I may have made a wrong move somewhere, which makes things a little trickier."

"You don't need a big lead up," I tell him. "We're not your men, we're your sons. Just talk."

He nods. "You boys are aware our world extends beyond our territory. There are several families, like us, that lead lives as we do, each offering something different in their zones, but serving the same purpose. We keep our towns clean, our people honest, and clear out the garbage. We do these things to not only protect the way of life we have chosen, but to punish those who decide to hurt our people."

"We know all this already," I say.

"You met the family from Riverside?" he asks.

"They came to warn us, said someone was looking to burn down the warehouses."

"Yes." He nods. "It was Vienna Sproud, one of the girls in the group home."

"Whoa, what?" Royce snaps.

"She was sent by Collins Graven, of course, but still. Seems she disappeared for now, but she'll be found and dealt with."

"She won't be back," I tell him and his frown meets mine. "Raven already banished her."

"Raven banished her," he draws out. "And how would she have the power to do that?"

"She earned respect before she learned who she was. Our people welcomed her when she was nobody to them."

"Good to know." His brows furrow, an irritated look crossing his face, and I grow tense.

He didn't like hearing that, but why?

"I've got a meeting set tomorrow," he announces. "You'll miss class and accompany me out of town where you'll meet the head of each family."

"Why tomorrow?" Captain asks, stiffness in his tone. "What's the rush?"

"Things are moving rather quickly, which brings me to my next concern." His eyes bounce between us again. "I asked you to keep Raven from the Gravens and you failed to do so."

I take a step forward, but Cap's eyes hit mine, a warning burning, and I force myself calm.

"He showed up at our game, we were in the locker room. We—"

"The why doesn't matter at this point, son. Fact of the matter is, Graven has laid eyes on her earlier than planned, so now we are out of time. Things will move."

"What things," I force past clenched teeth.

"If you'd have done what I asked," our dad repeats himself. "We'd have more time. You would have more time. I needed it to be on our terms, but what's done is done."

"Why keep her from them if you expected them to find out anyway?" Royce asks him.

"To ensure the same actions would be taken, to solidify the terms and make sure, this time around, it was solid proof."

"You need to give us more than that! I'm tired of this

roundabout bullshit!" I demand, my anger threatening to boil over.

"Ravina Brayshaw," he booms, not one to be over spoken. "Was promised to Felix Graven."

My head snaps back.

"The deal was set, the plans made, and then she ruined it. She left."

"What the fuck does this have to do with anything?" I growl. "What the hell are you saying to me right now?"

"A Brayshaw and a Graven," Cap whispers, his eyes hitting mine.

"Holy shit." Royce gapes at our dad. "That's why you brought her here. She was a fucking means to an end for you!"

My heart pounds against my chest so hard it might just rip right fucking through.

No fucking way he's saying what I think he's saying.

"No, son, she is the end. She is the pawn." Our dad speaks as if he didn't just threaten to tear apart our fucking world.

As if his words are final.

As if we're supposed to nod and accept his explanation.

As if we'll blindly let him lead us into what comes next.

As if ... we won't stand against him, our father, head of the Brayshaw name.

He just fucked up, and he doesn't even know it.

He has no idea what she means to us, no fucking clue what we'll do to protect what's ours.

And Raven. Is. Ours.

Eyes on the ground, I shift to stand in front of him, my brothers moving to stand beside me.

With my head dipped low, my eyes slice up to lock with his, and slowly my chin rises until we're eye to eye, chin to fucking chin.

I raise mine higher.

"No."

TO BE CONTINUED ...

Quick note from the author

YOU GUYS!!! Are you okay??? LOL!

When I started this series, I thought I knew what was to come, but I was so wrong! Raven took me on a journey I never expected. She is so much more than I ever imagined her to be, and the boys! I die! They're so incredibly similar, yet so very different. Thank you for coming on this journey, and I hope to heck you'll be here for Raven and Maddoc's final book! I can promise you, you have NO IDEA what's coming!

ARE YOU READY
FOR MADDOC AND RAVEN'S
FINAL BOOK (don't worry, the boys have their own too!)???

Find REIGN OF BRAYSHAW on Amazon now!

Want to read the first few chapters now? Read below!

Want to be notified about future books releases of mine?

Sign up for my Newsletter today @ www.meagan-brandy.com

Be the FIRST in the know and meet new book friends in my Facebook readers group. This is a PRIVATE group. Only those in the group can see posts, comments, and the like!!

Facebook Readers Group @ Meagan Brandys Readers group

REIGN OF BRAYSHAW

Maddoc

My father's eyes turn a shade of dark I've never seen.

All these years we have followed his every move, stood tall with his presence in mind and fought for all he taught us to believe in.

Family are the ones we chose.

Loyalty is given where gotten.

Trust only those who earn it.

His words were engraved into our bones before we even understood the meaning, and we've lived and breathed them ever fucking since.

Only one free pass was ever given, and without realization.

To *him*.

Instinctively, fully. With every fucking inch of who we are we believe in the man standing in front of us.

Bad move on us?

As if sensing my thoughts, our father's eyes tighten with his form.

I swear we stare at each other for a solid five minutes before he so much as blinks.

Finally, he speaks.

"No?" he repeats my last word. Slowly. Cautiously.

Good, he's getting it now.

I don't bother responding. He said Raven is the end, and no damn doubt about it, she is.

But she's *my* end.

My everything.

Above all. Before fucking all.

Raven Carver, or shit, Raven Brayshaw will forever be at *my* side. Period.

"I'm afraid this isn't up for negotiation." He eyes us carefully.

"*I'm afraid* you're dead fucking wrong." Royce pushes forward.

Our dad's eyes slide to him, only to move directly back to me.

"You'd go against me, for the girl?" He gives a mask of anger, but we're his sons, so we see the truth. Nothing but distress and uncertainty stares back.

He has no fucking clue. None. And, how could he? He hasn't been here.

"I don't know what you expected to happen." I give a slow shrug, shaking my head. "We feel like you know who we are, you say you do, but if that were true, we wouldn't be having this conversation." I level him with a hard look. "You may not have known what she became to us, I get none of your

319

watchers could break it down for you in a way to make you understand, it's some next level shit you have to witness up close to fully comprehend. Thing is, though, you've been up close, and you *have* seen, Dad. I know you have.

"You've studied, dissected really, our every fucking move with her. You've caught all of Captain's subtle shifts toward her when he senses she needs to feel him. You see how Royce clings to her, how his anger and need for a real connection drives him where she's concerned, helping him to open parts none of us thought we'd see. We don't even need to talk about me. You're just like I am, you know a possessive asshole when you see one.

"All the shit over the last few months, the way we grew as a unit. Stronger, bolder, fucking braver. She did this. *She* came in and reminded us without even speaking why we want this world. Why this town and lifestyle is important to us. We want what we were born for, Dad, what you groomed us for, the life you earned and promised to us, and we will have it."

"We told you." Cap steps forward. "She's not just some girl, never was, and now we know she was never meant to be." He confirms the answer to our dad's initial question – Raven comes first.

"There's a way around this," I say what I'm one hundred fucking percent sure of. "And I'm bettin' it's a lot less messy than the route we'll take." I look to my brothers a moment before turning back to him. "Tell us what you know. If you don't, we'll find the answers ourselves, even if it means walking through you to do it."

"And you think you're ready to hear it, hm?" he edges, and Royce cuts me a quick glance. "What if it's more than you can handle?"

"We can handle anything." I answer.

He nods, his eyes dropping to the floor before slowly returning to ours.

"There is a way." He speaks slow, a hint of resentment laced in his words. His features harden. "But I can promise you this, when I tell you, it will not serve as motivation. It will be a knowledge you wish you never asked for. The thought of it alone will haunt you at night, I swear it."

The conviction in his voice has the three of us pausing, our eyes briefly meeting before resolve is all that's left.

We're ready.

"Raven stays with us," Royce declares. "Now, tell us what we need to do to make sure this happens."

Our dad pushes to his full height and leisurely walks around his desk. He lowers himself into the leather seat, casually leaning back.

His eyes hold a hardened glare, but his hands lift as if to say *simple*. His words that follow are anything but.

"Give them Zoey instead."

-

Chapter 2 - RAVEN -

I groan, rolling over and slowly peel my eyes open.

The sun has finally set and I blink to refocus.

Slapping my hand beside me, I find Victoria is gone and Maddoc has yet to make his way in.

The second I push up on my elbows, my head starts to pound, my stomach both growling and turning at the same time.

Alcohol and being drugged by a dumb bitch doesn't mix.

I lick my dry lips, cringing at the bad taste in my mouth.

"Uh, fuck."

I toss my blankets off and strip my bed bare – I was sweating like crazy. Thank God Maddoc's not in here, I'm fucking disgusting.

Clammy and queasy, probably have puke in my hair.

Clothes in hand, I drag myself into the hall bathroom,

locking the door behind me just in case Daddy Bray is still home and for some reason comes back this way.

Why was he in Maddoc's room?

I sigh as the steaming water hits me, but my body is still so heavy, so I quickly wash my hair, leaving the conditioner in it, and plug the tub.

I've never taken a bath before, but this oversized one is calling my name right now.

The water on my feet is too hot when it's pouring like it is, so I turn down the heat, grab some shampoo and pour it against the running water like you would in a bucket for a carwash. Instantly, the bubbles start forming.

A small grin takes over my lips as I watch it fill, and finally, I lower myself into the warm water.

I reach over, grab a towel from the rack and roll it up behind my head like a pillow.

After a few minutes, the tub is full, so I turn off the water and close my eyes.

Wow. This is the shit.

My muscles instantly start to calm, the tautness vomiting created finally soothing out.

It's simple things like this people from my neighborhood will never experience. Not that this tub is any kind of simple, but still.

Bathtubs, in general, aren't something you find in low-grade trailers. We were lucky to have running water, let alone a working water heater.

A few blocks from the trailer park, where the railroad tracks meet the highway, there's a small truck stop with showers.

The city keeps the water running for the sinks and toilets and things, so a cold shower is free, but you can pay extra for heat. A lot of the people from the park go there to clean up and fill jugs for drinking. Wheeling it back is a pain in the fucking ass, but most have shopping carts or beat up strollers stashed behind their places for shit like that. Of course, cans or random shit found along the way that could potentially bring in money was priority over water.

I smile to myself at the thought of Gio making it out of there.

He was good to me, would hang out in the broken train carts until my mom's louder clients would leave. I would never invite him in, though.

He may have only been older than me by a few years, but that didn't stop her from trying to entice him.

I told her he was gay once when she wouldn't let up, kept trying to convince me it was time for me to 'grow up' – she wanted me fucking my friend at eleven years old – but she said his sexual preference didn't matter, that he was still a horny boy who would love the feel of his dick inside a "fresh vagina." Sick bitch.

Wait...

I try and shake off the thought, but it's useless and already growing deeper.

Ever since the day I started my period in fifth grade, my mother would push and push and *push*, constantly hounding me about being a prude.

She'd tell me to "get it over with already" talking about my virginity, said hanging on to it so tight would only cause me problems later.

She failed to see I wasn't holding on to anything – I was simply a fucking kid who wanted no part of the things I hated her for.

I knew what she was doing, saw people fucking on movies and even on picnic tables or in backseats of cars in our lot.

Grown men would walk out of her room naked, not sparing me a glance – if I was lucky – as they'd come fish a beer or what the fuck ever from the mini-fridge, so I'd seen dick before, pussy, too, for that matter.

I was disgusted by it.

The sounds they'd make, the smells. The way they acted as if my mother was a fucking queen while their wives or husbands sat at home probably wondering where the fuck their partners were. Betrayal and disregard for any and everything around.

So, no. Sex wasn't something I wanted.

For a long time I saw sex as a tool for manipulation, and I had no reason to use it. It wasn't until I was desperate to erase what I knew sex to be, dirty and shameful, painful, that I was interested.

Crazy thing about all the shit popping up, my mom trading me for money in her pocket doesn't surprise me in the least. There were tons of times I thought she would, and honestly, if it didn't offend her when her men would make sleazy comments about me, she probably would have.

Or maybe not since I was technically already owned by another – bought by a rich man who posed as a commoner, who used to bring me ice cream and movies to keep me busy while he spent an hour in my mother's room, supposedly talking about me. A man I knew to be good as far as good went in my world, who gave me my knife for protection before he was gone, only to make his way back into my life as my man's dad eleven years later.

How much more twisted can this shit get?

With a sigh, I sit up and reach for the body wash, but the second I pop it open, my senses are assaulted with the over-powering aroma of coconut and something else as equally disgusting.

I quickly shift to my knees, open the shower door, and lean over the toilet.

My stomach is damn near empty, so liquids and dry

heaving it is. A chill runs through my body as sweat beads form at the crown of my head.

Fuck!

I hate this. The shit Donley had Vienna inject me with is taking its day-after toll – one of the many reasons I touch nothing harder than the green.

As soon as I wipe my mouth, I submerge myself underwater and run my hands over my hair, using the bubbles in the water to wash my body off – thank hell the shampoo and conditioner were unscented.

I drag myself from the tub and dress as quick as I can without getting sick again, then drop onto the toilet to brush out my wet hair.

I feel like I got hit by a fucking truck. Still, conversations must be had today.

***

Maddoc

I swear to God you can hear the hard hit of our pulses echoing against the high ceiling and bouncing back, wrapping around our throats and cutting off our airways.

Give them Zoey instead.

What. The. Fuck.

My chest aches and I can't even fucking force myself to look at my brother, but I do when he stumbles a bit, falling back and dropping to his ass on the leather ottoman.

His hands slide through his blond hair, coming back to drag down his face. His skin is pulled tight, hands still covering half his face as his tortured eyes hit mine.

My lungs fucking fold, not an ounce of oxygen left to feed my body.

Cap isn't breathing either, his face starting to turn colors, and Royce cusses, quickly dropping in front of him.

He shakes his shoulders, but Cap never breaks my stare.

"Breathe, brother," Royce tells him, his head snapping my way, worry in his eyes when Cap refuses.

Doubt he's hearing Royce right now, he may not even be seeing me, even with his gaze locked on mine.

"Cap," I rasp, and unsure if it was loud enough for him to hear, but suddenly his hands fall, his arms flopping to his sides as his chin meets his chest.

He knows.

He *knows*, never in a million years would we turn our backs on our niece, my brother's daughter, for anything.

For anyone?

My chest stings. I'm pretty fucking sure a knife right through it would hurt less than the realization of what's in front of me.

My baby... or his.

I drag my eyes back to my dad, who now sits forward in his chair, eyes taut and face pained.

"I'm sorry, son. I was hoping you were still simply my boys who would take my word as gold and let me make the move, then allow me to be here for you during the aftermath. I never wanted this to hang over your heads. This is not how it was supposed to be."

"But this *is* what you planned when you brought her here."

He hesitates, but only for a second before giving a curt nod.

"So why not take her straight to them?" I ask.

If he had, we wouldn't know her as we do, wouldn't care who she was or the reason behind any of this shit. It wouldn't matter, Zoey wouldn't be at risk. We wouldn't be standing here cracking on the inside, facing decisions we could never make.

Acid lining my tongue as I say, "I wish you never dropped her here."

"Maddoc!" Royce snaps. "The fuck, man?"

I ignore him. "What's the reason behind all this? Why wasn't she with Graven the second you found out she existed?"

"I was waiting, hoping Collins would find someone else and we'd be clear until the next generation came, worry about it then, bring her home without telling her who she was, watch out for her, offer her a place here, but then..." He trails off, looking toward Captain.

I follow his line of sight, finding Cap staring right at him.

"But then Zoey was born," Cap rasps. "The first female Brayshaw in decades, or so they would have thought."

"Yes, son," our dad whispers. "Everything changed in that moment."

"Tell me the fucking truth," Cap speaks, but his words don't match the defeat in his tone. "Did you do this? Did you have a hand in Mallory giving her away, hiding her from me? Are you the reason I almost lost my daughter completely?"

My head snaps toward our dad.

"No, son." He shakes his head slowly. "I knew nothing about her until you hired our men to watch out for her. As soon as I learned, I brought in Maria. I made sure she was the one who would care for her. I knew she was the only person whom I could trust with my granddaughter, if not us or Maybell."

Cap shoots to his feet. "Maria Vega, you know her? She's good? She's... she's safe?"

"You had her checked out, have had her watched. You know this, Captain," he tells him.

Cap slams his palm against his desk, dipping into his face. "I know what I'm told. I don't know the truth. We know better than anyone, anything could happen behind closed doors."

"If you really believed that, son, you never would have put her back in her car."

"Say it," Captain demands.

He relents. "She is safe, loved, and will be very much missed by that woman once we bring her home."

"And when will that be?" Cap pushes.

Our dad winces, his eyes hitting mine briefly and I drop my chin to my chest before meeting Cap's stare.

This is why the decorator thought she'd be preparing the room across from Captain's for Zoey – it would be empty for her.

"Madman," Royce whispers and Cap's eyes tighten.

"No..." he whispers, shaking his head, eyes pleading and completely fucking wrecked.

He loves her like I do. They both do.

I give a small nod, gut twisted and tight. "She can come home when Raven is delivered."

No one speaks for several minutes, but it's the loudest silence we've ever suffered.

Our dad is the first to break it.

"Do you understand now, why she must go? Why I had to bring her here now? Why I could no longer protect her by keeping her away?" our dad asks.

Royce scoffs. "Man, don't start with the protecting her bull-shit. If you really cared, you'd have sent someone there to guard her."

"You think I didn't try?" He narrows his eyes. "I sent many people, but Raven trusted *no one*, no matter what role I tried to place them in her life."

"'Cause she's fucking smart," he throws back. "Still could have had someone making sure she was fucking fed, something—"

"She had that Gio guy," Cap interrupts. "I'm bettin' he didn't end up with the Riveras by accident. Why not set him up there, have him pull her in more?"

"I thought about it, though I'm not sure it would have even worked."

"Why?" I ask.

"For one, he was her friend, yes, but she still held back. And two, kids like them don't pin against each other when outsiders ask, not even for money. They'll take it, then show their loyalty to each other," he says. "I couldn't afford curiosity from either of them. As far as where he is, no, he didn't. I led Trick Rivera, Oakley's father, to Gio after I saw and decided his character was pure." Our dad looks across us. "The only person we saw Raven grow a liking to outside of him, was her last principal. He would have looked out for her but leaving her there was no longer an option. Collins learned she existed, and he was determined to find her. Our only move left was to bring her here, throw her in with the other girls and hope he didn't figure out who she really was."

My brothers and I share subtle looks. We're not fucking stupid – he's hiding something.

He had to bring her here, fine. He had to protect Zoey, good.

So, why not take her straight to Graven?

"I am not the villain here, boys. I was simply protecting my family. She was never supposed to be expendable. I was saving her for one of you, I planned to bring back the power having someone from the bloodline provided, but I had to make a rash decision and I chose my granddaughter." He shrugs, unapologetically. "Had I explained this to you in the beginning, we wouldn't be having this conversation. She never would have set foot in this home, and she'd be at Collins' side already. You'd have agreed in a heartbeat."

"This is what Collins meant when he kept telling her she didn't belong with us. He knew she was meant to be his," I growl.

"You put her in the Bray house to try and distract them." Captain frowns. "How did they figure out the new girl was Raven?"

"Besides the striking resemblance?" our dad asks, his tone off, softer than normal. "People searched for Ravina, their runaway princess, for years. Many believed she was killed, others thought she was locked in a dungeon somewhere..."

"Someone saw her," Cap offers.

I look to him then back to our dad. "She told Raven she couldn't be in this town long. She knew people would spot her."

He nods. "It was the first time she set foot here in eighteen years."

"Let's back the fuck up a minute," Royce snaps but his shoulders fall. "Raven... what do we do? I mean we can't..." He trails off, licks his lips and looks away.

"We can't tell her," Captain stresses, his eyes hitting mine.

"Cap." I glare. "Don't."

"I'm serious." He steps in front of me, pleading eyes and fucking all. "Maddoc, we can't."

"Cap, we can't keep this shit from her, man." Royce steps closer, but his tone disagrees, and his next words prove it. "I mean, can we?"

"Graven made a move on her," I tell them, filling them in on the bit they missed when Cap went after Perkins. "Donley drugged her, and he got a girl from our fucking group home to do it. He had a doctor waiting, pulled Raven's fucking pants off, and stuck shit inside her, checked her. They could have done worse. She needs to know."

Captain's temple ticks. "If you tell her, she will be gone quicker than you can fucking run."

My head draws back, my jaw locking shut a moment. "She won't run from me," I growl.

He gives a slow, mocking nod, eyes widening. "I know, brother, trust me, I fucking *know* what she'll do. So do you. Don't refuse to accept it."

"Fuck!" Royce shouts and starts pacing, dragging my atten-

330

tion to him. Hands folding over his head, his beaten eyes smash into mine. "She's too fucking loyal, brother," Royce whispers and it hits me. "Too fucking loyal to sit back and do nothing."

My face pales, my eyes slicing to my dad's.

He gives a rueful smile. "She didn't grow up here, yet she embodies who we are. She is Brayshaw by blood, at heart and will. She'll do whatever it takes to save one."

My facial muscles constrict to the point of pain, an instant pounding in my head taking over and dulling my vision.

I swallow, dropping against my dad's desk, fucking struck for the first time I can remember.

"Nothing we say will matter, no move will make a difference. She'll go to them willingly."

Royce turns to our dad. "We need time. Can you make it happen?"

Regret washes over his face, his stare quickly cutting to Cap before returning to Royce. "There is nothing you can do, son."

"Just fucking try to delay!" he yells, his moves growing frantic. "Can you do this for us or not?!"

"It will delay Zoey's homecoming," he says.

We look to Captain who gives a tight, instant nod.

"Delay, not prevent," Cap rasps, looking away. "We have to try. We owe it to Raven."

I keep Cap's eyes on me, masking my face as they shift, reassurance and promise now staring back at me. His eyes beg me to see what he won't say.

What do you know, brother?

Our dad nods. "I'll cancel the meeting I set with the other families, but we can't avoid Donley forever. He wants to collect what his family is owed, and I can't promise they'll stay away. Collins knows she's to be his and he likely won't be quiet about it."

"So it's settled." Captain makes sure to meet and hold our

331

eyes, our dad's too. "Raven can't know she's promised to Collins."

"Wow."

All our heads whip around to find her in the doorway, arms crossed, glare on me.

Fuck.

— Find Reign of Brayshaw on Amazon today!

Stay connected

Head over to www.meaganbrandy.com or search Meagan Brandy on any of the platforms below!

Book List
Newsletter
Amazon
Instagram
Facebook
Twitter
Pinterest
Bookbub
Facebook Readers Group
Goodreads

FAKE IT 'TIL YOU BREAK IT

Fake.
That's what we are.
That's what we agreed to be.

So why does it feel so real?
I thought it would have been harder, convincing everyone our
school's star receiver was mine and mine alone, but I was
wrong.

We played our parts so well that the lines between us began to
blur until they disappeared completely.

The thing about pretending, though, someone's always better at it, and by the time I realized my mistake, there was no going back.

I fell for our lie.
And then everything fell apart.

It turned out he and I were never playing the same game.

He didn't have to break me to win.
But he did it anyway.

FUMBLED HEARTS:

He's the persistent playboy who refuses to walk away. I'm the impassive new girl with nothing left to give.
Things are about to get complicated...

After months of refusing, I finally agreed to make the move to Alrick Falls. My family thought it was best - that a new scene would be good for me—and I was sick of having the same conversation.
So here I am, and the plan is simple. Smile through each day and avoid her at all costs.
It's perfect.

Until the cocky quarterback comes into play.

The last thing I want is his crooked grin and dark brown eyes focused on me.
Yet here he is, constantly in my space, pushing me, daring me to care. Telling me what I think and feel, as if he knows.
He doesn't know anything. And I plan to keep it that way.

DEFENSELESS HEARTS:

After months of silence, here she stands on my front porch, waiting to be let in again. But it's the same play every time, and I know how this ends - I give her all I have and she carries it with her on the way back to him.

I should turn her away, but I won't. Couldn't do it if I tried.

Because no matter how many times she pops back up, pulls me in and drags me under, it will never be enough. I'll always want more.
More of her.
More for us.

And she'll always choose him.

WRONG FOR ME:

They say to keep your enemies close, but 'they' never had to deal with the likes of Alec Daniels, the broody bad boy next door who loved to make my life a living nightmare...up until the day he disappeared.

See, Alec was a thief.

He stole my happy.
My sanity.
My first kiss.

I told myself I was glad the day he went away, and I'm reminded of why not five minutes after his sudden and unexpected return.

Now he stands before me with a heavy glare and hard body.

But those greedy green eyes, they're darker than I remember, and brimming with a secret...

A secret I didn't discover until it was far too late.

Because this time, he didn't steal a simple kiss.
This time... Alec Daniels stole my all.

Find these titles and more on Amazon!

Playlist

Dark Side – Bishop Briggs
Frustrated – R.LUM.R
Whatever it Takes – Imagine Dragons
Gangsta – Kahlani
Ghost – Badflower
Let's Get Lost – G-Eazy
Dazed and Confused – Ruel
Natural – Imagine Dragons
Human – Rag'n'Bone Man
Hard Place – H.E.R.
Him and I – G-Eazy and Halsey
Wheels Fall Off – Jelly Roll
Issues – Julia Michaels
Headstrong - Trapt

Acknowledgments

So – I'm laughing while typing this – the first line in my acknowledgments for Boys of Brayshaw High is, "I have never been more terrified for a release!! No joke!!" Well, guys, I HAVE NEVER BEEN MORE TERRIFED FOR A RELEASE! I thought I was scared before? Ha!

In all honesty, I was completely and utterly blown away by the response to book one. Truly. It served as the biggest motivator to stay true to the characters and storyline, even if it isn't what's expected, and I hope you felt that while reading! These boys and Raven own a piece of my soul! But, of course, it wouldn't be what it is without having an awesome team to help make it happen!

First, as always, to the man of my house, thank you...for not only putting up with my brand of crazy, but encouraging it!

Thank you to my editor, Ellie, for putting in the extra hours to ensure everyone got the best version of the boys! Told you you'd get used to the pain that is me!

Stefanie and Kelli! Thank you for staying on me and giving

me a safe place to send my words when they are nothing but bones! I trust you wholeheartedly!

Monica! I'm so glad we connected! Having you as a writing partner through this made the process that much easier! Thank you for talking me down when nerves would get the best of me and for being just a solid ass friend I know I can run to! Can't wait to hug you in Vegas!

Sarah! GIRL! You are such an incredible human! Thank you for challenging me and pushing me to give more! You are so great at what you do, and you do it with pride (rare AF). Respectful and honest and kind. A true class act! Never change!

To my main Bish, Melissa!!! I don't even know what to say to you anymore. You're amazing and one of my closest friends! I'd be lost in this amazing world if I didn't have you in my corner! Thank you!

Serena and Veronica, I love you girls! We've got a solid tribe going between the four of us, and I'm so thankful for it! Thank you for allowing me to attach you guys at the hip and don't ever try to get free! I need you!

Street Team! Heeey! Thank you for going on this journey with me! I'm so excited to see what noise we can make together!

To my review team, thank you for loving all my worlds and being open to different styles of writing from me! It means so much to have your support!

Bloggers and Bookstagrammers, thank you for participating and helping spread the word! I hope you love this crew even more with book 2!

And to my readers, I am forever in your debt! Thank you SO MUCH for your insane love for the boys and Raven, I cannot even explain what it means to me! I hope you loved Trouble at Brayshaw High as there is still more to come!!

About the Author

USA Today and Wall Street Journal bestselling author Meagan Brandy writes New Adult romance novels with a twist. She's is a candy crazed, jukebox junkie who tends to speak in lyrics. Born and raised in California, she is a married mother of three crazy boys who keep her bouncing from one sports field to another, depending on the season, and she wouldn't have it any other way. Starbucks is her best friend and words are her sanity.

About the Author